# I DREAMT
# OF TREES

★ ★ ★ ★ ★ ★ ★

★ ★ ★ ★ ★ ★ ★ ★

## GILLES DECRUYENAERE

Cover design by Gilles DeCruyenaere

Cover photograph copyright © Dml5050 | Dreamstime.com

Interior design by Gilles DeCruyenaere

Published by Gilles DeCruyenaere

For Joanne

## Acknowledgments

A big thank you to David McConnell for taking the time to read his brother-in-law's book and offering excellent (not to mention very encouraging) feedback.

Thanks also to Huguette Létourneau, Robert & Karen Létourneau, Patrick Letourneau and all the wonderful people who contributed so generously to the "I Dreamt of Trees" Indiegogo campaign.

Last but definitely not least, a very special thank you to my wife, editor and best friend in the whole wide world, Joanne DeCruyenaere, for her continued love and support through-out this project. It is by no means an exaggeration to say that "I Dreamt of Trees" would not have happened without her.

PROLOGUE

# September 20, 2734

## 7:58 pm

Drake Mathers stood transfixed as the energy beams claimed yet another victim, a little girl in a red jumper. Buzzing and crackling, the glaring white light enveloped the toddler, bright forks of energy shooting in all directions as the child's mother screamed in horror. Drake looked down at the package of NicoStix he had just purchased, blinked, then looked again towards the grief-stricken woman, who was now clawing desperately at the empty spot where her child had once stood.

## September 20, 2734

## 7:54 pm

Standing before the counter at the GoMart, Drake hummed and hawed over the selection of nicotine inhalers on display. Though the sign above the shelf promised "Twelve Delicious Flavours!", the only ones presently available were "Emergent Energy" and "Joyful Release". He crossed his arms and sighed, then glanced at the young woman behind the till.

"This all you got?"

"Yeah," the girl replied, reaching out to straighten one of the few packs on display. "Shipment's late again."

Drake frowned. Though he had tried all the flavours at one point or another and thought they were all pretty good, he was particularly fond of "Mindful Relaxation", which had a nice, spicy-sweet edge to it.

"No 'Mindful Relaxation'?"

"Nope. Just what's there."

He sighed. "Ok, then, I guess I'll take a 'Joyful Release.' "

The woman plucked a package from the shelf and tossed it onto the counter. "Anything else?"

"No, I guess that's good."

Drake smiled self-consciously as he dug around in his wallet. "I guess we could all use a little 'joyful release' once in a while, huh?"

The woman was not impressed. "Yeah, you older guys just love that joke, don't you?"

Drake laughed sheepishly, then paid and hurried out the door, chastising himself for his poor behaviour; it was bad enough that he was buying nicotine against his wife's wishes —he didn't need to be a lecherous old bastard about it.

In the car, he pulled out a Stix and hid the pack in the glove compartment, away from his wife's prying eyes. He had never really understood her fear of nicotine inhalers; the chemical itself was harmless, and thanks to a few carefully-chosen additives, less addictive than caffeine. Part of her fear was based on the rather dubious concept that people on Earth had once "smoked" a plant which naturally contained nicotine. They would supposedly chop it up, roll a piece of paper around it, then light it on fire and suck the smoke into their lungs. This bizarre, messy and overly-complicated way of delivering nicotine apparently resulted in terrible illness, and sooner or later, death.

Drake had long ago given up arguing the point; if Linda couldn't see how ancient Earth mythology had absolutely no bearing on present-day life in general, or NicoStix in partic-ular, then so be it.

He took a drag off his inhaler, then sighed as some of the tension in his shoulders melted away. Though it was far from his favourite, "Joyful Release" was actually not all that bad. The initial flavour was a little bitter, but there was a nice tangy aftertaste that reminded him of a cocktail his mother had been fond of.

Like his wife, Drake's mother had been interested in Earth folklore, but to a much lesser degree. While Linda looked to Earth literature for guidance on several aspects of her life, from spirituality to health to fashion to dinner party etiquette, Drake's mother had been mostly interested in the alcoholic aspects of Earth culture; apparently, people on Earth had devoted a ridiculous amount of time and resources to the art of cocktail making.

Shaking his head slightly, Drake took another hit off his inhaler and considered the bizarre concept of Earth worship. He had learned about the planet in school, and had listened with an open mind when hard-core Earthers had spoken to him at great length of the benefits of worshipping the astral sphere which had birthed them and sent them on their cosmic quest, but to him the whole concept seemed pretty farfetched. Of course, the vast city-ship on which they lived had to have come from somewhere; at some point in the distant past someone or something had constructed the mighty USS McAdam and sent it on its way, supposedly with some ultimate destination in mind. But to think that anyone on the ship actually knew its true origins was just ridiculous; too many centuries had passed since the ship had launched; too many computer malfunctions, human errors, and political shenanigans had transpired for any real proof of Earth to remain. Better to deal with the realities of today, Drake believed, and leave the mysteries to the past.

Drake was pulled out of his reverie by a child's shrill cry; across the parking lot a small girl tugged insistently at her mother's skirt while pointing up and to the east.

"Sky pretty!"

He smiled. The huge bank of lights which orbited the ship once every 24 hours did so without deviation - though the eastern sky did take on a pretty purple hue as the lights dipped toward the horizon in the west, it was the exact same pretty purple hue every single day; only a child or a simpleton would find it exciting. Drake dropped the NicoStix into his pocket and put his little car into reverse.

As he checked his rear-view mirror, he caught sight of a young couple staring wide-eyed at the darkening sky. *What the heck* ... Drake put his car in park and stepped out onto the pavement, squinting towards the east for any sign of whatever these people found so interesting. He stared at the pretty purple sky for a full sixty seconds, finally grunting in annoyance and turning back towards his car. As he placed his hand on the door handle, a chorus of oohs and ahhs arose from the people in the parking lot, and he spun around just in time to catch a bright splash of colour coruscating across the eastern horizon.

Drake gasped audibly. The shield surrounding the ship was designed to absorb harmful radiation, converting it into harmless light energy. The multicoloured light generated was usually barely visible, and only at the darkest time of night; for the light to show so vividly at sunset would require an absolutely enormous amount of radiation.

He pulled out his phone and called up a news site, hoping to find out just what the fuck was going on. His finger shook as he scrolled through the headlines, none of which made any mention of what was causing the light show. Shoving the phone back into his pocket, he looked up at the shifting colours, which were now glowing continuously. He took a deep breath, struggling to control his trembling.

Truth was, there was probably nothing to worry about; the shield technology was robust, and just about everything on the ship had been over-engineered, with built-in redundancies in all of the major components, as well as many of the minor ones. In theory, the ship should be able to take just about any kind of radiation that came its way. Still, Drake couldn't help but feel alarmed at this sudden drastic change in his heretofore dull, but relatively safe, environment. He had just about gotten his trembling under control when the thought occurred to him that the whole ship might be getting hit; just because the colours couldn't be seen in the relative brightness above and to the west didn't mean they weren't there.

Concerned for his wife, Drake spun around and pulled open his car door, then froze as a white flash of light appeared in his peripheral vision. He turned and saw two consecutive pillars of energy appear between the sky and some point behind the convenience store. They were gone again in an instant, but the light was bright enough to burn a temporary image into his retinas, and everywhere he looked he saw the ghostly outline of white fire.

There was another bright flash, much closer, and a terrified scream. Drake jerked his head up towards the sound, trying to blink away the images which still floated before his eyes. The young girl who had been admiring the sky with her boyfriend was now alone, staring in horror at a slightly discoloured spot on the pavement where her companion had stood. She turned towards Drake, and her pleading eyes met his just as another pillar of energy touched down, enveloping and, as far as Drake could tell, vaporising her completely.

An elderly gentleman and the GoMart girl hurried out of the store, the old man fainting as the young lady fell victim to one of the beams. By the time the little girl in the red jumper disappeared, Drake had fallen into a strange stupor; everything around him had taken on a surreal sharpness, a vividness he would have heretofore thought impossible. He stood with his hand on the car door, part of his brain screaming for him to flee, while another part experienced guilt for the feeling of excitement which coursed through his tingling, paralysed limbs. *Is this what it's like to really be alive?*

He was smiling when the beam hit him.

## November 8, 2734

Linda's residential recycler had gone on the fritz seven weeks earlier, the same day her husband Drake had died. A week later, after the funeral, Linda had contacted a recycling tech, only to be told that household recycler repairs had been relegated to low priority as most of the ship's technicians were still scrambling to stabilise the shields. She had made a half-hearted attempt at speeding up the process, then, worn out and overwhelmed with grief, had simply given up.

When a tech finally appeared, Linda Mathers had forty-eight days' worth of household waste decaying in her tiny kitchen.

"Hello, ma'am," the young man said as he hauled his equipment crate over the threshold. "Sorry about the delay. What with all the … Whoa!" The tech quickly set the crate down, opened the lid and retrieved what looked like an industrial strength gas mask. He put it over his face and switched on the communicator.

"Sorry about that. Like I was saying, sorry about the delay. Busier than fuck with the shields and all, if you'll excuse my French."

"Yes, of course," Linda whispered. She was mortified—she had no idea the smell had gotten so bad.

"Don't worry, ma'am," the tech said, sensing her distress. "Lots of folks with busted units out there. You're certainly not the only one with a smelly house right now."

"Oh," she replied, fiddling nervously with the top button on her checkered blouse, "I guess that's probably true ..."

For a moment both were silent. Linda could feel all the misery, grief and frustration from the past seven weeks beginning to creep towards the surface. Just as she was sure it would burst forth in an uncontrollable fit of crying and screaming, the tech cleared his throat.

"Well, then," he said, his voice taking on a slightly muffled, mechanical quality as it passed through the mask's com system, "where's this recycler of yours?"

Linda smiled meekly, then let out a small sound which was halfway between a giggle and a sob. "Of course ... right over here."

The tech smiled behind his mask. "All right. Have 'er fixed in a jiffy."

After about fifteen minutes of tinkering, the tech handed Linda a small plastic bag containing a slimy oblong object about the size of a deck of cards. It was her cell phone, which had coincidently gone missing the same day her recycler (and her husband) had died. Though she had no idea how it had ended up in the recycler, she really wasn't all that surprised—she had had a lot on her mind at the time.

Once the kitchen had been cleaned and most of the rotting goo flushed down the newly functioning recycler, Linda took the phone out of the bag and ran it under the faucet, hoping to at least salvage the protective (and decorative) outer casing which her late husband had given her on her last birthday. To her shock and surprise, the phone lit up as she flipped it open. There was an alert on the screen: *One missed call—from Drake—voice messages (1)—sent September 20, 2734, 7:59 pm—length: 17 seconds.*

Linda gasped and held a hand to her mouth. Security cameras at the GoMart had captured her husband's demise; the footage had been all over the news for weeks after the event. In most cases, the newscasters would freeze the video at the moment the beam touched down, so as to better study it, or perhaps to use it as a backdrop while various scientists, technicians and politicians discussed at length the ramifications of that day's events. Though she was notoriously bad at remembering dates and times, that grainy black and white image, complete with timestamp, would forever be burnt into Linda's memory.

*Camera 2c – 09/20/2734 – 19:58:22.*

Linda closed the phone and dropped it onto the coffee table. Surely this had to be some kind of mistake, some sort of malfunction. Her husband had died at 7:58 pm; how could he have possibly sent a message at 7:59? She briefly considered the possibility that one of the clocks, either the GoMart camera's or the phones, was off, then quickly dismissed the idea; every single clock on the ship was linked to a central timekeeping device deep beneath the ship's core, making it technically impossible that any of them could ever be out of sync. Still, being hit by a mysterious energy beam could have conceivably caused any number of malfunctions in her husband's phone; perhaps the message notification was just a weird glitch, some digital nonsense blurted out during the phone's final death throes.

Linda stared at the phone for a moment, then got up and paced around the living room. She stopped by the huge picture window, where a small brass telescope stood mounted to the floor. Linda brushed absently at the dust that had accumulated on the brass tube, smiling sadly as she recalled her husband's reaction to this addition to the home's decor.

Though he had always tried to respect, or at least tolerate his wife's beliefs as an Earther, he had often struggled to understand the rituals associated with her faith, shaking his head and sighing as she pointed her little telescope towards the dim point in the sky which most Earthers believed to be the birthplace of the human race. The fact that no definitive evidence remained of the exact location, nor even the existence of Earth did not deter her in the least. She believed she was looking at Earth, and that was good enough for her.

Of course she wasn't able to see much of anything anymore, what with the shields now glowing as they did every single night ...

Mrs. Mathers marched back to the coffee table, picked up the phone and, fingers shaking, punched in the message retrieval code. There was a moment of silence, then a beep followed by series of dreadful, hacking coughs. "Linda," Drake's voice gasped, "I need help!"

"Oh, my dear Earth ..." she moaned under her breath. "Drake ..."

"Don't know where I am ..." the voice continued. "Can hardly breathe," There was a pause, followed by more hacking. "I don't know what happened ... oh, fuck ... I was standing outside the GoMart ... I was buying NicoStix, Linda, I'm sorry." She flinched as static burst through the phone's speaker, followed by a series of heartbreaking sobs. "Oh, I'm such an asshole ... I was flirting with the girl too ... then there were these fucking flashes of light ... this little kid got killed right in front of me." Linda squeezed her eyes shut, a mixture of tears and mascara running down her face. "I don't know where I am. There's machines and wires, and it's cold!" Another wheezy gasp. "Air smells like ammonia ... my eyes are on fire!"

There was one final beep, and then silence.

# February 7, 2737

The hand-painted sign over the steel gate read: "Alternative Transportation Research Centre". Below was a smaller sign: "Volunteers report to Security". To the right of the gate was a small shack. Inside, an armed guard sat perusing a digital notebook.

Kevin Delacroix shuffled nervously for a moment, then dug the crumpled pamphlet from his jeans pocket.

### Anti-Poverty Initiative: Program 537-A
(Subject to Ship's Council Unilateral Limited Information Act Section 32-2-55.2)
### Volunteers Needed:
for Dome Defence Initiative 37-D.
Food, beverages and stipend will be provided to all applicants following selection procedure.
Successful applicants will be rewarded with a monthly stipend and a permanent shared residence within the Core.

Kevin stepped up to the security shack, bending down slightly to speak through the small hole in the plexiglass window. "Hi. I'm here to volunteer?"

The guard, a plump, grey-haired man in his fifties, fur-rowed his brow. "Is that right?"

Kevin shrugged. "Well, yeah. You're taking volunteers, right?" He held up the pamphlet.

The guard glanced at the brochure and shook his head, chuckling. "Yeah, we're taking volunteers all right. Hang on." He stepped out of the shack and opened a small shutter in the heavy steel fence which surrounded the compound. He waved toward one of the guards on the other side, who waved back, then came trotting over.

"What's up, Pete?" the guard said, peering through the opening.

"Got another volunteer for ya." He motioned toward Kevin, a bemused smile playing at the corners of his mouth.

The younger guard barked out a harsh laugh. "Wow, they just keep comin', don't they?"

"That they do."

Kevin frowned. He had attended his share of government cluster fuck cattle calls in the past, and the people in charge were generally polite, if not quite friendly. These guys ... these guys were just being weird.

He waited nervously as the older guard poked around on his information pad, taking the time to marvel once again at how far downhill the Rim, and thus his life, had gone.

There had always been an economic divide between the inner and outer areas of the ship, but the difference had once been fairly minimal, with the less-affluent citizens of the Rim still having a decent shot at living a comfortable life. Over the past two decades, however, a newly elected Head of Gov-ernment had begun diverting resources from the Rim to the Core as part of a much touted "Ship Restructuring Initiative". The citizens of the Rim had grudgingly gone along with the plan at first, mollified by promises of wonderful things to come if they just agreed to live with a little less for now. By the time anyone realised these wonderful things would never actually come to fruition, it was too late; the Initiative had gained an unstoppable momentum, leaving the Core-dwellers holding all the cards. Nowadays crossing the sewage moat which separated the Core from the Rim was like travelling to another world; on one side lay happiness and boundless prosperity, on the other, misery and abject poverty.

Kevin was debating whether or not to leave when the younger guard grunted, shook his head, and said: "All right, let him in." Pete the Security Guard gave Kevin one final glance, then stepped back into his shack. A buzzer sounded, and the gate rolled open.

Kevin blinked, raised his eyebrows, and walked into the compound. He gazed curiously about as the guard led him towards a small group a few yards past the gate. There was a huge hangar-like structure a few hundred feet away, with several smaller buildings surrounding it. He knew enough to guess that it had once been some kind of factory complex, but what it might have once produced was beyond him.

As Kevin studied the larger building, he was practically blinded by a flash of forked white light, followed in quick succession by two more. Though the beams seemed to be striking the structure's roof, there was no smoke or fire or signs of damage of any kind. Of course from his vantage point he couldn't actually see the roof, so he couldn't be sure. The guards certainly didn't seem too concerned.

"Wait here," his guide said, shoving him towards the other volunteers.

As he stumbled towards the small group, a young woman wearing an old garbage bag ran up to him. "Look at my feet!" she whispered hoarsely, not making eye contact. "They're smaller than they were, but they're still too big!"

Startled, Kevin turned and pushed deeper into the crowd. Most of the volunteers were dirty and smelly, and by the looks of them, only slightly more sane than the garbage bag woman. Did they even understand what was going on here?

Just as Kevin was preparing to pry a little more information from the guard, the gate rolled open and a large armoured truck rumbled in, coming to a stop a few feet away. The truck's rear doors banged open, and two more guards jumped out, followed by a dozen harried-looking individuals. Machine guns levelled, the guards shepherded them towards the first group.

Things were starting to look a little clearer to Kevin.

"Listen up!" a burly, middle-aged guard bellowed as the empty truck pulled away. "This is your lucky day!" A few of the Rim-dwellers turned towards him to listen, but most of them just kept milling about. "First, you are all going to receive food!"

This pretty much got everyone's attention. The crowd surged towards the speaker, crying "Food! Food!" or "Give it to us now!" The other guards were quick to hold them back, striking a few of the louder ones with the butt of their machine gun.

Once they had settled down a little, the speaker continued. "After you've eaten, we're going to ask you a few questions! Your answers will be of great value to Ship's Council, and as a reward for your cooperation you will be relocated to the Core!"

There was a moment of stunned silence, followed by a mini-riot. The bedraggled citizens began yelling, screaming and crying, some jumping up and down, some running around in circles. Amazingly, a few let loose and started pounding on each other. Those that ran towards the guards had their course corrected, and none too gently.

After a moment the speaker fired his weapon into the air. The crowd quieted down somewhat, and he continued. "Disorderly conduct will not be tolerated! Those who cooperate will be rewarded—those who cause trouble will be shot!"

Shaking her fist in the air, an old woman in a dirty blue housecoat yelled: "Fuck you, lying shit licker! Give us our fucking food!" and began pushing her way towards the guard. He levelled his weapon and blew five holes through her chest. The crowd grew silent.

"All right, here's how it's going to work!" the guard bellowed, scowling fiercely behind his riot helmet. "You will line up single file, and we will escort you one at a time into the food centre!" He pointed at the huge building, just as two more energy bolts flashed silently from the sky, eliciting cringes and excited cries from the crowd. "Once there we will tell you what to do! Do not push or cause any disturbance, or we'll put you down next to the dead lady!"

The guard pointed at Kevin. "You. You're first. The rest of you line up!"

Kevin took a step backward, the colour draining from his face. The guard levelled his gun at him. "Don't make me tell you again."

★ ★ ★

Kevin was led through a small door into a tiny cubicle barely large enough for him and the guard. Once the door was locked behind them, he was led through a second door into the main building.

The sheer scale of the place was almost overwhelming. Practically the whole building was one huge room, half-filled with people and equipment. At the centre was a huge gantry rising almost to the ceiling, where a large hole had been cut into the corrugated sheet metal.

The guard quickly passed Kevin over to a young woman in a lab coat and hardhat. She thrust a sandwich and a small cup of coffee into his hands and loaded him into a small two-person cart. Trembling, Kevin munched his sandwich and gulped his coffee, gazing about fearfully as the woman drove the vehicle toward the gantry. Though the cart moved fairly quickly, the trip felt impossibly long. This room truly was huge.

The cart came to a stop ten feet from the central structure. The woman disembarked and walked toward a large locker a few yards to the left. Kevin swallowed his last bit of sandwich and sat quietly, waiting for further instructions. After gathering up a few things from the locker, the woman walked back to the cart. "Show me," she said, indicating the beverage container with a nod of her head. Kevin paused, then held the cup towards the woman, eyebrows raised. She grasped his wrist and twisted it towards her, peering inside. "Okay. Put it in there," she said, indicating a plastic barrel next to the cart, "then follow me."

Puzzled by the woman's need to confirm that he had finished his coffee, Kevin added his empty cup to the scores already in the barrel, then followed her to a small bank of lockers a few yards away from the gantry. Once there, he was instructed to disrobe.

Kevin paused, glancing about. There were people everywhere, sitting at computers, working on machinery, talking into microphones. Other than the woman and a few armed guards who had been watching him constantly since he had entered the building, nobody seemed particularly interested in seeing him undress.

As he stood quietly contemplating his options (which were really very few), Kevin was suddenly struck by an all-encompassing sense of peace and contentment. He sighed heavily, then blinked and shook his head. He thought back to his little snack, and smiled dopily; they had dosed him with some kind of sedative. Some part of him deep down wanted to be outraged, but the rest of him just really didn't give a fuck. He looked at the woman, smiled, and got naked.

"Put this on," she said, handing him what looked like a thin white bodysuit. Smiling serenely, he pulled the outfit on, taking great pleasure in the sensation of the tight rubbery fabric sliding over his skin. Once he was "dressed" the woman gave him a small mask which fit over his nose and mouth, and a pair of goggles. Both had tubes connecting to a small apparatus which she strapped around his neck. Finally she handed him something that looked like a cell phone.

"All right," she said, "now say something."

Kevin giggled. "Do you have a mirror?"

The woman glanced over her shoulder at a man sitting at a nearby computer terminal. He gave her the thumbs up. She nodded at the man, then turned back to face Kevin.

"Okay, now listen carefully. You'll be stepping onto that pad over there." She pointed towards a small, raised concrete square directly below the huge gantry. "You'll see a huge flash of light, and you'll feel very tingly all over. After the flash, you'll be in a tiny room with lots of strange equipment around you. It'll be cold, but the suit will protect you. The air will be bad, so don't take off the mask or goggles, whatever you do. Understand?"

Kevin chuckled contentedly. "Oh, yeah … sure. Can I have another sandwich?"

"Later," the woman replied sternly. "Now pay attention, this is important. What I want you to do is describe everything you see and hear in the room. That device," she indicated the cell phone-type thing, "will pick up everything you say. You don't have to hold it to your face, just be sure not to drop it, whatever you do. Okay?" Kevin smiled down at the thing in his hand, then looked at the woman and nodded. "All right," she continued, "it's very important that you be thorough. The more useful information we get, the better the reward will be when you get back. Understand?"

Kevin's smile widened. "Fuck yeah! I'm gonna live in the Core!"

The woman sighed, then looked at Kevin with a hint of sadness in her otherwise stern eyes. "Yes, that's right. But you have to do what we say first. Do you understand everything I've said?"

"You're pretty."

"I'll take that as a yes. Now go stand on the pad and wait for the flash of light."

"Okay."

Kevin strode casually to the concrete square, turned to face the young woman, and waited. Nearby a group of men and women huddled around a bank of computer screens, carefully calibrating a section of the shields directly above the gantry, weakening it just enough to allow the energy beams to come through. Kevin grinned at the woman and gave her a thumbs-up.

Thirty-eight seconds later he was standing in a Squelcher ship.

Kevin winced as frigid air contacted the exposed skin on his face. Fortunately the suit was working as advertised, and he felt only a slight chill through its fabric. He blinked as his eyes recovered from the flash of light which had heralded his departure to … wherever this was.

To Kevin's right was an extremely narrow corridor which branched off after about three feet. To his left was a wall covered in tubes, wires and various blob-shaped projections. Random bits and bobs hung from the ceiling, mere inches above his head. Under his feet was a small circular pad of rubbery red material. He glanced at the phone device in his hand.

"Oh, yeah …" He cleared his throat, and held the phone up to his face, knocking it against his mask. "Oh, wait," he said, giggling nervously, "I don't have to do that …" He let his arm drop to his side. "Um, hello?" He paused, waiting for a response. When none was forthcoming, he shrugged. "Um, this is Kevin," he said, then shook his head, suddenly realising that no one had even asked him his name. He paused again, shivering; it really was cold in here. "Okay, so, this is Kevin, the guy you just sent … um, here. With the flash of light, and the suit and stuff ..." He frowned; of course they knew who he was. And what was he supposed to do again? *Oh, yeah* ... "Um, I'm standing in a small room. The walls are kinda purply-grey. There's a bunch of stuff, like wires and shit, and some tubes and stuff. Um ..."

Despite the cold, Kevin suddenly broke into a sweat. Whatever sedative they had given him seemed to be wearing off. He took a deep breath, shuddering slightly as he let it out again.

"Um, okay ..." he blurted, studying the branch at the end of the corridor. "Okay, there's a hallway in front of me, and it splits off at the end. Uhhh ..."

Kevin froze, suddenly overwhelmed. He reached up and touched his cheek, which was now painfully cold.

*I'm going to screw this up.*

"I ... I'm sorry," he croaked as his eyes welled up with tears. "Give ... give m-me a second ..."

Just then something turned the corner. At first Kevin thought it was a mass of blue rubber, or maybe plasticine, oozing and glistening in the dim light of the corridor. Whatever it was it seemed to be moving under its own power, expanding and contracting as it approached, various lumps and bumps crawling around beneath its surface. Multiple tentacles hung limply around the thing, one of them slowly becoming erect, exposing a row of ghastly looking black spikes.

Kevin's knees turned to water. "Oh shit," he groaned.

Turning to run, he stumbled off the lip of the rubbery pad and fell headlong into a mass of wires and tubes blocking the way behind him. He scrambled to his feet and turned back towards the rapidly advancing whatever-it-was. Practically insane with fear and panic, he threw the phone, which hit the wall to his left, then bounced across the hall, striking the opposite wall before finally landing between Kevin and the rubber-thing.

He stood for a moment, eyes flicking between the phone and the blue blob oozing its way towards him.

The woman had told him not to drop the phone.

"Fuck!" he cried, diving desperately for the device, hoping beyond hope that it wasn't broken. "There's a fucking ... thing in here!" he gasped as he snatched the phone from the ground.

The moment he made contact, the device delivered a small shock to his fingertips, causing him to drop it in surprise and dismay. It bounced as it hit the floor.

Kevin stared at the phone, wondering if they would shoot him when he got back.

*If* he got back.

"Fuck," he mumbled, tears freezing to his cheeks. "No fucking sandwich is worth this."

Suddenly a shadow fell over him. He looked up into a mass of blue, writhing goo which twisted and wriggled to-wards him, all the while emitting a soft squishing sound. He grabbed the device, gritting his teeth against the painful electric shocks it continued to deliver, and shouted: "Bring me back! Bring me back!"

The thing's erect appendage flailed suddenly, a large glossy spike scratching Kevin's exposed cheek. He screamed, turn-ing his head and jabbing out blindly with the phone. It made contact twice. The first time the blob paused, recoiling very slightly. The second time the device hit it just beneath the stiff tentacle, and the thing quickly retreated, its appendage deflating as it did so.

Kevin hazarded a terrified glance at the blue abomination which, unbelievably, seemed to be backing off. He scrambled to his feet and made a dash for the pad, hoping beyond hope it would send him back. As his foot touched the rubber, he stumbled, reaching out to the wall to steady himself. The phone made contact with a bumpy mass of wires, and there was an incredibly bright flash of light.

★ ★ ★

In the abandoned factory a group of technicians busied themselves monitoring and recording the information which flowed in from the Squelcher ship above. In addition to the cries and screams of their hapless volunteer, they were receiving temperature levels, atmospheric analyses, and a gamut of other readings provided by the jumped up cellphone they had given him.

Then, exactly twenty-three seconds after Kevin had been sent off on his little adventure, he was back on the ground, sprawled out on the square concrete launch pad.

"Holy shit," one of the techs whispered. "He came back."

★ ★ ★

There was a moment of awed silence as the techs absorbed what was happening. During this time Kevin struggled to his feet and gawped at the phone in his hand, which thankfully was no longer shocking him. His eyes found the woman who had sent him off, and he held the device out in her direction.

"S-sorry," he stammered, "I think I broke it."

As if on cue everyone came back to life. Those who were not busily flicking switches or punching buttons ran up to Kevin and herded him over to a nearby chair, where they proceeded to question him for exactly two minutes and fourteen seconds.

On that day, Kevin had helped them learn three very important things: First, that the rubbery blue things (hostile alien creatures which the scientists had dubbed Squelchers) were susceptible to small amounts of electrical energy. Second, that the same small amounts of electrical energy where the key to triggering the Squelchers' travelling apparatus. And third, that the Squelchers' thorns contained a fast-acting, horrendously lethal venom for which there was no known antidote.

PART I

## May 17, 2769

Jason Crawford watched calmly as the Squelcher closed in. The thing was ugly, awkward yet strangely fluid in its motion. Jason took a series of rapid, shallow breaths, the bio-membrane stretched over his mouth and nose extracting oxygen from the atmosphere while removing most of the poisons. He drew in only as much air as the confined space would allow; trying to inhale any deeper would serve only to increase the pressure against his back and chest, creating the illusion that he was suffocating. Of all the skills needed for combat in a Squelcher ship, the ability to move efficiently in extremely tight spaces was the greatest.

The creature approached slowly, its amorphous body expanding and contracting to accommodate the nooks and crannies of the cramped passageway. A spiked appendage extruded itself from a mass of blue tissue at the thing's base, rapidly lengthening and stiffening like some obscene sado-masochistic sex toy. Jason took one last shallow breath, held it for a count of two, then quickly released it, moving forward as far as the narrowing corridor would allow. Holding his breath (he would not have been able to inhale had he wanted to), Jason raised his right foot, pulling his knee tightly against his chest. He then kicked out, planting his heel between two ghastly spikes and pushing the appendage up and against the creature's yielding mass. He leaned forward and, bending his fingers at the second knuckle, struck out with his right hand, his metallic implants making contact just below the point where the creature's "arm" met its body. There was a small zapping sound as the tiny devices released a quick burst of electricity into the Squelcher's flesh, causing it to shudder and withdraw.

The creature paused a foot away, its appendage deflating rapidly, its entire body quaking obscenely. Jason backed off just far enough to breathe normally, carefully studying the creature to assess its condition. The Squelcher's shuddering eased up, then stopped altogether, and for a moment the thing was perfectly still. Jason smiled and moved forward, flexing his gleaming knuckles in anticipation of the final *coup de grâce*. As he once again evacuated his lungs so as to jam himself into the narrow part of the corridor, the creature suddenly sprang to life, flailing at Jason with its flaccid appendage. One of the spikes grazed his wrist, leaving a shallow scratch.

A buzzer rang as the walls began to move apart. High above, bright flood lights sprang to life. Jason looked unbelievingly at his wrist, then glared upward to a point approximately five feet above the lifeless blue blob. *You old fucking son of a whore* ... A small, grey-haired man was leaning over the top of the wall, fiddling with a set of cords which ran from a control box on his chest to the Squelcher puppet below. He was idly whistling to himself beneath his bio-mask. "You old fucking cunt!" Jason yelled, lunging towards the rubber Squelcher and grabbing a handful of control cords. The old man blinked in surprise as Jason yanked, sending the puppet-tech over the edge of the wall. The power umbilical snagged, and the man was left hanging, his face mere inches away from the floor. Jason kicked him in the mouth, then reached down and pulled off his mask. The old man cried out, then began coughing uncontrollably as powerful irritants flooded his nose and mouth.

Jason spun on his heel and strode away, tugging angrily at the thin insulating body suit which covered nearly his entire body from the neck down. Behind him a sim-tech was frantically trying to replace the puppet-tech's bio-mask while calling over his shoulder for assistance. "Crazy fucking kid," he said, none too quietly, as he finally managed to get the the old man's mask back on. Jason stopped in his tracks, the top half of his suit dangling around his waist. His exposed muscles were small, but well defined and powerful looking. They tensed as he opened and closed his fists, his implants gleaming through the access holes in his thermal gloves.

Just as he was about to turn around and deal with the loudmouth bastard sim-tech, a deep voice boomed over the loudspeakers. "Private J-538, report to Command Office B immediately!" Jason closed his eyes and mumbled something vile between his clenched teeth. After a few moments of creative visualising (he imagined himself stabbing the sim-tech in the crotch with a screwdriver) Jason finally managed to get his anger more or less under control. He began pulling his suit back on and headed for the airlock.

It took nearly 2 minutes for the cycle to complete, fans blowing in warm, clean air while vents along the floor sucked out cold, dirty low-oxygen stuff. Halfway through the cycle Jason pulled off his bio-mask, relishing the burning sensation as the diluted chemical irritants flowed into his nose and lungs. Had these been actual Squelcher toxins, Jason would have suffered permanent damage to his lungs. This being a simulation, he had nothing more to fear than a possible coughing fit. Finally the various whooshing and humming sounds quieted around him, and the exit door irised open.

The adjoining room was long and narrow, with lockers along one wall, and a flat metal bench along the other.

Monitors near the ceiling showed various views of the simulation room. Nearly a dozen young men milled about, waiting for their shot at the rubber aliens. "Yo, Gay-Jay! You in trouble, boy! Daddy's gonna whoop your sorry ass!" It was his buddy Isaac, who had obviously heard the captain's message through the prep room loudspeakers. The fact that Captain Halford had breached protocol by patching the summons through here was an indicator of just how mad he really was. Jason grimaced, anticipating a particularly humiliating round of verbal abuse as he ran the gauntlet from the airlock to the exit at the far end of the room. He was not disappointed.

"Attention Private J-538!" Isaac continued, his dark blue eyes sparkling as his fellow Flashers-in-training cheered and guffawed. "Report immediately to Command Office B for a big, hard ass-fucking!"

Two lockers down, Private Claude Creston tossed his towel at Isaac. "All right, man," he said, smiling, "we get it. Give the guy a break."

Isaac caught the towel in mid-air and sneered at Jason's would-be saviour. "Hey, Jason!" he called, waving the towel in the air. "I got a rag for ya! I'm pretty sure you're gonna need this!" He tossed it back at Claude, who caught it in an awkward, gangly sort of way. "Seriously, though," Isaac continued, his voice taking on a more somber tone, "you better get a good mop, cause you're gonna be leakin' the captain's cum out your ass for a week! No joke. Cum all over the place!"

"You can all suck my cock," Jason said between clenched teeth, struggling mightily to control his anger as he finally reached the door and punched in the code.

"Help us find it and you got yourself a deal!" Isaac called back, amidst various other insults and catcalls.

The door slid open, and Jason strode out.

★ ★ ★

"Close the door," Captain Desmond Halford said as he stared down at his computer monitor. Jason did so, then stood before the captain's desk and waited. The room was silent except for the odd tapping sound from Halford's keyboard.

"You wanted to see me, sir?" Jason asked, struggling to hide his irritation at being called into the old man's office.

Halford looked up. "Yes," he replied. He then hunched over his keyboard and continued typing.

*Fucking cock gobbler.*

Of all the faggot-assed so-called "superiors" he had to deal with, Jason hated Halford the most. They all gave him shit from time to time, but most of them seemed to recognise Jason's innate value to the Corps, delivering their tongue-lashings in a very business-like, *sorry, it's just my job* kind of way. Halford, on the other hand, actually seemed to enjoy crapping on Jason, taking every opportunity possible to call him into his office and give him an enthusiastic dressing-down. Jason suspected it was some kind of inferiority thing. Or maybe the old faggot was just gay for him.

Jason stewed quietly for a few moments longer, occasion-ally turning to glance at a small plastic chair to the right of the door. Though his meetings with Halford were never ex-actly casual, Jason was sometimes allowed to sit while the old man yelled at him. He looked down at the floor for a mo-ment, then took a step toward the seat.

"Did I tell you to sit?" the captain roared, rising from be-hind his desk.

Jason stepped back, snapping to attention. "No, sir, you did not sir!"

"Damn fucking right I didn't! And you know what else I didn't do?"

Believing this to be a rhetorical question, Jason remained silent. Halford strode around his desk and stood inches away from the young soldier, practically screaming in his face: "I said do you know what else I didn't do!"

"No, sir!" Jason replied, a hint of defiance showing in his eyes. "What else didn't you do, sir?"

"I didn't tell you to assault the puppet-techs, that's what I didn't do! In fact, I distinctly remember telling you *not* to assault the puppet-techs! Do you remember me telling you that, Private J-538? Do you remember me telling you *not* to assault the puppet-techs?"

Jason paused, struggling to keep his temper in check. "Yes sir!" he replied after a moment. "I remember you telling me not to assault the puppet-techs, sir!"

Just as Halford was drawing in a breath in preparation for his next verbal assault, the door chimed, simultaneously opening a crack. Halston's young secretary poked her head in. "Captain Halston?"

He looked over Jason's shoulder. "Yes?" he snapped.

"There's a haemo-tech here looking for Private J-538. He says he needs to give him his Q4 shot."

The captain glared at Jason. "Did you get your Jabber on the way here?"

"No sir," he answered between clenched teeth. "The captain requested that I report to him immediately, sir." The haemo-tech had actually intercepted Jason as he was leaving the simulation prep room, but the look on the young trainee's face had caused him to pause, missing his chance.

Captain Halford scowled at Jason for a moment, then shook his head and sighed. "Send him in, Carol."

The secretary left, and for a moment the two men stood silently glaring at each other. Finally a middle aged, white-smocked man poked his head in. "Sir?"

The captain kept his eyes on Jason. "Come on in."

The haemo-tech glanced nervously at the back of Jason's head, then hurriedly stepped in and closed the door behind him. He took another step, stopping just behind and to the left of the young soldier. "I need to give Private J-538 his Q4 shot, sir," he said, rather sheepishly.

Halford nodded. "You go right ahead."

The haemo-tech glanced nervously at Jason, then back at the captain. The tension in the air was palpable, nearly overwhelming. "Right here, sir?" He asked, the slightest hint of a tremble in his voice. The young trainee was obviously being chewed out, and having a haemo-tech in the room to witness the event might not be safe, especially for the haemo-tech. Unfortunately he was running out of time. Jason had received his daily Q4 shot that morning, but discharging his implants had caused a chemical reaction which would reduce the drug's effectiveness dramatically. If he didn't get a top up right away, his body would begin to reject the implants, and then the real trouble would start …

The captain turned and circled back around his desk. Once again locking eyes with Jason, he removed the thin leather glove from his right hand and tossed it next to his keyboard.

While Jason had implants on the first and second knuckles of both hands, the captain's were present only on the first two fingers of his right. They were slightly larger than Jason's, and delivered a considerably larger jolt of electricity; Jason's were designed to disable Squelchers, the captain's were designed to disable cocky young soldiers.

"Yes," Halford said, "right here."

The haemo-tech swallowed nervously, emitting an audible gulp which might have been humorous under other circumstances. He took a step closer to Jason and fumbled in his utility belt for a syringe containing the synthetic haemoglobin which served as a suspension medium for the anti-rejection drugs.

Halford sat behind his desk. "Now, where were we?" The haemo-tech glanced apprehensively at Jason, who turned his head slightly to glare back at him. The technician quickly averted his gaze. "Look at me, Private!" the captain yelled. Glowering, Jason snapped back to attention. "I said, where were we?"

Jason clenched his jaw. "We were discussing my memory, sir," he replied, a tinge of sarcasm in his voice.

The technician hastily produced a vial from his belt and proceeded to suck a tiny amount of anti-rejection drug into the syringe. He paused a moment as the blue compound mixed with the haemoglobin.

"Yes we were, smart-ass!" The captain bellowed. "As I recall, you said you remembered me telling you not to assault the puppet-techs! Funny thing is, your sim video shows you doing just that! Care to explain that, you fucking useless piece of shit?" He looked at the haemo-tech, who was holding the syringe and glancing nervously between Jason and the captain. "Belay that!" He snapped, then nodded to the tech, who quickly moved in to administer the shot. His hands trembled slightly as the needle punctured the young man's neck. Once the syringe was empty and the needle safely extracted, the haemo-tech took a step back and looked at the captain expectantly.

"You stay here," Halford said, his implants glinting menacingly beneath the fluorescent lights overhead. The tech emitted another audible gulp.

"Sir!" Jason blurted, glancing angrily at the Captain's balled fist. "The puppet-tech breached simulation protocol, sir!"

"Is that so? Please explain."

"Sir, the puppet-tech attacked me after the Squelcher was disabled, sir!"

The captain grunted derisively. "The Squelcher was disabled, was it?"

"Yes, sir!"

"And you're sure of that?"

"Yes, sir! I administered an electrical current to the lateral meta ganglion at the base of the Squelcher's second proximal appendage, sir! The Squelcher displayed all the proper signs of a successful disablement, sir! There was no way it could have hit me like it did!"

"All the proper signs, you say?"

"Yes, sir!"

"Was the distillate mandibular fold yellow?"

Jason blinked. "Sir … I assume it was not, sir!"

Halford looked away momentarily, then took a deep breath and once again faced the young man. "You *assume* it was not."

Jason swallowed, then averted his gaze. "Yes, sir!"

"But you didn't actually *look* at it?"

Jason paused as his anger gave way to uncertainty. He had, in fact, neglected to check the colour of the creature's mandibular fold. Though he had been told several times during training that a yellow fold was sometimes a sign of incomplete disablement, and that a creature displaying said yellow fold was apt to attack in unusual and unexpected ways, he had also heard from seasoned veterans of the Squelcher war that these conditions simply never occurred in actual combat situations. As such, Jason had considered it safe, not to mention logical, to ignore this indicator and concentrate solely on what he perceived to be actual threats. He was just now starting to wonder if he had made a mistake. "No, sir, I did not look at it, sir! Yellow distillate mandibular folds do not happen in actual combat, and …" He looked at the captain, then, stiffening visibly, quickly looked away. "And I believe the puppet-tech was wrong to incorporate that particular element into the training scenario, sir!"

Captain Halford practically flew around his desk, once again placing himself face to face with the young soldier. Jason flinched, a drop of sweat flinging off the tip of his nose. The haemo-tech emitted a little yelp. "And what if I told you I instructed the puppet-tech to incorporate that particular element into the training scenario?" he howled. "What if I told you that the yellow distillate mandibular fold does in fact happen in actual combat situations? What if I told you that you were a useless, cocky, stupid-fuck cock sucker? What would you have to say to that?"

Jason's eyes blazed with anger. "I would say the captain couldn't possibly know that, since he's never set foot on an actual Squelcher ship, and I would also say that the puppet-tech is a hopeless old cunt, and he'd be more useful wiping my ass than fucking up my training sessions!" He paused, breathing heavily. When he continued, his voice practically dripped with derision. "Sir."

For a moment the room was silent, save for the sound of the beleaguered technician's feet shuffling nervously on the floor. Finally, the captain relaxed and returned to his desk, where he picked up his glove and began carefully placing it back over his hand. He turned toward the haemo-tech, who looked like he might throw up. "What's your name, tech?"

"Frederick Jallison, sir," he sputtered.

Halford sat down, once again studying his monitor. "Thank you, Mister Jallison. You can go now."

"Thank you, sir," said Frederick, turning and exiting so quickly that the captain had to stifle a chuckle.

"Tell me, Private," Halford said after a moment, "how long until you're eligible for active duty?"

Jason stared at the floor, frowning. "Eleven days, sir."

"Uh huh," The captain switched off his monitor, then leaned back to look at him. "Listen, son, this is how it is— you're one of the best trainees we've got, and we've put a lot of money and effort into making you what you are. More than you know. The puppet-tech you assaulted is one of our best. We've also put a lot of money and effort into making *him* what he is. Now granted he's easier to replace than you are, but that's not the issue here. The issue is that your cocki-ness is a liability to us and to the war effort. We can't afford to have people screwing up in battle—it's just too hard getting you there in the first place, and there's just too much at stake to risk losing the fight. Do you understand?"

Jason took a deep breath and answered grudgingly. "Yes, sir."

"Well, I hope you do. But I think you should know that you've got one foot over the line here. There have been several occasions when I've suggested to the brass that you have consequences for your asshole behaviour. I've pushed to have you grounded, or even have your Booster Brigade privileges revoked, but the powers that be thought it would be unwise to deny our star pupil the chance to blow off a little steam. They wanted to just watch you for a while, see if you didn't shape up on your own. Well, you obviously haven't. I'll be filing a level 3 probationary order against you today." Jason's eyes went wide. "With my recommendation," the captain continued, "and that of a military haemo-tech, the order will automatically be put through without the need for review. After witnessing your insubordinate behaviour here today, I'm sure tech Frederick Jallison won't hesitate to back me up. And by the way, you so much as look at him sideways and I'll have you tossed into the Rim. That goes for the poor old guy you put the boots to today. Do you understand?"

Jason had to struggle to keep his jaw off the floor. *You sneaky faggot son of a whore.* When the captain had asked the tech to stay, Jason had assumed it was because Halford was planning on dispensing some discipline, in which case the captain would need a quick Jabber himself. Turns out what he had really needed was a witness—taking his glove off had just been a ploy to get Jason even more worked up than he already was. Well, it had worked; Jason had gotten just angry enough to dig himself a nice big hole, and now he was on probation. That meant at least another month before he could graduate. One more screw up and he could actually be out for good.

Jason stood motionless for a moment, the anger which

had just recently started to ease now suddenly returning with a vengeance, threatening to send him over the edge— quite possibly ending his career as a Flasher before it had even truly started.

Halford watched patiently as a cavalcade of emotions played across the young man's face. Eventually, Jason's expression turned slack, and his shoulders drooped. "Yes, sir," he said quietly, "I understand, sir."

"Good," the captain said, once again powering up his monitor. "Dismissed."

Jason stalked through the halls of the training facility stark naked, his training suit balled up in his hand. Heads turned as he entered the medical unit, several female staff pausing to admire the young man's physique while most of the males simply shrugged, shaking their heads. When Jason stopped in front of one of three "Privilege Suites" which lined the hall past the nurses' station, Martin Baker, the hae-mo-tech assigned to the rooms, rushed to intercept him.

"Whoa, Jason, hang on a second," he said, throwing a quick glance behind him. Several nurses were watching nervously.

"That's 'Private Crawford' to you, fuckwad!" Jason barked, thrusting his training suit towards him.

Baker grabbed the garment from his hand. "Yeah, yeah … okay … Private Crawford." He paused for a second, fidgeting with the suit as Jason punched in his access code. "Look," he said, his expression pleading, "you gotta take it easy on this one, okay?" The door panel chimed as the code was accepted, and Jason pressed his thumb on a pad beneath the keys.

"Fuck you," Jason replied, as the computer processed his genetic information, confirming both his identity and his account standing. Baker glanced at the nurses again. One of them was almost in tears.

"Wait! Wait … listen," the tech said hurriedly as the door unlocked itself with a muffled *clunk*, "she might not get pregnant if you rough her up too much." Baker immediately frowned and looked away, disgusted at himself for what he felt he had to say to appeal to the private's particular way of thinking. The door irised open, revealing a small privacy alcove and a second door beyond.

Jason shot Baker a furious glance. "Did you give her a fucking fertility shot?" he growled through clenched teeth.

"Well yeah, of course I did, but …"

"Then she'd better fucking get pregnant, you useless prick!" he shouted. "Or it'll be your fucking *cock* on my mother's mantel!" And with that Private J-538 strode into the alcove, stroking his half-erect penis as the door sighed shut behind him.

Haemo-tech Martin Baker, looking beaten and ashamed, turned and left.

## June 12, 2769

It was another beautiful evening on the USS McAdam. The ship's artificial sun was just below the western horizon, and a glorious, multicoloured light show was once again beginning in the east, courtesy of the Squelchers' energy beams cascading across the ship's photonic shields high above. Families strolled contentedly through the residential streets nestled safely within the ship's Core, adults stopping to chat as children ran about, often kneeling by the large curbside vents, relishing the sensation as warm, oxygen-rich air rushed past their face.

In a modest, well-kept bungalow at 68 Waterford Cove, one small family (the members of whom had taken their stroll earlier that day) was expecting company. The father, a slightly overweight, balding middle-aged man, helped his thin, pretty and also middle-aged wife set the dishes for the evening meal, which was to be held tonight in the formal dining room. A boy of about 11 tossed sofa cushions at his older sister, who, having spent the last hour before the mirror, was now watching anxiously through the living room window for the arrival of their guests.

"Angie!" the mother called from the other room. "Mind yourself, now! I can see right up that skirt of yours!"

The 13-year-old sighed dramatically, climbing down from her vantage point on the couch and pulling her skirt down as far as it would go, which was not very far at all. "Mom, you told me to wear this!"

"Yes I did. But I didn't tell you to go flashing your panties to anyone who might happen to be looking in your direction."

"Yeah, Angie," the boy said, tossing one final cushion at his sister's head. "the only person who's supposed to see your panties is Super-Sexy Private Jason Studly-Butt, remember?"

The young girl threw the cushion back at the boy. "Shut up, you little puke! I am so going to rip your face off!"

"All right, now, settle down, the both of you," the father said, settling into a recliner and switching on the news feed.

"Dexter!" the mother said. "Shut that thing off! They'll be here any minute!"

"Don't worry dear," he replied, "I'm sure they'll be late as usual."

"They most certainly will not! And I will not have you lazing about in front of the news feed when they get here."

Sighing heavily, Dexter switched off the television and struggled out of his chair.

"We need to show Claude we support him," the mother continued as she lit a candle for the table's centrepiece. "And we need to show respect for his friends."

"Yes dear," he replied, wandering over to the fireplace and gazing idly at the assorted knick-knacks on the mantel. "What's this doing here?" he asked, picking up a small acrylic cube. "You know Claude hates it when you put these out."

"Oh, pshaw!" his wife replied. "He's just too modest. Besides, we want to show our guests how proud we are, don't we?"

Dexter shook his head, frowning. "No, we can't leave this out." He turned towards the couch where his youngest son sat fidgeting. "Raymond, go put this in your brother's room."

"I'll do it!" Angie said, springing to her feet.

"No, let Raymond do it."

"Yeah, let me do it!" Raymond said, bouncing up and down on the couch. "I know where all his stuff goes!"

"Well somebody take it!" the mother exclaimed. "They'll be here any minute!"

Skipping over to where her father stood, Angie reached up and grabbed the cube. "Be right back!" she said as she trotted off towards the hallway.

Alone in her brother's room, the young girl took a moment to study the item. Measuring 3 inches on all sides, the cube was cast in crystal clear acrylic, with a glossy black base. A bronze plaque on one side read: "In Honour of Private Claude Creston, Trainee, Elite Flasher Squad", and on the next line, the Flasher motto: "Strength, Courage, Virility". Deep within the cube was a tiny human embryo.

Angie turned the thing over in her hands, eyes wide with wonder ... and fear.

For the past two years, Angie had been part of the West Henderson Legion of Boosterettes, spending her weekends doing community work, as well as learning the skills she would need when she became a full-fledged Booster Girl.

Pleasuring the young Flasher Cadets in the Privilege Suites was a very high-profile, not to mention, very rewarding career. As exciting and prestigious as it was, however, the job did have some drawbacks; though the cadets were technically not allowed to harm them, the Booster Girls were expected to do everything in their power to please the young men, and if that included soaking up some of their left-over aggression after a simulation, well ...

Angie held the cube close to her face, squinting to make out the details of the little plastic-coated person. At 32 days, the embryo was little more than a lump of mottled pink tissue, its various bumps and ridges bearing little resemblance to anything human. It was more than large enough to see, however, and as such was deemed suitable for display as proof of the Flasher cadets' boundless strength and virility.

Though Angie had been assured repeatedly that the procedure was painless, she still became breathless at the thought of having a machine thrust into her, and a piece of her insides ripped out.

"Angie, will you come out of there!" her mother cried, exasperated. "They've just pulled up!"

Surprised out of her morbid reverie, the young girl quickly placed the cube onto her brother's desk and ran out of the room.

Outside, three young men where boisterously piling out of a small vehicle. Resplendent in their formal Cadet uniforms, all three sported new hairstyles, their short locks gleaming with a variety of iridescent colouring products. Jason, the first one out, immediately stomped through the artificial river stones covering most of the front yard, stopping just short of a small circular picket fence. Inside was a tiny shrub with thick glossy green leaves and bright orange flowers. "Hey, don't touch the bush, man!" Claude called as he pried himself from the back seat of the electric car. "My mom'll kill me!"

"Fuckin' relax, man," Isaac said as he closed the driver's side door. "Nobody's gonna touch your mom's bush."

"Come on, Isaac, that's not funny," Claude replied, looking slightly wounded.

"Yes it is," Jason said conversationally, leaning over the fence until his nose was just barely touching one of the leaves. "This thing's looking pretty good. Finally got your dad to stop pissing on it, eh?"

Claude blinked, "What? That doesn't even make sense!" He joined Jason by the fence, checking to make sure nothing untoward had been done to the little bush. They were the only house on the block to have a real plant in their yard (one of the many little perks which came with having a family member in the military), and Claude's mother was more than a little attached to it.

"Come on guys, let's go!" Isaac called from the front stoop. "I'm starving!"

"All right, all right, hang on." Claude trotted towards the door, glancing over his shoulder to make sure Jason was following. To Claude's surprise and relief, he was. He pushed past Isaac, took a deep breath, then rang the doorbell. A moment later Mrs. Jennifer Creston appeared, looking radiant in a bright blue, ankle-length dinner gown.

"Welcome to the Creston household," she said demurely, reciting the age-old traditional dinner greeting as was the duty of every respectable wife and mother. "It is my pleasure to have you join us for this evening meal, and it is my utmost wish that you do not leave this evening wanting."

"Many thanks, good woman," Claude replied self-consciously. He found these stupid little rituals fairly embarrassing. His mother did love them though ... "Please allow me to introduce my party." He cleared his throat, then paused, catching a glimpse of his sister standing in the foyer. She was dressed in bright red stilettos, a ridiculously short skirt, and an extremely tight sweater made of some thin, stretchy fabric. Her nipples were so erect he wondered at how they didn't poke holes in her top. Obviously her mother, always eager to make a good impression when company was over, had iced them down while she helped her daughter get dressed. He cleared his throat again, and continued: "I, of course, am Private Claude Creston, your eldest son, Member in Good Standing of the USS McAdam Special Corps, presently in training with the Elite Flasher Squad. With me are Private Isaac Masters, Member in Good Standing of the USS McAdam Special Corps, presently in training with the Elite Flasher Squad, as well as Private Jason Crawford, Mem-

ber in … um …" Claude glanced nervously at Jay, who shot
him a meaningful scowl. "I mean, soon to be a full member
of the Elite Flasher Squad," he finished quickly. After a brief
pause, the three young men bowed in unison.

"Please come in" Jennifer said, standing aside. The boys
entered the foyer and lined up to the right, from shortest to
tallest. This put Jason first, with Isaac, a mere inch taller,
second. Claude, who stood a good six inches taller than
Isaac, was third.

As slightness of build was an important sign of status
amongst the Flasher elite (not to mention a huge benefit
while fighting in the tight confines of a Squelcher ship), this
particular tradition was meant to represent the cadets' standing relative to each other. Though it was mostly symbolic,
Claude firmly believed that the tradition should be modified
to allow for other considerations. After all, it was plainly
clear that physically, Claude just barely qualified as Flasher
material; he saw no good reason to have to humiliate himself
by advertising the fact in his own home.

"Please allow me to introduce my family," Mrs. Creston
said, oblivious to her son's discomfiture. "I, of course, am
Jennifer Creston, matriarch of the Clan Creston. This is Dexter, Husband and Adjunct Councillor, Department of Non-
Organic Waste Reclamation." Dexter bowed slightly, a small,
embarrassed smile touching his lips. "Next to him is Angie,
Daughter and Member in Good Standing of the Booster Brigade's "Little Boosterettes". Angie giggled and waved. "And
next to Angie is Raymond, Youngest Son and Member in
Good Standing of the Crestview Valley Branch of the 'Flash
Tots." Ray stuck out his tongue.

After a few moments of silence, Mrs. Creston burst out
laughing, and opened her arms to embrace her eldest son.
"Come here, my little boy, give your mommy a kiss!" Claude
obliged as the others filed into the dining room, laughing
and exchanging greetings of a less formal nature.

The meal, having been laid out before the guests' arrival, began immediately. "Well, Jason," Mrs. Creston said as she scooped a large steaming gob of carbohydrates onto her plate, "when is your first assignment?"

"Well, I'll be graduating in a few weeks," he replied. "Then I'll be on call, so it could be anytime after that."

"Isn't it exciting!" she gushed, glancing across the length of the table to where her husband sat, quietly poking at a small chunk of protein. "A Flasher in our home! At our very own table no less!" She reached to her right and grabbed Angie's hand, giving it a little shake. Angie glanced up at Jason, then looked down and giggled. Next to her, Raymond made a little gagging noise, which everyone ignored. "A Full Member of the Elite Flasher Squad!" Mrs. Creston exclaimed, this time reaching to her left to grasp Jason's hand. "And only seventeen years of age! Can you imagine!"

Jason smiled with false modesty, his bright blue, gold-speckled eyes, dancing mischievously. "Oh, Mrs. Creston, it's no big deal, really ..."

"Oh, goodness!" she enthused, fluttering a hand above her breast. "Of course it is! It's just too exciting!" She gazed intently at the young man for a moment, then turned to face Claude's other friend. "And you, Isaac," she said, rearranging the napkin on her lap, "I imagine you'll be finished your training soon as well."

"With any luck I'll be done in a couple of months," he replied, giving Angie a little wink.

"That is just fantastic! Ooh, I am so proud of you boys!"

For a moment everyone sat quietly smiling at each other, except for Claude, who was looking downright crestfallen. Apparently noting his friend's unease, Isaac gave him a friendly jab with his elbow. "Claude's been tearing it up in the sims himself lately," he said. "Been puttin' the Squelchers down with style." Claude cast a suspicious glance towards his fellow cadet; though Isaac was generally a good guy, he usually didn't put up with Claude's self-pitying ways. He decided Isaac probably just felt bad for him, what with his mother gushing over everyone but her own son.

"Do you think he'll finish in time to do this year's parade with the two of you?" asked Mr. Creston, a note of cautious optimism in his voice.

Isaac looked at Claude, then opened his mouth to respond. Claude beat him to it. "Yes," he said, glaring at his father, "I think he will."

Mr. Creston cleared his throat. "No offence, son, but you'll be twenty next month. Someone your age who's already been through the program twice … Well, all I'm saying is maybe you could look into haemo-tech training. Or maybe a government position. I mean, you've always been interested in politics, and I could get you a couple of meetings with …"

"Dexter, that's enough," Mrs. Creston interrupted, her authoritative tone punctuated by an icy stare. "If our son says he'll make it, then he'll make it." Claude looked morosely at his father, then down at his plate. "Besides," she continued gamely, "we didn't raise our children to be failures, now, did we? And with Jason and Isaac around to show him the way …"

"Fuck!" Claude exclaimed, pounding the table with his fist. "Can we please change the fucking topic?"

Mrs. Creston was momentarily startled into silence. "Well of course, son," she said. "No need to be rude in front of company." She glanced around the table, made a nervous little coughing noise, then leaned back into her chair, quickly rearranging her dress. "If you want to talk about something else, then by all means we'll talk about something else. Why not?" She picked up her knife and fork, and began cutting into her protein. "We'll talk about Angie," she said, brightening visibly at the thought. "How on Earth could we not talk about her? Our little angel has just been promoted to Senior Boosterette!"

Jason looked at Isaac, eyebrows raised. He then turned towards Angie. "Congratulations!"

"Thanks," she replied, blushing furiously.

"Of course she just has the title now," Jennifer said, once again reaching out to grasp her daughter's hand. "She won't be starting her Privilege Suite duties until she turns fourteen."

"Of course," Jason said, grinning. "She will be in this year's parade though, won't she?"

"Oh, yes!" Mrs Creston replied gleefully. "I spoke with her Brigade Mother, and it's all set! She might even be on the same float as you!"

"Well, wouldn't that be great!" Jason said cheerfully. He nudged Isaac with his knee, then, pretending to rearrange the napkin on his lap, made a small masturbating motion. Isaac winked, then smiled and raised his glass in Angie's direction.

Claude sighed.

★ ★ ★

As Claude dug through his closet for a fresh uniform (his little brother had "accidentally" dumped a bowlful of savoury sauce on his pants), Jason browsed through the books in his friend's room. Mixed in with the graphic novels and works of popular fiction were a few more questionable titles, such as: "The Squelcher Fallacy" and "Shielding the Truth: Are We Really in Danger?". Though these books questioned the basic beliefs behind the Flasher system, they were actually required reading for all trainees; one had to learn the opposing viewpoint before one could be convinced of its incorrectness.

On a shelf next to Claude's bed were a pile of art books. Jason grabbed the one on top, a collection of paintings and sketches called: "I Dreamt of Trees". He flipped through it quickly, then went back to the title page.

## I Dreamt of Trees
*A Speculative Vision of Plant Life on Earth*
Paintings and Sketches by Michelle Bantam
Foreword by Terrence Gordman-Liev

The page had been signed by the artist, complete with a tiny sketch of what she imagined a pine tree might have looked like. Beneath the signature was a hand-written message from Jason.

> To Claude: I hope you enjoy this beautifully bound collection of homo erotic artwork. Just don't get too carried away, because I'm not getting you another one once the pages start sticking together.
>
>    Happy Birthday!
>
>    Jay

Jason smiled. "Hey, Claude," he said, bouncing the book on his knee, "I heard this bitch has some paintings on display at a gallery on the other side of the Core. Wanna go with me Sunday and check it out?"

Stripping off his stained trousers, Claude paused, then shook his head. "Nah, can't. My mom's taking me out for some mother-son time. Dinner and a movie kind of thing."

"Is that so?" Jason replied, frowning slightly. "Well how about Monday then?"

Claude tossed his pants into the laundry hamper and pulled a clean pair from the closet. "Uh, yeah, well … I don't know. I'll have to see what's going on."

Jay's frown deepened. "What? You're going to see some paintings is what's going on." He shook his head and grimaced. "Whatever. I don't want to hang around a bunch of faggotty art-types anyway."

Claude sighed. "Look, I'm sorry. I'll see, okay?"

"Yeah, whatever." Jay grabbed a pen from Claude's desk and scrawled an erect penis next to the artist's signature. He was adding cartoon semen when Claude snatched the book from his lap.

"What the fuck are you doing, you prick?" he said, glaring at his friend.

"What?" Jason said, feigning injury. "I thought you liked art."

Claude shook his head in disgust. "Look," he said, placing the book out of Jay's reach, "just don't touch anything, okay? That goes for both of you."

"What'd *I* do?" Isaac exclaimed, throwing his hands in the air.

"Whatever. Just leave my stuff alone."

"Whatever."

Claude shook his head, then began poking moodily through his sock drawer. He liked Jason well enough, despite his usually unpleasant nature. Truth was, neither of them had many real friends, and putting up with each other's differences was generally better than being alone. Claude figured it was just some kind of insecurity that caused Jason to lash out like he did. Case in point, Jay had once confided in him that most people only wanted to hang around with him because he was a big shot Flasher cadet, and otherwise didn't give a shit about him. Claude couldn't bring himself to believe that he fell into that category; he was a Flasher cadet himself, for crying out loud. Yet he had to admit that being seen with Jason did make him feel validated as a Flasher-in-training. Still, a person who would buy you a gift one day and deface it another ... Claude sometimes wondered why he bothered even speaking to the guy.

After a while Isaac wandered over to Claude's desk and peered at his collection of Booster Cubes. "Hey Claude," he said, picking one up and turning it over in his hand, "you're getting pretty good at faking these things. This one almost looks real."

"What looks real?" he asked, still frowning into his dresser drawer. "What the fuck are you talking about?"

"What he's talking about," Jason interjected as he leaped onto Claude's bed, stretching out with his hands behind his head, "is that a useless little faggot like you with half an inch of shrivelled pecker couldn't possibly procreate, fertility drugs or no fertility drugs."

"All right, enough! Just shut the fuck up!" Claude shouted, grabbing a pair of socks and stomping over to his desk. "And you!" he barked, snatching the cube away from Isaac. "I said *don't fucking touch!*"

"Whoa, whoa, little buddy!" Isaac replied, stepping back with his hands in the air. "I got it. No touchy the blocky. No problem." Isaac stepped carefully around his friend as Claude collected his trophies and placed them carefully into a drawer.

"Why do you keep hiding those, anyway?" Jason asked as Isaac took a seat on the end of the bed. "Some people might start to think you're a little low on the old Flasher pride."

Claude pushed the cubes tightly together, then moved the whole group over to the back corner of the drawer. "I got all the pride I need," he grumbled.

Like most children on the McAdam, Claude had been caught up in the Flasher hype from an early age. The thought of one day being zapped up to an alien ship and fighting for a just cause filled him with an electric kind of excitement. He recalled his fascination at seeing his first Booster Cube. The awards, the Privilege Suites, the "added bonuses" had all seemed fairly abstract to his young mind; these things were just decoration, fun in the way that a hidden prize in a box of candy was fun. As he grew older, however, his under-standing of the world, and the Flasher agenda, had begun to change; the abuse of young women, the killing—and even worse, displaying—of tiny, unborn children ... these things which he had once seen as exciting symbols of the Flasher war had more recently become a source of shame and inner turmoil.

"I guess I'm just not a big show-off," he mumbled, carefully placing a magazine over the cubes, "so just drop it."

"What do you mean, 'show off'?" Jay persisted. "Why wouldn't you want people to see these? A memento of time well spent in the Privilege Suites!" When Claude didn't reply, Jay sat up and looked at Isaac, a mischievous smile tugging at the corners of his mouth. "Don't you want to give Little Sis a preview of days to come?"

Claude's face abruptly twisted with rage as he spun around to face Jason. "Fuck you, man!" he cried, spit flying from his lips. "You stay away from her, you hear me, you sick fuck!" Jason and Isaac looked at each other, stunned. Jason chuckled quietly.

"Hey Isaac," he said, "you think I hit a nerve?"

Claude balled his fists, "I mean it, Jason! I'm not fucking around!"

"All right, all right, relax," Jay said, getting up to place an appeasing hand on his friend's shoulder. "I was just joshing. Skanky little cunt sisters are off limits." He turned towards Isaac, smiling. "Isn't that right, Isaac?"

Isaac glared fiercely. "Ok man," he said quietly. "You should probably shut up right about now." Claude glanced at him, grateful to have someone on his side for once.

"C'mon, guys!" Jay said, grinning. "Lighten up! We're supposed to be having a good time here!" Far from mollified, Claude glared, while Isaac shifted from one foot to another, refusing to make eye contact. "Fine then!" Jay exclaimed brightly. "Let's go get drunk!"

★ ★ ★

It was a typical Friday night at Core Plaza. Thousands

upon thousands of happy citizens wandered about the mall's perimeter, some in search of food and drink, some looking for entertainment, and others simply soaking up the festive atmosphere.

Of course, no trip to Core Plaza was complete without a stroll across the huge circular glass floor commonly known as the "Star Walk". Measuring exactly one mile in diameter, the Star Walk spanned the upper end of the USS McAdam's primary waste chute. Used mainly as a vent for the insanely dangerous radioactive gas created by the McAdam's PNTPD (photo-nuclear tri-phasic drive), the chute also served as a conduit for any unpleasant waste which could not be re-claimed by the ship's many complex recycling mechanisms. As the tube, by necessity, pierced the ship's photonic shields, the star walk now offered the populace their only truly clear view of space. On any given day, hundreds of people could be seen gazing in wonder at the breathtaking view below, from time to time emitting a small group cheer as a Squelcher ship would inexplicably fly below the mouth of the vent, only to be summarily torn apart in a maelstrom of glowing blue plasma. For many of the residents of the Good Ship McAdam, a Friday night "Star Stroll" was truly the highlight of their week.

For those who found the family friendly atmosphere a little too saccharine for their tastes, the plaza's second level offered a fine selection of taverns, brothels, drug dens and tattoo parlours, each catering to its own specific flavour of free-minded individual. At the moment two such free-minded individuals were tending to their comrade as he vomited over the second level balcony onto the happy Star Strollers below.

"Oh, man," Claude said, grasping his friend's arm in an at-tempt to prevent him from tumbling over the rail, "I think we might have overdid it a bit, ya think?"

Isaac, somehow managing to look suave while holding

Jason's other arm, smiled broadly. "Relax, man! Jason wanted to celebrate, so we're celebrating! You wouldn't want him to go out on his first mission without a proper send-off, would ya?"

Claude looked over the balcony and grimaced. A little girl was squawking loudly as her mother busily cleaned vomit from her hair. The father was speaking to a security guard, gesticulating enthusiastically towards the puke's apparent point of origin. "Oh, shit," Claude said quietly, "we'd better get out of here."

"You bet," Isaac replied as he grabbed Jason by the waist and hauled him over his shoulder, a thin stream of vomit running down the back of his shirt. "Follow me!"

Claude grunted in surprise as Jason's head flopped over onto his shoulder. Swearing under his breath, he gently shoved his friend aside. "C'mon, Isaac!" he said, looking past Jay to where his friend sat sprawled on the taxi's back seat. "Seriously, where are we going?"

"Don't worry about it," Isaac replied, winking. "Trust me, you're gonna love this."

"Yeah, well … I just don't like going this close to the Rim," Claude said, glancing nervously out the window.

Isaac tilted his head back and closed his eyes. "Yeah, well … you don't like fucking your mother either, but …"

"Hardy freakin' har!" Claude replied, turning his attention to the navigational display mounted behind the driver's seat. He was alarmed to see that they were now only a few blocks from Capston Bridge, one of the eight colossal structures joining the Core to the Rim. Though neighbourhoods in the Core were generally very clean and safe, conditions tended to deteriorate the closer you got to the Moat, with the areas near the bridges leaving quite a lot to be desired. "Seriously, this area seems kind of sketchy. And it stinks."

"It does *not* stink," Isaac replied, rolling his eyes. "I keep telling you that's all in your head."

"It's not all in my head!" Claude snapped. "*I* keep telling *you*, the closer we get to the Moat, the more it stinks. I mean, c'mon! It's full of shit for fuck's sake! How can you possibly not smell that?"

"Please ..." Isaac said, waving a hand dismissively, "the Moat is a freakin' marvel of engineering. Don't you read the Infrastructure Updates in the papers? Seriously, man, whatever you're smelling, it's not coming from there."

Claude crossed his arms, frowning. He had in fact read the Updates on several occasions, and they always said more or less the same thing: that all of the stinky air from the moat was being collected and purified, ensuring a safe and pleasant atmosphere for every one of the 700,000 citizens of the Good Ship McAdam. Well, whatever the papers said, his nose said different.

Claude looked at Isaac, then reached across Jason to punch him in the shoulder. "Chill out, man!" he said. "I mean, hey! Does Jay look worried to you?"

Claude grudgingly turned towards their friend, who was sprawled out between them, deeply unconscious. "No," he grumbled, "Jay does not look worried ... more like dead if you ask me." He sat in silence for a moment, staring morosely at his intoxicated comrade. "Actually," Claude said quietly, "he really does seem out of it. Do you think there's something wrong with him?"

"Well, he likes to jerk off in his dad's underwear drawer. I guess you could say that's wrong."

"Come on, man, I'm serious! I'm getting a little concerned here."

Isaac sat up. "I swear, Claude," he said, "you have got to be the biggest little crybaby faggot in the Core! There's nothing wrong with Gay Jay. He just had a couple of snoozers out at the Plaza."

Claude spun to face him. "You gave Jason *snoozers*? Are you fucking crazy?"

"What? I only gave him two ..."

Claude bent forward and buried his face in his hands. Snoozers were high potency sleeping pills; one snoozer would give you a solid, restful night's sleep, while two snoozers would put you into a kind of coma which lasted anywhere from eight to twelve hours. "Ah man, Isaac ..." he groaned, "that shit's dangerous! And mixed with alcohol ... Fuck! What were you thinking?"

"Oh, relax, Claude!" Isaac replied, rolling his eyes. "Jay can handle it. Besides, when you see what I have planned, you'll change your tune. Trust me." He looked at Jason, then made a show of carefully adjusting the collar on his sleeping friend's shirt. "Why do you care so much anyway? You're the one who's always saying what an asshole he is."

"Yeah, well, you're an asshole too."

"Granted," Isaac said, grinning. After a moment he leaned toward Claude. "Listen," he said quietly, "we both saw how he was eyeing your sister,"

Claude tensed instantly, eyes blazing. "Don't even fucking go there!" he growled.

Isaac quickly leaned back, hands in the air. "Whoa, big boy, settle down. You know I'd never touch her. And I'm sure Jason probably wouldn't either. I'm just sayin' is all."

Claude relaxed, but only slightly. "Yeah," he said, crossing his arms and gazing out the window. "Maybe we should just not talk for a while."

"All right buddy," Isaac replied, flashing his best conciliatory smile, "you got it."

★ ★ ★

Bert Lasalle leaned against the side of the truck, sucking on a NicoStix and nodding his head to the tunes drifting from the driver's side window. Things were generally slow for him when he worked this close to the Moat, and tonight was no different—only six bodies so far and less than 30 minutes until he crossed the bridge into the Rim. Bert didn't mind. In fact, screwing the pooch on company time suited him just fine.

He liked his job all right, but he didn't like his bosses; they tended to dress a little fancy for his taste, and had a habit of drinking their caffeine drinks with foamy protein solution and little bits of candy shit on top. *Fucking queers.*

He thumbed a button on the inhaler, ejecting the spent cartridge into his pocket, then looked to the east, where jagged white bolts of energy flashed and danced near the horizon. "Flash 'em up, boys," he muttered under his breath as he pulled another cartridge from the pack. "Flash 'em up and fuck 'em up."

Headlights momentarily illuminated the side of Bert's truck, rousing him from his lazy reverie. "Bout fucking time," he muttered, tucking his NicoStix into his pocket. He wasn't really irritated at his cousin for being late—not like he had much else to do anyway. What really irked him was that Isaac was pressuring him into doing something stupid and risky. He liked his cousin, but there was such a thing as asking too much. If Isaac hadn't promised to sneak him into a Privilege Suite next week, he would have probably told him to shove it. *Fuckin' right.*

He walked around to the back of the truck and watched as Isaac and some tall gangly guy dragged a little blond guy out of the cab and laid him on the sidewalk. The cab driver seemed hesitant to leave the kid out here in such an obviously unconscious state, but a little cajoling and a fat tip from Isaac saw him merrily on his way. Once the cab was safely out of sight, Isaac and the other guy grabbed the kid and carried him over to the back of the truck.

"It's about fuckin' time you guys got here!" Bert complained, swinging open the heavy double doors and climbing into the back of the truck. "You think I got nothin' better to do than wait around here with my thumb up my ass?"

Isaac smiled what he hoped was his most winning smile. "Ah, don't be like that, Bertie old boy. Aren't you glad to see your favourite cousin?"

"I'd rather see the inside of a fuckin' Privilege Suite," Bert grunted.

"Okay, okay, just relax. I promise I'm gonna make this worth your while."

"Yeah, well ya' fuckin' better," Bert replied, quickly undoing the latches which held the stretcher in place. "If I don't smell me some Booster Girl pussy next week, there's gonna be trouble. I ain't fuckin' around here."

"Okay, okay. I got it," Isaac said, shaking his head. "By the way, this is my buddy Claude, and the sleepy guy there is Jay."

"Don't care."

Sighing, Isaac turned to Claude. "C'mon, help me get Jay closer to the truck."

"What? What the fuck are you talking about?" Claude said. "What the fuck's going on?" Frowning, he stepped closer to the vehicle and peered through the doors. Inside were several rows of shelves, mostly empty. A few held large black plastic bags with zippers across the top.

"Are you fucking kidding me?" he exclaimed, obviously alarmed. "Is this a fucking *meat truck*?" His eyes went wide as a new thought hit him. "Holy shit, Isaac," he cried, "you're not gonna fucking kill him, are you?" Please, tell me you're not gonna fucking kill him!"

"Hey!" Bert bellowed. "Keep it the fuck down!" He stuck his head out the door and looked around nervously. Taking his own advice, he lowered his voice. "This ain't exactly supposed to be no fuckin' public event!" He glared at Isaac. "Didn't you tell this guy what's going on?"

"No, he didn't," Claude said, eyeing his friend reproachfully.

"All right, just chill," Isaac said. "Bert, you set up your stuff, and Claude, follow me and I'll explain everything." He took his friend's arm and began guiding him towards the sidewalk.

"Just fuckin' hurry it up!" Bert grumbled as he man-handled the gurney off the back of the truck. "I have to be across the Shit in twenty minutes!"

Isaac raised a placating hand. "No worries."

Isaac led Claude to a phone booth about forty feet from the truck. He glanced back at Bert, then guided his friend around to the other side of the booth. Once he was satisfied they would have an acceptable amount of privacy, he leaned his head towards Claude's and spoke in a conspiratorial whisper. "Listen, Claude, all we're doing is pulling a prank on Jay, right? We're gonna put him on the truck, he's gonna wake up in the Reclamation Centre." Clearly agitated, Claude opened his mouth to object. "Whoa, whoa, hang on a minute," Isaac said, placing a hand on his friend's shoulder. "Let me finish. He's gonna wake up in the Reclamation Centre, then he's gonna laugh like crazy and get someone there to drive him home. Okay?"

Claude blinked. Surely Isaac couldn't be serious. "Is this a joke?" he asked slowly.

"Yeah, I told you, it's a joke! A prank!"

"On me."

"What? No, man! On Jay. Trust me, he's gonna love it!"

Claude shook his head, frowning fiercely; he couldn't be-lieve Isaac would actually consider doing this. Sending a Flasher into the Transitional Zone was no joke.

Before the Squelcher crisis, citizens of the USS McAdam had enjoyed great freedom to travel just about anywhere on the ship. Soon after the first attack, however, residents of the Rim were discouraged from crossing into the Core while, under the guise of the continuing Ship Restructuring Program, the powers that be began truly plundering the Rim's already depleted resources to support the fledgling Squelcher War. Within five years, the Rim had been completely sealed off from the Core, with highly-guarded police outposts being built on the inner side of every bridge to ensure the increasingly disgruntled Rim-Dwellers stayed put.

The only exception to this was the bridge leading to the Transitional Zone, a small, walled-off neighbourhood at the Rim end of one of the bridges. Though physically located in the Rim, the Zone was technically part of the Core, housing several important government offices and a few less-palatable utilities, such as the Infectious Disease Centre and the Reclamation Centre, whose main job was to recycle human corpses into food. The area was also home to the Transitional Zone Work Program, a government initiative which offered jobs to Rim-Dwellers with the goal of eventually integrating them into Core society. Though there existed a police outpost between the Transitional Zone and the Rim proper, there was also a smaller outpost on the Core side of the bridge, whose main concern was controlling the flow of Core-Dwellers into and out of the Zone.

As a rule, the general population was not allowed into the Transitional Zone, for both safety and security purposes. One group, however, was flat-out forbidden from entering the Zone. These were the Flashers and Flashers-in-training, who, though generally held in extremely high esteem by residents of the Core, were mostly despised by Rim-Dwellers, and as such were considered a possible target for unhappy clients of the Work Program. Though most Core citizens, as well as some government officials, believed the danger to be minimal, those at the highest levels of power, i.e. Flasher High Command, claimed that even the smallest risk was absolutely unacceptable, given the Flashers' immense value in the battle against the Squelchers. As such, any Flashers unlucky enough to be apprehended in the Transitional Zone were subject to severe punishment.

"No, no, no …" Claude blurted, shaking his head, "no way! He's not gonna love it—he's gonna be pissed! And no one's gonna just *give him a ride home*! Isaac, he's gonna get *arrested*—you gotta know that!"

Isaac shook his head and smiled. "No one's gonna get arrested, Claude. Why are you so uptight all the time? Tell you what, after this I'll take you back to the Plaza and buy you a couple of drinks, whaddya say?"

"I say fuck you! He probably will get arrested, and you know what, we'll probably get arrested too! My mom'll kill me! And Jason will probably get kicked out of the Academy, then *he'll* kill me! And you too!" Claude brought his hands to his head and made a small, strangled whining sound. "Isaac, he's on probation, for fuck's sake! What the hell are you thinking?"

Isaac sighed heavily, then looked down at his feet. "All right," he said, straightening up and looking Claude in the eye, "this is how it is. Jason probably *will* get in trouble for this, and I say good for him. That little prick's had this coming for a long time."

"What the fuck are you talking about?" Claude whined, near tears.

"You know what I mean."

Claude swiped a hand across his eyes. Truth was, Jason *did* have something coming … but *this*? "I know," he whined, "Jay's done some pretty bad shit, but this is too much! We *all* do bad shit! We're Flasher Cadets, for fuck's sake! We're practically *supposed* to!"

Isaac stepped closer. "Yeah, you're right," he said, lowering his voice. "We're Flasher Cadets, and we do bad things. But we don't do *really* bad things. And we don't do them to each other."

Claude's shoulders slumped. He thought he knew what

was coming, but he hoped he was wrong. "What are you talking about, Isaac?" he whispered.

"I'm saying he did my sister."

Claude emitted a strangled sob. "Oh, man ..."

"Yeah that's right," Isaac continued through gritted teeth. "He'll smile and swear up and down that friends and family are off limits, but it's all bullshit! That's why Cindy *really* had to quit the Booster Brigade! And it's his fault she can't fucking see out of her left eye! That cock sucker nearly killed her!"

"Oh, man ..." Claude was crying freely now, big tears rolling down his cheeks and dripping onto the sidewalk. He had been told that Isaac's sister had been hurt in a car accident. It had been a hard time for Isaac's family, dealing with Cindy's injuries, her withdrawal from the Booster Brigade, the family's loss of status and reduction in benefits ... "Are you sure it was him?" he pleaded. "I mean really, *really* sure?"

Isaac nodded soberly. "Yeah, I'm sure. She told us when we saw her in the hospital. We talked to Halford, but he decided we should fucking pretend it never happened. 'In the best interests of the Corps and their families' bullshit. Then he said some crap about secretly kicking Jay's ass over it, but ..."

Claude wiped his nose with the back of his hand, then shook his head. He had always liked Cindy. And Angie ... he worried a lot about Angie.

"What if *we* get in trouble?" he said quietly. "Messing with Jay is one thing, fucking up our own lives is another story."

Isaac leaned closer to his friend. "We won't get in trouble. We were all drunk and we got jumped by a bunch of guys. Don't know who they were, can't really remember what happened. Right?"

Claude dried his face with his sleeve. "Well ... what about your cousin?" he said uncertainly, pointing back in the direction of the truck.

"What, that dumb fuck? He's an asshole—don't worry about him."

Claude gave him a look. *Seriously?*

"All right, all right, fine," he said, rolling his eyes. "Look, we've got him all worked out too. He was loading a body when a bunch of yahoos rushed him. He ran around to the front of the truck when one of them tried to get into the driver's seat. The others must have loaded Jay into the truck while Bert was wrestling with the guy up front. After a few minutes the yahoos took off, Bert wasn't hurt, and he figured everything was hunky-dory. Sound good?"

Claude relaxed a little, but he still didn't seem convinced. "Oh man, I don't know … They're gonna question us. We'll have to get our stories straight …"

A tentative smile played at the corners of Isaac's mouth. "Don't worry, Claude old boy. Me and Bert have got everything squared away, and you and me'll practice our story on the way home. I'm sure we'll even have time to go over it a few more times before they question us."

"Well …" Claude said, rubbing his temples. His head ached. Things were moving too fast, and he wasn't entirely convinced this was a good plan.

Still, he *was* starting to like the idea of putting Jason in his place … especially after Isaac's revelation.

"All right," Claude said finally. "All right."

Isaac clapped his friend on the back and grinned.

## June 13, 2769

Jason groaned and turned on his side. He felt incredibly tired and unwell, and his head was pounding like a jackhammer. He tried for a few moments to go back to sleep, but the pain was simply too great. He opened his eyes to absolute darkness, then tried to sit up. His head got caught in the blanket, holding him down. After a brief struggle, he gave up and flopped onto his back.

His bed felt hard this morning. Actually, it felt really hard. And come to think of it, his blanket felt kind of weird too—sort of rubbery and slippery. Jason reached down to scratch his belly, and realised that he was still fully dressed.

*What the fuck's going on?* he thought, alarmed and now slightly more awake. He struggled to remember the events of the night before. He remembered going to the Plaza with Isaac and Fag Boy, drinking at a few bars, getting a blow job from some big-titted skank, more bars, then … nothing.

Jason once again tried to sit up, the tiniest inkling of panic germinating deep within his mind. Once again the blanket grabbed his head, and as he felt around he realized he was actually in some kind of rubber sleeping bag, with the zipper done up.

"All right, take it easy …" he muttered to himself as he

fought to stay calm. "You're just camped out ... *some-where* ... open the bag and you'll be good." He felt along the zipper for the pull, but could not find one. After a little more searching, he finally poked his finger through a small opening above and behind his head, where the zipper had not been fully done up. Little did he know that this small opening was the only thing between him and death by suffocation.

He pushed the end of the zipper apart until the opening was big enough for his hand, then reached out and grasped the outer pull. He yanked it down and sat up, gasping. The air that filled his lungs was startlingly cold. He blinked, trying to figure out just where the hell he was.

Truth was, this was not the first time he had woken up in a strange place, with no idea how he got there. More often than not, however, there was a girl (or two) next to him, and enough light to at least see his hand in front of his face. He was also usually in a more comfortable bed, with regular fabric covers. This weird rubbery thing he was in made him think the evening may have taken a particularly kinky turn.

Swivelling his aching head from side to side, he noticed what seemed to be a door a few feet away, with thin slivers of bright light flowing in through the cracks. Over to the right, a few tiny coloured lights floated in the gloom.

Jason quickly unzipped the bag as far as it would go, then lifted his legs out and swung them around to the side. His thighs came to rest on what felt like round metal bars, and his feet dangled below him. Judging by the angle of the light coming in under the door, he figured he probably wasn't very far up. Hoping that he wasn't being fooled by some hangover-induced optical illusion, he carefully lowered himself down, his feet touching the ground before his butt had fully slid off the metal bars.

His head pounding as fiercely as ever, Jason took a deep breath, then let it out slowly. After a moment, he began taking small, careful steps toward the door. Not being able to see his feet gave him the sensation that he might be stepping over some cliff into an abyss at any moment. The sensation was similar to one he often got in dark theatres, trying to find his seat without stumbling and spilling his movie snack. *I give this movie 0 stars*, he thought, waving his hands blindly before him.

After what seemed to him like an eternity of tiny shuffling steps, Jason was finally able to reach out and touch the door. He quickly felt around it for a light switch, and flicked it on.

★ ★ ★

Private J-538 had always imagined his first and only trip to the Reclamation Centre would be several years from now, after a brief but stellar stint as Flasher Extraordinaire, followed by a very long period of heavy drinking and fucking.

He was wrong.

Jason stood facing what looked like an operating table, complete with lights, equipment trays, various machines and computer monitors. To the left and right were several rows of gurneys, each bearing what could only be dead bodies in bags (except, of course, for his gurney, whose bag was now empty.) The tiled walls were lined with counters, shelves and cabinets, home to more equipment and monitors. In the far corner stood a battered cart labelled: "Protein Conversion – Muscle Tissue Only – No Internal Organs". Directly above it was a small security camera, pointed directly at him. Jason quickly flipped the light switch off, then stood silently for a moment as the gravity of his situation settled in.

Though he had never heard of any Flashers actually being caught in the Transitional Zone, the list of supposed punishments for such a transgression was very long, ranging from demotion to corporal punishment to dishonourable discharge (though the latter seemed unlikely given the fact that the laws were supposedly written to protect Flashers so they could keep killing Squelchers). Still, considering the fact that he was presently on probation, not to mention the general lack of respect shown him by Commanding Officer Captain Homo Halford, Jay thought it entirely possible that the cock gobblers at High Command might actually give him the boot.

Gritting his teeth, Jason swiped a hand across his eyes. His head throbbed relentlessly, and his stomach churned. For the first time in years, he felt on the verge of tears.

What the fuck was he doing in the Reclamation Centre? What the fuck was he doing in a *meat bag*? Was this some kind of a fucked-up *joke*? He squatted down and wrapped his arms around his chest as a wave of shivers took hold of him. Why weren't his friends looking out for him? Or did *they* do this? *Would* they do this? Just beneath his headache there appeared a faint buzzing, setting his teeth on edge.

"Oh, shit …" he mumbled under his breath. The shivers, the buzzing, the empty, dreamless hole in his memory … these were all symptoms of snoozer withdrawal. Someone had dosed him and somehow gotten him onto a meat truck. But who could arrange that?

Jay leaned heavily against the wall as it all clicked into place.

*Fucking Isaac.*

Isaac's cousin drove a meat truck, and Isaac's cousin was a knuckle-dragging sack of shit—it wouldn't take much to convince him to do something like this. And Isaac had bought Jason drinks last night, which at the time had struck him as odd, because Isaac was usually a cheap-ass son of a bitch. He must have dosed him at one of the last bars they went to.

"Fuck!" Jay hissed between his teeth. He had long ago accepted the fact that none of his "friends" really liked him, and as such expected little from them in the way of decency —but for Isaac to do something like *this* … And Claude?

Where was Claude when all this was happening? Jay hugged himself tighter as a fresh wave of shivers took hold.

*Fuck 'em*, he thought, struggling to contain the sobs which welled up unbidden from his chest. *They'll get theirs. They always do ...*

Taking a deep breath, Jay turned his mind to more immediate concerns.

Though his situation appeared dire, there was still a chance, albeit slim, that he could get out of this. If the person manning the Centre's security station happened to have been watching the monitor during the few seconds when the light was on, then of course it was game over. Jay would just have to hope the guard had been looking elsewhere, and work from there.

His first order of business was to get out of the building unseen. Once he was in the Transitional Zone, he might stand a chance of bluffing his way through the gate to the Core, or at least of disappearing amongst the crowd while he figured out his next move.

At least, he could if he weren't dressed in full casual Flasher attire.

He supposed he could just ditch his jacket, which was adorned with several symbols and details unique to the Flasher uniform. His t-shirt and pants, though expensive and well-tailored, were not too different from the more common fashions worn in the Core, and probably would not attract too much attention. Of course his hair screamed Flasher, as did the custom-fitted, Flasher-crested gloves which concealed the equally attention-grabbing implants beneath. Maybe he could just stick his hands in his pockets, and as for his hair ... keep his jacket, turn it inside-out and put it over his head?

Jay tensed as he heard footsteps approaching down the hall. Standing quickly, he pulled the glove from his right hand and, holding his breath, cocked his fist, ready to zap anyone who might come in. He exhaled slowly as the footsteps receded, simultaneously coming to the conclusion that he had to leave now, attire be damned. Truth was, a stranger in the Reclamation Centre was likely to attract attention, Flasher outfit or no Flasher outfit.

His first impulse was to simply open the door and make a break for it. Of course, the rational part of his mind knew better; he had no idea where the exits were, and there was too great a chance of running into someone on the way out. Besides, even if he made it all the way to the door unscathed, there would certainly be at least one guard posted there. No, he had to find a more unorthodox means of exiting the building. Unfortunately, that meant turning the lights on to see what he was working with. It was a risk, but he had no choice; he would just have to be quick about it.

Jason stripped off his jacket, turned it inside out and pulled it over his head, then yanked his t-shirt up over his nose, effectively hiding everything but his eyes. He considered his gloves for a moment, aware that he couldn't simply stick his hands in his pockets and still get anything done.

Fashioned out of thin white vinyl with the fingers exposed beyond the second knuckle, the gloves were in many ways similar to those worn by the young fashion-conscious Core-dwellers of the day. Turned inside-out, they actually might be all right, assuming they were only seen for a moment (any longer and someone might notice the padded areas over the implants, or the suspiciously Flasher-crested shape of the seams on the gloves' back).

Having convinced himself this was the best way to go, Jason quickly stripped off the gloves, turned them inside out, and slipped them back on.

After a final adjustment to his shirt, Jason took a deep, shaky breath and turned on the lights.

Finger still on the switch, Private J-538 scanned the room, quickly locating an air vent on the right hand wall. He then turned his attention to a set of medical tools laid out next to the operating table, and after a quick inventory, flicked the lights off again.

Yanking his shirt and jacket back down, Jason quickly but carefully walked over to the operating table, guiding himself along its edge until he reached the tool cart. Gingerly moving his hands from one item to another, he managed to find the small flashlight he had noted amongst the medical tools. He clicked it on, then quickly ran the beam over the cart's other contents, finally grabbing a small selection of tools and stuffing them in his pocket. Concealing the light in his palm, he walked carefully towards the wall where he had seen the vent, holding his arms before him and using the gurneys to help guide him.

When his leg bumped the edge of the counter, Jason uncovered the light, using it to locate the vent and assess the space available on the counter beneath. After clearing a few items away, he climbed onto the counter, took a small step to the right, then stuck the flashlight in his mouth. He pointed the beam towards the screws securing the vent, then pulled the tools from his pocket and held them up to the beam of light. Choosing a small spatula-shaped object, he stuck the other tools back into his pocket. Then, after testing the object on one of the screws, Jason snapped off the light and stowed it with the rest of his purloined gear.

It was only a matter of seconds before Jason had all four screws out, and the cover came off with the tiniest of clicks. He leaned it against the wall near his feet, then took the flashlight out for one more peek.

The air duct was relatively large, with only a few small pipes running along the inner wall. Putting the flashlight back into his pocket, Jason easily pulled himself up and in, gathering his knees under his chest and twisting his body around to face the opening. He then reached out and down to retrieve the vent cover, snapping it loosely into place.

★ ★ ★

Jason lay on his stomach for a few minutes, cursing his friends and longing for his bed at home. Though his head-ache had abated somewhat, the small exertion required to climb into the vent had ramped up his nausea to the point where he thought he might actually puke in this dark, con-fined space. Not wanting to crawl through a puddle of his own vomit, Jason closed his eyes and breathed deeply, doing his best to think of anything non stomach-related.

When the worst of the wooziness finally passed, Private J-538 lifted himself onto his elbows, then slowly dragged him-self toward a shaft of light about seven feet ahead. Peering out into a hallway, he saw a door marked "Fluid Reclamation Prep Room", with a short stretch of empty hallway on either side. He continued down the ventilation shaft, pausing to glance out of several similar openings, none of which offered any obvious hope of escaping undetected. Eventually the shaft made a right turn, ending abruptly at a small "T" inter-section.

Jason wriggled to the left, peering down through the opening at the shaft's end, a mere 4 feet away from the inter-section. Directly beneath the vent were a series of carts heaped with unidentifiable meat and tissue. A label on the side of one read: "Protein Conversion – Grade C – Commer-cial Use Only".

Jason recalled his last meal in the Plaza; cubes of chewy grey protein with spicy brown sauce. His stomach churned and he retched loudly, acid rising up and burning his throat. He swallowed quickly and repeatedly, then once again breathed deeply, trying more or less successfully not to ima-gine a stream of puke splashing across the mass of people meat below him. When his stomach finally settled once again, he squirmed around and crawled over to the other branch of the intersection.

This shaft went straight for at least forty feet, then turned sharply to the left, continuing for another thirty feet before flaring out, ending at a huge vent. From the opening came a low chugging sound, accompanied by various clicks and beeps. Jason pulled himself forward, pausing suddenly as someone below him spoke.

"You check the lines?" It was a deep male voice, the owner of which was a big fan of NicoStix, judging by the harsh way his words left his throat.

"Yeah, they're all good." This was a female; young and kind of sexy-sounding. "Eight was a little wonky, but I fixed it. Might have explained the weird readings on the heart monitor."

His elbows aching and his arms weakening from fatigue, Jason carefully laid himself flat against the bottom of the vent. Not daring to move backwards or forwards for fear of being heard, and with no way of knowing how long these people would stick around, he figured the best thing to do was to just relax for a while and try not to cramp up.

"Well, let's hope that's all it was," the man said. "I guess we'll just keep an eye on it and see if it stabilises. If the yields go down, though, we'll have to run some diagnostics."

"Gotcha," the female answered. "Last thing we need is Delenchek chewing our ears off. Last week the yields went down five percent and she nearly had a stroke."

"Huh, no kidding? Was that on my day off?"

"Yeah. Don't you wish you had come in?"

Jason lay listening for a while as the pair continued discussing yields and levels and such. His headache and nausea now just about gone, he was beginning to feel drowsy. If this went on much longer, he thought, he might actually fall asleep right here in the ventilation shaft.

He perked up a few minutes later when the woman mentioned something about lunchtime.

"I'm going upstairs," she said. "You coming?"

"Nah. My wife made me some fungus cakes. I think I'm just gonna go to the lounge and eat there."

"Suit yourself. Don't forget to lock up."

"Hang on, I'm leaving too."

There was the sound of footsteps, then a loud *clunk* as the door swung shut.

Jason listened a moment longer then, reasonably certain that the two had indeed left, dragged himself over to the vent and peered through the grate.

Against the opposite wall stood a row of hospital beds, most of them occupied by what appeared to be elderly men. A large array of tubes and wires led from their bodies to various pieces of machinery, which were apparently the source of the chugging and beeping sounds.

Jason furrowed his brow in confusion. He had never imagined that there would be a hospital wing in the Reclamation Centre; there were plenty of hospitals in the Core, and they were never full. He wondered if these patients might be Rim-mers, but that made even less sense—as far as he knew Rim-dwellers were barely fed, let alone cared for medically.

Shrugging mentally, Jason focused on more immediate concerns, such as finding a way to get the fuck out of the building. Closing his eyes, he lay his head on his fists and con-sidered his options, which were few. None of the many vents and openings he had found seemed particularly promising as far as escape was concerned. Still, having spent a good chunk of time fully exploring this particular stretch of ducts, he figured his best bet might be to just pick one and go.

The room he had awakened in only had the one vent, so there was no point in going back there. The opening into the hallway was far too risky; there was just too great a chance of dropping right into someone's line of sight. Though the Pro-tein Reclamation room could possibly offer a way out, the vent opened directly above a cart full of people meat, and though he felt pretty good at the moment, he doubted his di-gestive system would tolerate a head-first dive into a pile of slimy human remains.

That left the room he was presently lying above. Though it seemed empty other than the apparently unconscious patients, there was always a risk that one of them would wake up, possibly raising the alarm as the bedraggled Flasher dropped unexpectedly from a vent in the wall.

Further inspection of the patients helped ease his mind a little on that point. They were all lying on their backs, perfectly still, some with their eyes open and staring sightlessly at the ceiling; these people seemed barely alive, let alone strong enough to warn anyone about anything. Besides, try as he might to travel silently, he could not avoid making at least a little noise as he dragged himself through the ducts; it would probably be best to just get out while the getting was good.

Jason pushed experimentally on the vent cover which, to his great surprise and delight, snapped open with ease, swinging almost silently on a pair of hinges at the top. He slid forward a little and stuck his head out for a better look at the room.

To his left was a series of carts and shelves, stacked with supplies. To his right were a few more beds, and a wash station next to a large metal door.

Strangely, there seemed to be no cameras in the room that he could see.

Jason pulled himself back into the duct, twisted his body around to face the other way, and backed out of the opening, hanging a moment by his fingertips before finally dropping lightly to the floor. He backed up a few steps to study the wall, which was basically blank save for the door, the vent he had just exited and a second, slightly smaller vent just above.

Jason frowned as he considered the second vent. Perhaps he should try the ducts one more time, regardless of the noise. After all, he hadn't been in that one at all yet—maybe it led outside. It certainly couldn't be any riskier than opening the door and walking into … well, who knows what?

He hurried over to the second opening and, jumping up with his arms outstretched, just managed to grab hold of the cover, his fingers curled into the grid-work. Unfortunately, it soon became apparent that he would not be able to open the cover and crawl inside without some kind of support from below. He dropped back down and trotted to the group of carts at the end of the room, choosing one that was waist-height, and spun it around on its wheels. He froze in his tracks as he caught a glimpse of the patient on the far end of the row of beds.

The man was horribly disfigured, his scalp missing from his eyebrows to the top of his head, exposing the smooth white surface of his skull. His left ear was gone, as was his left eye; the socket was crusty and cracked, and oozed a thick yellow liquid. His right eyeball was swollen, bulging sightlessly from his ravaged face. On the side of his neck was a small tattoo.

Jason blinked and, fighting against a brand new wave of nausea, stepped closer to the man's bed. Though it was faded and distorted by the patient's shrivelled, yellow skin, the design was unmistakeable; a fist holding a stylised energy bolt, surrounded by a blue circle.

Jason's jaw dropped. This man was a Flasher. What in the world was a Flasher doing in a hospital in the Rim? He glanced nervously around the room, then backed away hurriedly, snatching up the electronic chart hanging at the foot of the bed. Jabbing a finger at the home screen, he opened the patient's file. A line at the top of the page read: "Flasher Squad Special Operations: Asset Management Initiative: Patient D-268 – Hep Leipsic".

Jason blinked; surely he wasn't reading this right. He was hungover and stressed, after all. He read it again, very carefully, and shook his head, frowning. If this information was correct, then one of his greatest childhood heroes, Hep Leipsic, was lying before him, hooked up to a mess of ma-

chinery and missing half his face. Hep Leipsic, who had survived two hundred and twenty seven missions during his
four year rotation. Hep Leipsic, whose heroic actions had
aided tremendously in the destruction of twenty-eight
Squelcher ships. Hep Leipsic, whose poster to this day hung
in a place of honour in young Jason Crawford's bedroom.

Hep Leipsic, who had died on a Squelcher ship over
twenty-two years ago.

★ ★ ★

Below the patient's name was a menu for navigating to the
various sections of the chart. Among the common items one
would expect on a medical chart ("Cardiac Function", "Pul-
monary Stats", "Kidney Function", etc.), were more unusual
items such as: "Yield Projections", "Yield History", "Genetic
Plotting" and "Product Quality Tracking". At the bottom of
the list was an item which simply read: "Offspring". Jason selected it and was rewarded by a list of names: "E-478 – Mark
Rettengard", "E-888 – Henri Falston", "F-197 – Zachary
Gent-Mathers", "F-201 – Jacob Hurley" …

Jason felt his heart racing. Flashers, every last one of them.
Even more surprising, he actually knew some of these
people. One of them was in his Cadet group.

What the hell was going on here?

His hands shaking, Jason activated a search bar at the bottom of the chart, and typed in: "J-538 – Jason Crawford".
What came up turned his blood cold.

**Subject:** J-538 – Jason Crawford
**Date of Birth:** April 16, 2752
**Age:** 17
**Rank:** Private, Cadet – Flasher Squad
**Supervising Officer:** Captain Desmond Halford
**Source Donor:** C-114 – Lieutenant-Commander Derek
Stanfield

**Status:** On Disciplinary Probation. Graduation from Academy pending resolution of Probationary Status.

**Anticipated Performance Level:** Very High

**Estimated Combat Productivity:** Seven Hundred Fifty-Eight Minutes, over Four Years.

**Probability of Donor Status:** Extremely High

**Genetic Analysis Results:** Highly Viable. For detailed results, *press here.*

**Negative Trait Indicators:** Present but Acceptable. For more information, *press here.*

**Estimated Yield:** 75ccs/day, indefinitely (assuming continued viability of specimen).

**Estimated Number of Viable Offspring:** Insufficient Data Available for Estimate at this time.

Jason dropped the chart onto Hep Leipsic's legs and pressed the heels of his hands against his eyes. After a moment, he grabbed the chart and took another look at the line which read: "Source Donor". He threw it down again and, grim-faced, strode purposefully down the aisle, scanning the names on the charts. He stopped at the foot of Patient D-224's bed.

What he saw when he looked at the man's face should have been overwhelming, but all Jason felt was a heavy numbness.

Derek Stanfield was a pitiful wreck of a man. His skin was yellow and stretched tight against his skull, making him look like speculative illustrations Jason had once seen of mummies back on Earth. His hair was white, thin and straggly. His chest raised and fell in time with the artificial respirator chugging away by his bed. A bag of urine hung by his side. It was impossible to tell how old the man was in his present state.

Jason bent over and studied the man's eyes. They were bright blue, and flecked with gold.

★ ★ ★

Gina Leblanc sat on a bench behind the sewage reclamation centre, eating her morning snack. Today it was crackers with protein spread—not great by Core standards, but abso-fucking-lutely awesome compared to what she was used to in the Rim. She brushed a few crumbs off of her bright orange jumpsuit, and smiled.

Life was much different for Gina since she had been accepted into the Transitional Zone Work Program. The first week had been extremely difficult—she had been malnourished and weak, and even the simple task of sweeping up the sidewalks had been a real challenge. After a few days of regular meals and exercise, however, things had started to look up. Now, one short month later, she felt happy and energetic. She had even started to gain weight!

Of course, life was still far from perfect; there were no residential facilities in the Transitional Zone, which meant she had to spend her off-work hours in the Rim proper. Still, this was pretty sweet. She could see why the Zone was often referred to as "Little Paradise" by the Rimmers.

She finished off her snack and tossed the wrapper into the small reclamation bin next to the bench. She then reached down and grasped her employee card, which hung from a clip on her right breast pocket. Gina ran her thumb over the raised Transitional Zone logo printed on the front and smiled. *My ticket to Paradise.* After a moment she carefully placed the card back over her breast, grabbed the handle of her little sweeping cart, and walked briskly towards the front of the building and the street beyond.

Stopping in front of the Secondary Human Waste Filtration Depot to pull on her gloves, Gina gazed wistfully at a billboard across the street. The words "Support our Troops" were printed in big, bright red letters, alongside a photo of a dashing young Flasher in full ceremonial garb.

Most of the Work Programmers, though pre-screened to weed out any full-blown Flasher haters, viewed this propaganda with at least some small level of disdain; the Squelcher war had taken huge amounts of resources from the Rim, transforming what was once a miserable slum into a full-blown hellhole. Gina, however, saw the war in a much more romantic light. To her, the war represented such positive things as courage, affluence, hope, and sex.

To put it bluntly, Gina would give her left tit to fuck a Flasher.

She sighed, pulled the broom out of her cart, and began carefully sweeping the sidewalk. Though there was very little to pick up (littering was a serious crime in both the Core and the Transitional Zone), even the tiniest speck of dirt had to be collected and processed; on a virtually self-sustaining city-ship travelling through the depths of space, waste was simply not an option.

It took her about five minutes to do the first section of sidewalk, after which she returned to the cart and carefully brushed a tiny pile of debris from her dustpan. Tilting the little trolley on its wheels, Gina turned and headed towards the next section of concrete. Three quarters of the way there she froze, staring incredulously at a vent on the rear wall of the Reclamation Centre.

There, against all odds, dangled something closely resembling a real-life, honest-to-fuck Flasher.

★ ★ ★

Jason took a deep breath, then let go. He landed hard, attempting to roll but only managing to thrust his hands before him, scraping his fingertips on the concrete. He glanced quickly in both directions, reassuring himself that the loading area was empty, then dashed across the pavement, finally taking cover behind a row of meat trucks.

Though he had managed to escape the Reclamation Centre, he was still in deep shit; there was no way he could get back into the Core without being detected, and even if he could, would he want to, knowing what was waiting for him at the end of his career? His stomach churned as he recalled the ravaged bodies in the hospital wing, doomed to some horrific kind of half-life as machines relentlessly sucked out the essence of what they had once been.

Willing his stomach to settle, Jason took one last calming breath then peered between two trucks, trying to get a sense of his surroundings. It was still early, and people were just starting their commute to work. Whatever he did, he would have to do it soon.

He looked down at his shirt and pants, which were heavily smeared with dirt, grease and rust from the vents. His first order of business was to—somehow—find a change of clothes; the sorry state of his attire was bound to attract attention. He glanced at his bloody fingertips, then squeezed his eyes shut and shuddered. Even with a less conspicuous outfit, Jason couldn't stay in the Zone for long; the area was only about twenty blocks square and filled to the brim with government buildings. He would almost certainly be found in short order—and he could only imagine what the High Command would do to a Flasher who had seen what he had seen.

There was only one place left to go.

Jason broke out in a cold sweat as a wave of nausea hit him. He doubled over and retched, bile streaming from his nose and mouth. He spat, then gasped as his bladder, which had not been emptied since the night before, threatened to let go. He fumbled madly with his zipper, opening his pants just as a heavy stream of dark urine shot out, splashing against the concrete and spraying back against his legs. Supporting himself on one bloody and painful hand, he sobbed as the stream wound down to a trickle, then, trembling un-controllably, did up his pants and struggled awkwardly to his feet.

"Hi there."

Jason spun around with a start. A few feet away stood a young woman in an orange jumpsuit.

"Oh, shit," Gina said, giggling nervously. "Did I scare you?"

Gina had worn her jumpsuit with her cuffs rolled up, which was good, as she was quite a bit shorter than Jason. Once they were unrolled, the uniform actually fit pretty well.

He fished through the contents of his discarded pants, retrieving his cell phone and haemo-pen and stuffing them into one the jumpsuit's many pockets. He paused for a moment, considering whether or not to take his wallet. Quickly realising that most of its contents would only serve to help identify him, he tossed it into the girl's reclamation cart, along with his pants, jacket, shoes and gloves.

He studied the girl's boots for a moment and, seeing there was no way they could possibly fit him, tossed them into the cart. He would look kind of strange walking around in the girl's sweat socks (which just barely stretched over his feet), but that couldn't be helped; the fancy, tailored shoes he had been wearing would have looked even more out of place.

The girl's work gloves were an uncomfortably tight fit, eliciting a twinge from his implants as he slid them on. The pain was an early sign of rejection; he was overdue for a Jabber. He considered the haemo-pen in his pocket, but was hesitant to use it yet; it contained only one dose, and the way things were going, he doubted he would be able to find another anytime soon.

This was going to be a serious problem, but there was nothing he could do about it now.

He looked down at the girl's ID card and frowned. Though Jason and Gina shared a roughly similar facial structure, her hair was a darker, dirtier blond than his, with not a hint of flashy iridescence; even a quick glance at the tag could be enough to expose him as the imposter he was. He quickly fished through the reclamation bin and retrieved a few used food wrappers; these he tore open and rubbed down the front of his jumpsuit, carefully smearing part of the picture without completely covering it. After tossing the wrappers back in the bin, Jason gave the card a few quick swipes with his hand, hoping it would look as though he had dirtied himself while eating, then made a half-hearted attempt at cleaning himself up.

Satisfied that he had done as much as he dared to conceal the image on the ID, Jason turned his attention to the half-naked girl lying unconscious before him.

Despite his attempts at concealing the most damning parts of his outfit, Gina had immediately recognised him as a Flasher in distress. His first instinct had been to run, but something about her manner had given him pause; there had been not a shred of anger or fear in her eyes—in fact, she had seemed genuinely happy to see him. Recognising Jason's confusion and apparent vulnerability, Gina had quickly lead him to a secluded area in a nearby alley, where she had cheerfully offered him help in exchange for sex.

Though the stress he felt had, as usual, left him tremend-ously aroused, his first reaction to her sexual overtures had been anger; he could have any woman he wanted in the Core, and for this scrawny little piece of Rim filth to even imagine he would be interested in her was beyond out-rageous. If she had had any respect at all for his Flasher status, she should have just helped him, letting *him* decide if she deserved anything for it. He had glared at her for a mo-ment, considering her request in the light of his present situ-ation, and his anger had grown.

"Fucking cunt," he had spat under his breath, bending her over her cart and fucking her aggressively from behind, cov-ering her mouth to silence her cries. While climaxing, he had made no effort whatsoever to curb the violent aggression which, also as usual, had welled up inside him like a raging fire. Afterwards, tears streaming down her face, the girl had threatened to expose him. The flame still roiling in his mind, he had kicked her repeatedly in the stomach, finally beating her to unconsciousness with her own broom as she lay curled up on the pavement.

He now knelt and rolled her onto her side, eliciting a small groan from her swollen, bloodied lips. His rage subsiding, he felt an abstract sort of remorse for what he had done to her (he usually did at times like these). Still, the fucking cumbucket had threatened him, and he already had enough to worry about. He grabbed her by the armpits and dragged her further into the alley, depositing her behind a large electrical box. Hopefully she would be out long enough for him to get away.

Jason trotted back to the cart and, grabbing the bright orange cap the girl had left hanging off its handle, pulled it down snugly over his head, concealing virtually all of his iridescent locks. He paused, then glanced at his filthy ID. With his hair hidden, maybe he didn't need to conceal the photo so much after all. Then again, this *was* a photo of another person; best to just let it be. After a few deep, calming breaths, he grabbed the trolley and, rolling it behind him, strode out onto the sidewalk.

The morning rush, though not yet in full swing, was definitely ramping up; at least a dozen people strode by as Jason stood next to his cart, nervously fiddling with his broom. Much to his relief, not one of them gave him a second look. He leaned the broom against the trolley and looked around, trying to get his bearings. There was a power arch to his left, meaning the Core was also that way; logically, the entrance to the Rim proper should be more or less in the opposite direction.

Turning to the right, Jason grabbed his cart and walked.

★ ★ ★

The exit from the Transitional Zone into the Rim turned out to be a relatively inconspicuous affair. Two small doorways were set in the concrete wall surrounding the Zone, about twenty feet apart. Between them ran a strip of chain link fence about forty feet long and ten feet high. Next to the right hand door was an unassuming little security structure, while the door on the left, which had no handle, seemed to be unguarded. Watching from a block away, Jason assumed the second door was how the workers entered the Transitional Zone from the Rim; any kind of serious security setup would probably be located on the other side.

Half a dozen orange-clad workers stood in a line a few feet away from the security booth by the right hand door, an armed guard leading them one at a time through what appeared to be some sort of scanner. A sign above the device read: "REMEMBER: Only take out what you brought in—attempting to smuggle contraband into the Rim will result in loss of Transitional Zone Work Permit and/or imprisonment." Workers seemed to be going through smoothly and quickly, with hardly a look from the guard. Jason supposed this was to be expected; these losers must have gone through some sort of risk assessment before being allowed into the Transitional Zone. And they were going into the Rim after all; he imagined the entrance back to the Zone would be a different story altogether.

Jason tensed as an elderly man shuffled by with a cart similar to his. Fortunately, the old guy showed no interest whatsoever in his fellow worker, turning quietly into a nearby alley and emerging a moment later sans cart. After pausing to scratch his ass, the old man wandered slowly over to the end of the scanner line.

Following the man's lead, Jason grabbed his cart and hurried towards the nearby alley. Turning the corner, he came across a short row of loading docks, the first two of which were filled to the brink with carts. He walked over to the third and, seeing a dozen or so trolleys neatly lined up at the back, pulled his up the ramp. Rolling his cart next to the others, he paused; this would be his last chance to get rid of any potentially incriminating items before going past the guards.

Jason hurried to the front of the loading dock and looked both ways down the alley. Confident that he was alone (at least for the moment), he trotted back to his cart and fished through his pockets. The first item he pulled out was his haemo-pen.

His heart sank as he stared down at the slim metallic cylinder. With his implants already showing signs of rejection, one final booster shot would have little effect; unless he found a source of Phenylbutalol in the Rim, he would certainly lose them.

Jason gripped the haemo-pen tightly, fighting back his anger.

How the fuck had his life suddenly come to this, he wondered. Yesterday he had had everything: prestige, money, family, friends … Now he had nothing. His career was over, his friends had betrayed him and he would probably never see his family again. For that matter, he wasn't really sure who his family was anymore. Was he even biologically related to them? Had his mother actually given birth to him, or had he been brewed up in a beaker somewhere in the depths of the fucking Reclamation Centre? Even worse, did his "family" know what would happen to him at the end of his Flasher career?

Of all the horrors of his new life, however, one stood out as the most egregious: the loss of his implants. The one and only true mark of a Flasher, they had been an immeasurable part of his life since early childhood, defining him in ways that nothing else ever had, or ever could. He could no sooner give them up than he could his arms or his legs; the thought of existing without them was nearly intolerable.

Squeezing his eyes shut, Jason held the pen to his neck

and pushed the button, gasping as the contents of the cylinder ejected themselves into his skin. Tossing the empty device into his cart, he leaned against the wall, choking back the bile which rose uncontrollably to his throat.

His throat burning, Jason angrily thrust his hand into his pocket and pulled out his phone.

He had so far resisted the urge to call for help, as every phone call and text message sent included very detailed tracking information. Besides, who would he call? His so-called friends? His *maybe* parents? He stared morosely at the device, then flipped it open and ran a gloved finger across the keypad. *I can't just give up totally,* he thought. *There has to be something I can try.*

Jason carefully stripped off his bulky work glove and scrolled through his list of contacts, pausing at Claude's entry. He clicked through to the profile picture, a photo of Claude with his eyes half-closed, drunkenly chewing a mouthful of protein-carb snack. Claude hated that picture, which appealed to Jason's slightly perverse sense of humour.

The corners of Jason's mouth twitched up momentarily, a brief wave of affection vying for space with the less positive emotions roiling through his mind. The little faggot was basically a good guy, and he was probably too much of a chicken shit to go along with Isaac's plans ... *and* his father had connections in the Council; if *anyone* could help ...

Of course, receiving a message from Jason right now could potentially get Claude in trouble ... but then again, how much trouble could *he* get into? *He* wasn't the one who had stumbled into a Flasher horror show; Claude would just have to be discreet when High Command questioned him, not say anything stupid ...

Setting his jaw, Jason composed a short message. When he was finished, he paused, his finger hovering over the "Send" button.

Was this really the right thing to do?

*Fuck it.*

Message sent, he switched the phone off and tossed it into the bin.

He started sliding the glove back on, then paused as a bolt of pain travelled up his hand to his wrist. Frowning, Jason pulled the glove back off and looked down at his bare hand. The skin surrounding his implants was red and swollen, and one of the metallic devices seemed to have shifted position slightly. Gritting his teeth, he prepared to pull the glove on again when a thought struck him.

*Damn.*

He had immediately thought of his phone and hemo-pen as risky items to take into the Rim, but he hadn't given his implants a second thought. After all, they would be well-hidden, and as far as he could tell, nobody going past the guards was being asked to remove their gloves. The problem was, he was so used to thinking of them as part of his body that he had temporarily overlooked the fact that they were at least partially metallic, and therefore quite likely to set off the scanner. Taking the glove off yet again, he stared grimly at his knuckles, silently cursing himself for his stupidity.

Just then Jason's bowels, which had been complaining since he had awakened in the Reclamation Centre, emitted a loud gurgling sound. Though he had, up to this point, been able to ignore the unrest brewing in his gut, last night's drinking and this morning's stress now conspired to push his system into overdrive; there would soon be an emptying, whether he liked it or not.

Jason took a deep breath, struggling to control his insides as he considered his options. He could try finding a bathroom, but that would take time; for all he knew there could be people out searching for him at this very moment. Besides, the way things were going down below, he probably wouldn't make it very far before disaster struck. Grimacing, he took a quick peek towards the alley and, seeing no one, pushed his way between the carts to the rear of the loading dock. Squatting in the corner, he frantically undid his jumpsuit and pulled it down to his ankles.

He barely had time to yank off his underwear before his bowels let go, noisily spewing a copious amount of runny shit onto the concrete. When he was sure it was over, Jason stripped naked and, still squatting at the rear of the dock, used his underwear to wipe himself, gagging slightly as he felt the loose, sticky crap smearing across his ass. Tossing the now useless garment under a cart, he was suddenly struck with a very disgusting, yet potentially brilliant idea.

Legs cramping, Jason pulled the jumpsuit back on, then reached under the cart and retrieved the dirty underwear. Carefully unfolding the fabric to expose a particularly soiled section, he gingerly smeared a thick layer of shit over the back of his hands, then slowly slid his gloves back on, hoping they wouldn't wipe too much of it away.

His implants stung as the wet, cooling shit worked its way into the crevices surrounding them.

Gord Upney gazed dreamily into the distance. His shift was winding down, and he was finding it harder and harder to concentrate. Not that there was much to concentrate on— the last employee shift rotation had been half an hour ago, and the only people going out now were a few stragglers who for some reason or another had been delayed at their post. Of course many of them were simply dallying, doing their best to avoid the shift monitors. Gord couldn't blame them, really—if he were in their place, he wouldn't be in a big hurry to get back into the Rim either.

He shifted his machine gun on his shoulder, then nodded to a middle-aged woman at the head of the line. She stepped up to the scanner mechanism, quickly sliding her employee card through the slot at the front of the arch. The card reader *bleeped* as the information from her I.D. was transmitted to the computer terminal in the small shack beyond. The woman looked at Gord, eyebrows raised.

"Go ahead," he said, waving the woman along. An indicator light flashed green as she hurried through the scanner, prompting Gord to push a button on his belt. The heavy door beyond the scanner arch unlocked with a loud *clunk*, and the woman hurried through.

Once the door had closed and locked behind her, Gord nodded to the next person in line: a sweaty, nervous-looking young man with no shoes. There was a big smear across the front of his jumpsuit, which the guy had apparently tried to clean, albeit in a decidedly half-assed manner. As a result, all that could be seen of his photo was a bit of dirty blonde hair and pale skin peeking out between streaks of grey sauce. The employee walked quickly to the arch, unclipping his card from his pocket and sliding it awkwardly through the slot. Nothing happened.

Gord's shoulders slumped, and he let out a loud sigh. The lazy little prick had probably just gummed up the card reader with his dirty fucking I.D. card. *I really should have asked him to clean that thing.* He was drawing in a breath to do just that when the young man flipped the card over and swiped it again. This time the slot flashed green. Gord sighed again, this time with relief.

The young man turned and looked at Gord expectantly.

"Where are your boots?" the guard asked. He was planning on turning a blind eye to this idiot's shoeless condition, but now that he was just standing there like a moron instead of walking through the scanner …

"Someone stole them," the young man answered, a little too loudly. He shuffled his feet a bit and shrugged. "Sorry."

Gord chuckled despite himself. He wanted to be professional, but sometimes these Work Program Rimmers were just so fucking *stupid*.

"Whatever," he said, shaking his head. "Just make sure you file a report on your way out."

The young man blinked, then pointed toward the door in the wall, "You mean on my way out there?"

Gord frowned. "At your fucking locker terminal!" he barked.

Anger flashed momentarily across the young man's face, then dissolved into a strange kind of frightened sheepishness as Gord adjusted his weapon across his chest. "Oh, right, of course," the young man replied quickly. "The terminal." He laughed nervously, then gave the guard a little salute.

Gord narrowed his eyes, studying the employee's pale, haggard face. "What the fuck's wrong with you?" he asked. "Are you sick or something?"

The young man cleared his throat. "Yeah ... I mean, no, I'm not sick." He paused, looking down at his feet. "Oh, yeah, but the guy who stole my boots just kinda beat me up a little, so I guess I don't feel so great after all."

"Oh, man," the guard said, simultaneously scowling and rolling his eyes. "Just be sure to get yourself checked out before your next shift. The last thing we need is some fucking Rimmer disease in the Zone."

The young man nodded vigorously. "Yeah, that's for sure ..."

Gord frowned as the employee just stood staring. *What the fuck is up with this guy?*

"Well," he said, pointing the barrel of his gun toward the scanner, "fucking let's go!"

"Oh! Yeah, right," the kid said, nodding enthusiastically. "Okay! See you later."

Gord shook his head as the young man turned and hurried through the scanner, then glanced up at the top of the arch and blinked. The light was red. "Whoa! Hang on a second!" he called out. "Get the fuck back here!"

The employee froze, then turned and walked slowly back

through the arch as the others in line watched with mild interest. The guard removed a wand device from his belt. "Stand here and put your arms out to the side," he said. The young man quickly complied. "You got anything you shouldn't have? Metal? Weapons?"

"No sir!" he replied in a slightly quavery voice. Sweat dripped from his forehead, and there were large wet marks under his arms.

Gord waved the wand over the front of the employee's body, then along his right arm. The device emitted a faint beep as it passed the young man's hand. The guard waved the device a few more times to be sure, then clipped it back onto his belt.

"Take off your gloves," Gord said, glancing over his shoulder to see if the guard in the shack was paying attention. His partner was looking at his feet, blithely yakking away on his cell phone. Gord swore under his breath, hoping this would turn out to be nothing; his headset was on the fritz, and he was in no mood to be running around like a moron trying to get the other guard's attention while wrestling some crazy fucking Rimmer. He sighed, then grimaced. Something smelled like shit.

The guard glanced down at the young man's hand only to find it smeared with faeces. "What the fuck?" he cried, taking a step back. "What the fuck is *wrong* with you?" He once again turned toward the security shack. "Denny!" he barked. "Denny, heads up!"

Just as Denny turned towards his partner, an alarm sounded from the direction of the Reclamation Centre. *Just fucking great,* Gord thought, glaring angrily at the stupid little prick standing before him. The kid was shaking visibly, and he looked like he was going to puke. The guard gagged as he caught another whiff of the guy's shit-caked hand.

*Fuck this,* he thought. Whatever metal the guy may or may not have hidden under that mess, it wasn't big enough to worry about right now; he would tell Denny to flag the fucker's employee card once this alarm business was dealt with, and then it would be some other schmuck's problem.

"Get the fuck out of here," he said, waving his gun towards the door.

The young man ducked his head and without another word, spun on his heel and scurried away.

The alarm still blaring, Gord shook his head and looked toward his partner, who was having an animated discussion with someone over his walkie-talkie. He then turned his attention to the short line of employees waiting to pass through the scanner, several of whom were snickering.

*Fucking, fucking, fuck* ... he thought grimly, *I'm getting way too fucking old for this shit.*

★ ★ ★

The room was large and brightly lit. To the left were toilets, showers and sinks; to the right were several rows of lockers. A few Rim Dwellers, male and female, milled about in various states of undress. At the other end of the room a solitary, bored-looking guard leaned near a thick plexiglass door marked: "Exit", with a solid metal door about three feet beyond. Below the exit sign someone had scrawled: "Abandon all hope, for through this door lies cataclysm!", punctuated by a small yellow happy face.

His socks soaking up dirty water from the floor, Jason hurried to the second row of lockers, out of sight of the guard. After quickly assuring himself that he was, for the time being, alone, he squatted next to a bench and closed his eyes.

*Fucking Isaac,* he thought, as his body was gripped by an uncontrollable bout of shaking, *Fucking shit sucker Isaac ...*

As the trembling slowly subsided, Jason leaned his head against a locker and considered his next step.

The easiest and most tempting thing to do at the moment

would be to simply bolt for the exit; once through the door he would most certainly find himself in the Rim proper, where he should be able to lose himself long enough to maybe make some bigger plans. Unfortunately, leaving in his work uniform would most likely attract the attention of the guard; the presence of lockers, as well as the number of people wandering around the room in civilian clothing, suggested that he was expected to change before leaving.

Jason took a moment to study the locker across from him. The grey metal door, chipped and dented from years of use, was adorned with a large number "38". In lieu of a handle, there was a card slot on the right hand side, next to a small keypad and speaker. Unclipping the I.D. from his pocket, he rubbed it briskly against his pant leg, then searched the card for some indication of which locker might be his. Below the girl's picture was printed her name, her fifteen-digit employee number, and the words "Transitional Zone Work Program – Card Must Be Worn At All Times". Jason frowned, hoping he wouldn't have to puzzle out his locker number from the employee number. Though he could probably manage after a little trial and error, even one attempt at opening someone else's locker might attract undue attention. He flipped the card over and, to his relief, found the number "15" printed above the magnetic strip.

Jason took a moment to study the numbers on the surrounding lockers, getting a feel for how they were organised. Once he had his bearings, he hurried over to the next row, homing in quickly on his target.

Jason wasted no time sliding his card into the slot, which immediately lit up. The speaker crackled momentarily, and a synthetic female voice announced: "Transitional Zone Employee Number 50432-45A-MCA332-Z acknowledged. You are not scheduled to leave for another six hours and fifty-seven minutes. If you have returned in error, please retrieve your card and have a guard escort you back into the Trans-

itional Zone. Otherwise, please listen carefully to the following choices."

*Fuck.*

Jason had harboured the naive hope that inserting his
card in the slot would simply unlock the door. Now, thoroughly disillusioned, he tugged at his collar while various
possible scenarios played out in his head, each one more
dreadful than the other.

After a brief pause the speaker crackled again, and the
voice continued. "If you have been instructed by a superior
to exit the Transitional Zone, press 1. If you are sick and/or
injured, press 2. Please make your selection now."

Jason hesitated a moment, then took a deep breath and
pressed 2 on the keypad below the speaker.

"If you are sick," the artificial woman said, "press 1. If you
are injured, press 2. If you are both sick and injured, press 3.
To return to the main menu, press 4."

"Oh, for fuck's sake ..." Jason growled under his breath.
"Just fucking open the door already ..." Sighing heavily, he
considered which number to press. Though he was definitely
feeling more sick than injured, he *had* told the guard outside
that he had been beaten up, so ... *All right,* he decided, nodding once, *injured it is.* He pressed 2.

"If the injury was the result of an accident, press 1. If the
injury was the result of an assault, press 2. To return to the
main menu, press 3." He pressed 2.

"All injuries resulting from an assault must be reported to
a senior member of the Transitional Zone Work Program
management team," droned the voice. Jason's heart sank; if
he actually had to explain all this to a real person, he was
probably done for. "If you have already reported the injury,"
continued the artificial woman, "press 1. If you have not yet
reported the injury, press 2. To return to the main menu,
press 3".

Jason frowned. If he chose 2, he ran a very real risk of

having to report to a live human being. If he chose 1, however, he might be caught in a lie, which could be just as bad (if not worse). Then again, reporting to a supervisor could mean leaving a recorded message, which might only be heard later …

Steeling himself, Jason pressed 2.

"If your injuries require immediate medical attention, press 1. If your injuries do not require immediate medical attention, press 2. To return to the main menu, press 3."

*Oh, please, please, let this fucking end already.* He pressed 2 once again.

"Please report the incident to a supervisor at the beginning of your next scheduled shift. Goodbye."

The door popped open with a loud *clunk*.

Jason blinked, then grabbed the edge of the door and slowly opened it, peering inside. On a hook to the right hung a pair of ragged cut-off jeans. To the left hung a long purple tank top which, upon closer inspection, turned out to be adorned with the words 'Party Bitch', emblazoned in big sparkly gold letters. A small cubicle at the top of the locker held a tiny pair of yellow runners and a big floppy green beret of some sort. *Of all the stupid fucking cunts I could run into,* he thought, shaking his head, *this one turns out to be a fucking fashion expert.* He reached into the cubicle and pulled out the hat. It was filthy and torn, but at least it would hide his hair.

Jason hastily switched his cap for the beret, pulling it snugly over his ears. He then fumbled with the zipper pull on the front of his uniform, yanking off his glove so he could get a better grip. The smell of shit radiating from his hand nearly knocked him over, and he quickly put the glove back on.

He looked down at his hands and frowned. He had been hoping to simply change and leave, but it was now apparent to him that he would have to deal with the faeces issue first.

He couldn't very well just walk past the guard with shit all over his hands; at the very least it would draw unwanted attention. He could probably just stick his hands in the pockets of the cut-offs, but he ran the risk of scraping shit onto the outside of the pocket, leaving him with dirty clothes as well as dirty hands. Of course, the tank top might be long enough to cover his pockets. But then there was still the smell to consider ...

*Ah, fuck it.*

There was no way around it; he had to get this stuff off before he left. Besides, considering where he was going, this might very well be his best and last chance to properly clean his implants.

*Not that it'll make much fucking difference ...*

Peering around the bank of lockers, Jason considered the showers on the opposite wall. As he watched, a nude woman walked into one and turned on the faucet. He looked over at the guard, who seemed fairly uninterested in anything that was going on.

*All right,* he thought, *looks simple enough.*

Ignoring the tiny yellow runners, Jason grabbed the shorts and shirt, then closed the door. Reaching for his I.D. card, he paused as the light around the slot began flashing; should he hurry up and grab it, or was the flashing a signal that he should wait? A moment later the light went out, and the card was sucked unceremoniously to who knows where.

*Well, so much for that.*

Hurrying (in what he hoped was a casual way) over to the nearest stall, Jason dropped the girl's clothes on a small bench opposite the shower head, then quickly stripped naked, except for the beret. It would undoubtedly get soaked, but there was no getting around it—he had to keep his hair hidden.

The fact that the enclosure had neither door nor curtains normally wouldn't have bothered him (he had always been kind of an exhibitionist), but right now he knew it was in his best interests to attract as little attention as possible. There were also his implants to consider; keeping them hidden while showering was going to be a challenge.

Reaching down, Jason pushed the shower's activation button, steeling himself for the cold water assault that would undoubtedly follow. To his surprise the shower was, if not hot, at least pleasantly warm. Keeping his back to the stall's opening, he carefully rinsed most of the shit from his hands, then, reaching over to the dispenser on the wall, squirted a small amount of liquid soap into his palm. Working the soap into a lather, he gingerly rubbed the red, swollen skin around his implants. *Let this be a lesson to you, Jason,* he thought, a small sardonic smile crossing his lips, *If you make it back into the Core, don't ever miss your jabber. And whatever you do, don't rub shit on your hands.*

Having spent as much time as he dared on his hands, Jason turned around and gave his ass a quick wash, finally switching the shower off and peeking around the edge of the stall in the hopes of finding a towel. To his dismay, all he could see were a couple of small blow dryers mounted on the wall a few yards away.

Not wanting to leave the limited cover of the shower stall until absolutely necessary, Jason squeezed some of the water out of the beret, then grabbed his work overalls and quickly patted himself down. He then pulled on the shorts, which were extremely baggy; they would have slid right back down around his ankles were it not for a length of plastic bailing twine hanging off the belt loops. Once the rope was tightened and secured to his satisfaction, Jason pulled on the "Party Bitch" shirt, which hung down almost to his knees, completely covering the shorts.

*Don't I fucking look beautiful …*

After pulling on his damp socks, Jason once again glanced around the stall. The security guard, who was busily chewing his thumbnail, seemed rather unconcerned with what Jason, or anyone else for that matter, was doing. Ducking back into the shower, Jason took a deep breath, carefully jammed his smarting hands into his short pockets, and resolutely strode out of the stall towards the exit.

Halfway to his destination, Jason caught sight of a Rimmer stuffing his work uniform into a large chute set into the wall. A sign above read: "All soiled work garments must be deposited in laundry receptacle prior to reentering the Rim." Suddenly uncertain, Jason glanced back towards the shower stall, where his jumpsuit lay balled up on the bench. Going back for it would be a risk; even if he wrapped the uniform around his hands, his implants would be exposed for a few moments after he dumped it down the chute ...

He turned back towards the guard, who was now watching him with mild interest.

*Well,* he thought, *I guess it's now or never.*

Head down and hands in pockets, Private J-538 strode awkwardly forward, looking for all the world like a drunk young woman.

A few steps from the exit, the guard placed a gloved hand on his shoulder. Jason's chest tightened, and he felt his bladder loosen, threatening to let go. When he looked up, the man was shaking his head, the hint of a smirk playing at the corners of his mouth.

"You lost, kid?"

Jason blinked. "What?"

The guard took his hand off the young man's shoulder, and rested it over his machine gun. "I said, you lost?"

"Um ... no," he said, his mouth twitching, "I don't think so."

"Well," replied the guard, spreading his hands, "seems to me you must be lost. This facility's reserved for Transitional Workers, and you obviously aren't one of those."

Jason coughed and quickly looked away. His throat began to close up. "What do you mean?" he croaked.

"I mean that even the stupidest fucking inbred Trans-itional Worker knows you're supposed to shower coming *out* of the Rim, not going *into* it. Now since I just saw you taking a shower, and now you're going into the Rim, I have to as-sume you're not actually a *Transitional Worker*."

"Oh, yeah …" Jason said quietly, his voice shaking, "I, I guess I shouldn't have done that … Had a long day, thought maybe I could sneak in a quick shower …" He cleared his throat, then looked down at the floor. "Sorry?"

"Sorry?" the guard bellowed, "You're fucking *sorry*? Well like they say, sorry don't pay the rent, do it? So what the *fuck* am I supposed to do with *sorry*?"

With an odd sense of relief, Jason realised it was all over. Though he didn't have a hope of successfully fighting his way out of this in his present condition, he figured he should at least go out swinging. He took a deep breath as he con-sidered whether to go for the face or the balls.

The guard chuckled. "You fucking Rimmers are something else, you know that? Now get the fuck out of here."

Jason looked up, eyes wide.

Just then the guard's walkie-talkie *bleeped*. "Yo, Miller. We've got a level 5 breach, Reclamation Centre."

Frowning, Miller grabbed his walkie. "Okay," he said, "hang on a second." Letting his arm drop, he glared at the pale young man still standing before him. "Well, what the fuck are you waiting for?" he barked. "Go home! And don't let me catch you disrespecting the rules again, or I'll shine my rod in your asshole!"

Jason quickly turned and marched to the plexiglass door, which opened automatically upon his approach. A sign in the small cubicle read: "Please enter completely – outer door will not open until inner door is fully closed". A moment later the door behind him hissed shut, and the metal door before him swung open, flooding the little room with artifi-cial sunlight. Partly blinded by the glare, he stumbled halfway out, then stopped and stared in horrified wonder at the desolate, broken-down wasteland before him.

"What are you, fucking retarded?" the guard shouted through the plexiglass. "Fucking move it already!"

Startled, Jason jerked forward, wincing as bits of broken concrete dug into the soles of his feet. Shabby-looking individuals watched speculatively as he came to a halting stop a few feet past the exit.

In the distance an alarm wailed.

"By the way," the guard shouted as the door swung closed, "nice dress!"

PART II

# June 14, 2769

A few blocks from his apartment, Gregory's eye was drawn to a brightly coloured object in an otherwise drab, grey alleyway. Though he rarely found anything of value just sitting out in the open, there was something about the object's appearance that intrigued him, and after a quick look around, he marched over to the alley to investigate.

What he found was a tiny scrap of plastic greenery, its smooth, glossy leaves gleaming in the ship's artificial sun. Kneeling down, he considered the strange way it had settled itself into a crack in the pavement, as though it were actually growing out of the sterile concrete. Had some crazed Rim-Dweller with a well-developed sense of irony placed it that way? Chuckling quietly, Greg pinched the thing between his thumb and index finger, plucking it out in one quick motion and holding it up to his eyes for a better look. The tiny stem, crowned by a cluster of bright green leaves, was soft and pliable beneath his fingers, its base branching out into a network of fuzzy, golden roots ...

Greg's eyes went wide.

Requiring a healthy dose of precious nutrients to survive in the sterile environment of the ship, live plants were the ultimate sign of one's wealth and social status, allowed only to the highest-ranking government officials and, of course, Flashers and their families. Plainly stated, one did not simply stumble upon a plant on the USS McAdam. And yet, here it was: a veritable live weed which, against all odds and prob‐ abilities, had managed to eke out an existence in one of the most barren and desolate areas of the city.

And with one careless act, Gregory had more than likely killed it.

Gripped by an intense mixture of grief and determination, Greg dropped the precious weed into his chest pocket and ran like mad towards home. At the rear of the apartment building, he rummaged through his bag, retrieving a spe‐ cially modified wrench; this he used to loosen a bolt at the base of the fire escape mechanism, causing the ladder to drop with a resounding *clang*. Heaving himself up onto the lowest riser, Greg stomped noisily to the third floor, where a hidden latch allowed him access into the building proper. Once inside, he raced down the hall and up the stairs, heed‐ less of the noise he was making, or the fact that he was leav‐ ing his carefully hidden series of secret doors and passage‐ ways wide open for all to see. Finally bursting into his apart‐ ment, Greg spared barely a second to secure the latches on the door before throwing his pack down and running for the sink. He grabbed a small tin from the counter and half filled it with water from the tap, then stood staring into the con‐ tainer as he caught his breath, wondering what else he needed to keep his little treasure alive.

Plants needed water, he knew, but they also needed soil and sunlight. Though the ship's artificial sun would probably have sufficed (actually had sufficed, evidenced by this plant's very existence), Gregory had boarded up all the windows in his apartment as a security measure. He thought some other kind of artificial light might work, but he couldn't be sure; his childhood Biological History classes had given him a ba‐ sic understanding of how to keep plants alive on a living planet, but had not mentioned anything about raising plants in an artificial environment, much less one as harsh and barren as the Rim. Fortunately he had several different kinds of lights in his apartment: fluorescent, halogen, LED, even a few ancient incandescent bulbs he had scavenged from the basement of a derelict antique store; he would just have to work with what he had and hope for the best.

Greg placed the tin onto the counter and carefully retrieved the plant from his pocket. It sagged visibly between his fingers, apparently showing signs of distress from having been so unceremoniously yanked out of its environment. For a moment he considered dropping it right into the water, but worried that completely submersing the thing might do it more harm than good; he needed some kind of soil substitute, something that would deliver water to the roots without soaking the rest of the plant.

His first thought was to use a few sheets of toilet paper; the stuff was soft and absorbent, and he had four and a half rolls of it stacked up next to his workbench. After some deliberation, he dismissed the idea outright; toilet paper was just too useful, and obtaining this particular stack had been far from easy. He would just have to find something else.

Gingerly placing the plant on the counter next to the tin, Gregory scanned the apartment, his eye falling on an old armchair with a particularly large rip in the cushion. Rushing over, he thrust his hand into the hole, yanking out a large mass of fluffy yellow stuffing. Hurrying back to the sink, he soaked the stuff under the tap then squeezed it in his fist, nodding with satisfaction as rivulets of water flowed freely between his fingers. He teased a smaller piece from the wad and jammed it into the can, then carefully lifted the plant and placed it upright onto the soaked stuffing, finally covering the roots with a few more bits of the soggy stuff.

Greg held the can up to his face and studied the little plant, which, though presently sagging against the rim, seemed still to be in reasonably good shape. Placing it back on the counter, he drew a deep breath and noisily let it out. Who would have thought he'd ever own a plant? And a miracle plant from the Rim, no less? Shaking his head and smiling, Greg carried the tin over to his makeshift laboratory table, where a small gooseneck lamp glowed with a warmth which, to his eyes, was reminiscent of the USS McAdam's artificial sun. He carefully moved aside the small assortment of beakers and glass tubes which he had set up in preparation for his next batch of "Rim juice", and gently placed his tiny charge beneath the light.

Though this little setup seemed promising, Greg was still worried; he had a virtually unlimited supply of water and light (assuming one of his lamps would agree with this little weed), but finding nutrients was going to be a big problem. Of course the weed seemed to be doing fine in the practically nutrient-free environment of the Rim, but that didn't necessarily mean it wasn't feeding off of something he just wasn't aware of— possibly tiny bits of the same organic material which supported the ship's surprisingly robust population of cockroaches? But then, unlike the plant, the roaches had legs which enabled them to search high and low for food. Greg blinked, then began quickly pacing back and forth across his apartment. Maybe that was the answer! Maybe the cockroaches were somehow unwittingly supplying the plant with nutrients, possibly sloughing off cells or dropping the tiniest bits of food as they brushed against it. Or maybe they were even attracted to it, engaged in some sort of symbiotic relationship where, in return for some benefit from the plant, the cockroaches would deposit their cells, or even faecal matter …

Greg stopped in his tracks. Faecal matter! Of course! His childhood instructors had spoken of beasts on Earth who were raised for food and who also excreted a substance called "manure", which was beneficial to plants. Of course he didn't have access to real "manure", but maybe human excretions would serve just as well? In any case, it was worth a shot. Next time he had a dump, he would save some and put it in the can with the water and chair stuffing, and hope for the best.

And now, almost three years later, the plant had more than quadrupled in size on a steady diet of tap water and poop, and bloomed regularly with tiny brilliant yellow flowers. Greg placed the weed (which he had eventually named "Joe") in its usual spot by the sink, then turned to consider the young man tied to the ratty old fold-out couch across the room.

★ ★ ★

"Hey Buddy, wake up." The voice was distant and fuzzy. Jason felt heavy, relaxed; he did not want to wake up. "Hey! Hey, Buddy!" the voice persisted, as Jay became dimly aware of someone far away shaking him gently by the shoulder. Sighing contentedly, he flexed his right hand, triggering a dull, throbbing pain in his knuckles. He tensed slightly, suddenly aware of various small discomforts throughout his body: his hands, his left elbow, his jaw, his ass …

Jason's serenity was suddenly imbued with a dreamlike anxiety and panic, as hazy, nightmarish sensations flooded into his brain. Whimpering, he struggled to open his eyes, groaning as the harsh light from a ceiling fixture assaulted his pupils. With what seemed like a gargantuan effort, he turned his head to the left, where a dark blur slowly resolved itself into a bearded man hovering a few feet away. The man's hair was long and greasy, and he had a ragged scar on his right cheek, partially obscured by a patch over his eye. Jason tried to ask the man who the fuck he was, and just exactly *where* the fuck *he* was, but all that came out was a pitiful, incoherent mumble. Temporarily defeated, he closed his eyes and let his head roll back.

"Ok, hang on," the voice said. "I'm giving you something to help you wake up a bit … there, give that a couple of seconds."

A few moments later Jason opened his eyes, turning his head to once again face the bearded man. "Where am I?" he croaked.

"You're at my place," the man replied, smiling slightly. "You're safe."

Jason studied his face for a moment, trying in vain to identify him. "Who are you?"

"My name's Greg. I found you in an alley and brought you back here." The man took a tentative step forward. "We're in the Rim. Do you remember how you got here?"

Jason blinked. In the Rim? In the fucking *Rim*? Agitated, he tried to sit up but for some reason just … couldn't. Confused and frustrated, he looked down at his body, most of which was concealed under a ratty old blanket. As he moved to pull the thing off, something tightened around his wrist, holding it back. A bright spark of anger flared up deep inside him, then faded almost immediately to a dull glow, like a flame trapped within a block of ice. He looked up at Greg.

"What the fuck happened to me?"

"You were attacked," Greg said, placing a hand on Jay's shoulder. Jay flinched, and he moved his hand away.

"Who attacked me?" Jay asked, struggling feebly to remember.

"I'm sorry, I don't know." Greg paused, scratching at his greying beard, "But don't worry, you'll be okay now."

Jay squeezed his eyes shut, struggling to think back on what had happened. All he could summon were vague sensations, emotions … fear … shame … "I can't really remember," he croaked.

"That's not surprising," Greg said with a small, sympathetic smile. "You probably blocked it out. You're lucky though, there were no serious injuries."

"Did I break anything?" Jay asked, shifting experimentally in his bed.

"No. A few cuts and some damn fine bruises, but that's mostly it."

Jason frowned. *Mostly?* He looked at Greg, who was fidgeting with an IV drip. "Why does my ass hurt so much?"

Greg continued to fidget. "Well, if I had to guess," he said, eyes locked on the medical equipment, "I'd say you got kicked pretty good."

"You think so?" Jay said quietly, a hint of fear in his voice.

"Seeing as how most of your bruises are suspiciously foot-shaped," Greg replied, finally turning towards the young man, "I'd say it's a pretty good bet."

Jason stared at the man, then quickly looked away. "Yeah, that must be it," he said tersely. "I got kicked. Fucking cock suckers kicked me."

Greg considered his patient for a moment, then turned and walked towards the nearby sink. Jason closed his eyes as the sound of running water drifted towards him. The man returned a moment later with a glass of water. "Here," he said, "drink this. Can you lift your head?"

Grunting with effort, Jason got his face a few inches above the pillow and allowed the man to pour a thin stream of water into his mouth. He gulped loudly, then let his head fall back onto the mattress, water dribbling down his chin and onto his neck. He sighed as the liquid soaked into his parched throat.

"What did you give me?" he asked, "I can barely fucking move."

"I gave you a sedative. I didn't want you thrashing around and hurting yourself."

Jason tried once again to move his arm, and once again felt the tightening around his wrist. He struggled feebly for a moment, then glared at Greg, eyes wide with sudden understanding. "Did you fucking *tie me down*?"

Gregory shrugged unapologetically. "Like I said, I didn't want you to hurt yourself."

"Is that so?" Jay growled. "Well, you can fucking *un*tie me now."

"Sorry," Greg said, shaking his head, "I can't do that yet. I have to wait a while till I'm sure you're not gonna throw a fit."

"Throw a fit?" Jason paused, frowning. What was this guy up to? "You want to see a fucking fit?" he growled, his anger rising, "Fucking untie me right fucking now, you fucking homo cock sucker, and I'll show you—"

Jason froze in mid-rant, his eyes suddenly going wide as a horrific thought took root in his brain. He shot Greg a furious, wide-eyed look. "You're not a fucking *faggot*, are you?"

"What ..." Gregory stared at Jason a moment, then shook his head and chuckled. "No, no, I'm not a homosexual."

"You sure?"

"Yes," Greg replied, still chuckling, "I'm sure."

"All right then," Jason snapped, "Fucking untie me!"

Greg studied the young man's face for a moment, finally shrugging and stepping to the end of the makeshift hospital bed. "Okay," he said. "Just remember you've got an IV in your arm. I don't want you pulling it out when you sit up or anything." After carefully removing the blanket, Greg leaned over and began untying the scrap of fabric around Jason's left foot. "Hmmm ..." he said, "I seem to have tied these a little too well. Hang on a second, I'll get a knife or something."

Jason watched Greg as he wandered into the kitchen, then looked down at his clothes. He was wearing a pair of baggy brown pants below a checkered, button-down shirt with the sleeves cut off. *Must be Beardy-Boy's clothes,* he thought, *cause they sure as fuck aren't mine*. He glanced at the IV in his left arm, then frowned as he considered the thick bandages wrapped around his hand.

"Shit!" he called out, twisting his head to look at Greg, "Did you give me a Jabber? I need a fucking Jabber!"

"Whoa! Whoa! Hang on a minute," Greg replied as he approached the bed, knife in hand. "Let me get those restraints before you hurt yourself."

"My—my implants!" Jason cried, his voice tinged with panic. "What did you do?"

Alarmed by Jason's mounting agitation, Greg paused a few feet away. "I don't have any Phenylbutalol," he said slowly, and not without sympathy. "I had to take them out."

Jason's eyes went wide. His face, naturally pale, turned dead white. Instinctively, Greg stepped away from the bed. "I'm sorry. I had no choice."

Jason strained against his bonds. "No choice?" he shrieked. "No fucking choice? You fucking faggot cock sucker! I'm gonna kill you! I'm gonna fucking rip your head off!"

Greg raised his hands. "Whoa, take it easy. There was really nothing I could do. Nothing. If I had left them in they would have gotten infected. You can die from an infection here."

"You had no right!" Jason bawled. "You fucking prick! Put them back!" His face went from white to red as he flailed against his restraints, screaming at the top of his lungs. Greg took another step back, hoping the kid would wear himself out before any serious damage was done. Fortunately, he did; two minutes later Jason lay still, quietly weeping. "I'm gonna kill you," he said between sobs.

"Listen, kid," Greg said, once again approaching the bed, "like I said, I'm really sorry. I'm trying to help you here."

"Fuck you, you f-fucking faggot rim-job! I'm gonna t-t-tear your dick off then jerk off on your face, you piece of shit!"

Greg sighed, then after a moment said, "Look, let's get something straight here. You're in the Rim. You're weak and injured. I don't know what your story is, but obviously the Rim hasn't been too good to you so far."

"I'm gonna shit on your face!" Jason cried, "Do you fucking know who I am?"

"I could have left you where I found you," Gregory said, raising his voice above the young man's rantings, "but I want to *help* you."

Jason lay still a moment, his face red and damp, his breath heavy and rasping. "I'm going to kill you," he croaked.

"Well, you can certainly try," Greg said, exasperated, "but that wouldn't be a good idea, and here's why: first of all, you're smaller and I would bet quite a bit weaker than I am, or at least you are right now. And while you're probably excellent at fighting monsters in cramped quarters in outer space, based on how I found you, I'd say you're shit at fighting real people in the real world. Secondly, if you do get lucky and actually kill me, you'll be back on your own in the Rim, and trust me, no one out there gives a single solitary shit about your well-being."

Jason blinked away an errant tear. "We'll see about that."

Greg sighed. "Yeah, I guess we will."

Jason sat at a small table a few feet away from the couch, the ratty old blanket hanging loosely over his shoulders. He lifted a cracked mug up to his nose. "This smells like ass."

"Yeah," Greg replied, chuckling, "I guess it does." He retrieved a small metal can from a cupboard and placed it on the table in front of Jason. "Try some sugar with it if you want."

Jason took a sip and grimaced. "For fuck's sake," he said, hastily reaching for the can. "What is this shit?"

"Vitamin tea. Hard to get. Trust me, your body will thank you." The young man dumped in two heaping spoonfuls of sugar, then stirred in sullen silence. Greg sipped his drink. "So," he said, "first things first. What's your name?"

Jason tentatively sampled his newly sweetened drink, then put the cup down and pushed it towards his host. "Seriously, I'm gonna fucking puke. Thanks but no thanks." He stared at Greg a moment, then crossed his arms and looked away. "My name's Jake."

"Jake?" Greg replied, eyebrows raised. "Hmmm ..." He blew on his tea, had a sip. "Look, kid," he said, leaning back, "I know you're in a tough situation here, but you've gotta believe me when I say I'm on your side."

Jason rolled his eyes. "Yeah, whatever."

" 'Whatever'? Hey, I saved your life!"

"Yeah," Jay replied, glaring. "And you fucking tied me to a bed and cut out my implants! Wow, how will I *ever* repay you?" He shook his head. "I still think you must be some kind of faggot or something."

"I *told* you, I *had* to take—" Greg paused, exasperated. "Listen Jason, I know who you are. You've been all over the news broadcasts today."

Jay's eyes widened. "The news? What are you talking about? What are they saying about me? Are they looking for me?" He paused, wondering if his message to Claude might actually be bearing fruit. "Did they mention anything about someone called Creston? Does it sound like ..." He trailed off as Greg shook his head, a sympathetic look on his face. "What? What's going on?"

"I'm sorry Jason," Greg said slowly. "They're saying you're dead; killed on your first Flasher mission."

Jason's jaw dropped. "Dead? Are you fucking kidding me?"

"I'm afraid not."

Jason blinked, then slowly lowered his head onto his hands. Since finding himself at the Reclamation Centre, he had held no illusions whatsoever that he would ever return to his old life. Still, despite his dire situation, he had continued to believe that someone, somehow, might eventually come to his aid, at the very least allowing him to return to the Core and lead something resembling a life worth living. Now that he had been declared dead however, the already vanishingly slim chance of his rescue had been obliterated outright; Jason no longer existed, and the powers that be would never allow anyone to prove differently.

"Jason," Greg said, leaning forward, "what happened? Why are you in the Rim?"

Jay sat silently for a moment, finally raising his head and slumping on his chair. "Fucking Isaac," he mumbled, angrily swiping tears from his cheeks.

"Who's Isaac?"

"My so-called fucking friend. I was out drinking with him and another guy, and I woke up in a fucking bag at the Reclamation Centre." Jason pulled the blanket tight around his shoulders and looked down, shaking his head. "Can you fucking believe it? Who would fucking do something like that? Fucking Isaac ..."

Greg nodded sympathetically, then frowned. "The Reclamation Centre eh? That's in the Transitional Zone ... How'd you wind up in the Rim?"

Jay took a deep, shaky breath, then let it out. "I was fucking hung over and freaked out. When I figured out I was in the Reclamation Centre I panicked ..."

"Yeah, I'll bet. Apparently a Flasher caught in the Zone is a pretty big deal."

"Yeah."

"So you escaped into the Rim."

"Yeah."

"Wow. Do you think the High Command is really *that* strict? I mean, seriously, even if they *had* caught you, it couldn't have been worse than going into the Rim ... could it?"

"Yeah," Jay replied, giving Greg a sidelong glance, "it could." *Especially if you've been seen taking a tour of the old*

*Flasher's retirement home.* He slumped a little lower in his chair. "It really, really could."

"Huh …" Greg leaned back and steepled his fingers. "So how'd you do it? I mean, you couldn't have just walked past the guards into the Rim."

Jay opened his mouth to speak, then paused, searching Greg's face. "You're a curious fucker, aren't you?" he said, frowning.

Greg chuckled. "Yeah, I guess I am. But you've gotta admit, you've got a pretty intriguing story there."

*Yeah, fucking fascinating.* Jason sniffled a few times, then blew his nose in the blanket. Greg winced slightly. "Tell you what," Jay said, balling up the cover and tossing it on the floor. "Why don't you entertain *me* for a minute, and tell me what the fuck *your* story is?"

"Well, sure. What would you like to know?"

"Well how about you tell me how you scored a place like this in the Rim?"

Greg laughed out loud. "Huh!" he exclaimed, grinning through his beard. "Impressed by my swanky décor, are we?"

"Well, no," Jay replied. "The place is a fucking dump. But still … you've got running water, power, medical shit. What's the deal?"

"Well, first of all, everyone on the ship gets power. The towers emit in all directions, and the Council takes care of the towers. Power's not a problem … getting the stuff that uses the power is the problem."

"Yeah, that's right." Jason said, shaking his head. "Man, I fucking knew that …"

Greg smiled sympathetically. "It's all right. You've had quite a shock. Things will clear up in time."

"Fuck you, you condescending faggot."

Greg raised his hands. "Sorry."

"Yeah." Jay glared at Greg, then looked away. "So, what

about the water then? You gonna tell me the pipes emit it in all directions, or some shit like that?"

Greg smiled. "No, no … well, not exactly. Thing is, the pumps that service the Core are the same ones that service the Rim, kind of like the power arches. They don't maintain the pipes going into the Rim, but they've never shut them off either, much as they'd like to."

"Fucking bleeding hearts would throw a shit fit if they did."

Greg sighed. "Well, maybe. Anyway, the pipes were built to last, so most of the buildings still get water. Even if some of the plumbing's messed up, it's pretty easy to tap into a main line somewhere."

Jay nodded. "Yeah, I guess that makes sense. But still … drugs? Syringes? Fucking *vitamin tea*? There's no way that shit's just lying around in this fucking place."

"Well, yeah, you're right. Or mostly right anyway. There *is* some stuff just lying around, but most of it's no good. I spend a lot of time scavenging though, and every once in a while I get lucky and find something good that got left behind when they cleared out the Rim. It's usually somewhere that's really hard to get to, or maybe it's a couple of small items buried under a pile of shit or something." Greg chuckled. "Actually, one time I did find something under a pile of shit. Seriously, a real pile of shit. It was pretty gross, but I got a fine piece of electronic hardware out of it." He paused, a faint smile on his face. After a moment he sighed. "Yeah. And sometimes I trade for stuff. Anyway, I find enough to survive." He winked at Jay. "I even have a little left over for the odd Flasher who happens to drop by."

"Yeah, well don't expect me to blow you or anything."

Greg raised his hands. "Hey, I told you already, I'm straight."

"Yeah, so you say. And don't fucking wink at me."

"Huh. *Anyway* … some of this stuff they let me bring in

when I got shipped out of the Core, and I also get supplies from my connections at the Reclamation Centre."

Jay suddenly sat up straight, eyes wide. "What do you know about the Reclamation Centre?"

"I used to work there."

Jay's eyes narrowed in suspicion "Really … doing what?"

"I was Head of the Nutrient Salvage Division of the Decomposed Human Tissue Reclamation Project."

"*Decomposed Tissue …*" Jay said, eyes flashing, "Are you fucking serious? Are you fucking telling me they've been feeding us *rotten fucking meat*?"

Greg chuckled. "No, no … well, not exactly, anyway. They've been feeding us 'reclaimed nutrients' from rotten meat. And don't worry, you haven't had any … um, yet. It's only used in food destined for the Rim."

Jason shook his head in horrified wonder. "Fuck me …"

Greg spread his hands. "Again … not gay."

"Yeah, yeah," Jay said, his voice dripping with derision, "Whatever … I get it."

Greg grinned. "Maybe so, but you won't get it from me, cause like I said …"

"All right!" Jason exclaimed, now smiling slightly despite himself. "Fucking enough already!"

Greg shrugged amicably. "As you wish." He paused, his eyes twinkling with mischief. "But not every way you wish, cause, you know …"

"Okay! I fucking get it! Just shut the fuck up!" Jay was surprised to find himself actually laughing. It felt good.

Greg raised his hands in mock surrender. "Okay, okay. No more. I promise."

"Good." Jay allowed himself a few more chuckles, then sighed. "So what's the deal?" he asked, turning to study Greg's makeshift laboratory. "Who did you fuck to end up here?"

"Nobody, really." Greg said, a touch of melancholy in his voice. "I guess it was my punishment for being too curious."

"Too curious. What does that mean?"

"It means if I were a cat I'd be dead."

"What the fuck's a cat?"

Greg chuckled. "Ancient Earth animal. Or possibly mythical Earth animal, or … well, never mind …"

"Seriously, man, what the fuck is wrong with you?"

"Okay, okay, here's the story: I was working in Reclamation, like I said, but what I really wanted to do was get into Research." Greg paused and raised a finger. "That's the curiosity part. So anyway …" he continued, lowering his finger and settling into his chair, "I made some connections and started learning more about the field—how things worked on that end.

"So everything's going great till one day I get invited for a meeting with the Head of Security for the Research Division. Old bald guy, smelled like farts. Anyhow he starts by congratulating me on my fine work with decomposed tissues, then tells me how much my superiors love me, and how some of the folks in the Division are all excited about the possibility of me going over to work with them.

"Then things get weird. He starts talking about the 'sacrifices' people have to make in the name of research. Asks me a bunch of ethical questions about what I would be willing to do to help strengthen the fight against the Squelchers. Wants to know what books I read, what my political leanings are. By the time I left, my head was swimming, but I knew one thing for sure—I no longer wanted anything to do with the Research Division."

"So what, you wouldn't bend over for this security guy, and … what? They just up and shipped you out of the Core?"

"Well, not exactly," Greg replied, once again steepling his fingers. "I was pretty careful about what I told him. We 'bleeding hearts' have to watch what we say." Jay snorted derisively. Greg smiled. "The Research Division actually took an active interest in me. When I didn't, um, 'bend over' they assumed I was just playing hard to get, no pun intended, and came back at me with bigger and sweeter job offers. They just wouldn't take no for an answer. That's when I started getting *really* curious, wondering just what on Earth these guys were up to. So I met with them a few more times, and started milking them for information, asking uncomfortable questions. They told me just enough to make me even more suspicious of their motives, claiming they couldn't tell me more until I was hired and had sworn an oath of secrecy. I started telling my friends what was going on, hoping to tease out some information or rumours. Then one day, I guess the Research Division decided I had become more of a potential liability than a potential asset and ..." Greg paused and spread his hands. "Here I am."

Jay nodded slowly. "Yeah," he said. "Here we are."

Greg sighed. "Indeed." He swirled his tea and took a sip. "This is cold, I'm gonna heat it up." He reached over to grab Jay's cup. "You're sure you're not gonna finish this?"

"Fuckin' right, I'm sure."

Greg chuckled as he poured Jay's tea into his. "Well, I'm not going to let it go to waste. Especially after you dumped half my sugar in it." He placed the cup into the microwave by the stove, and set it for 20 seconds. "So," he said, over the whirr of the appliance's fan, "now that I've told you a little about myself, how about you tell me how you got into the Rim."

Jay flexed his right hand, staring morosely at the bandages. He looked up at Greg. "I need you to tell me something else first."

"What? I just told you a bunch of stuff. It's your turn. Quid pro quo."

"*Quid pro* suck my dick. I need to hear some more."

Greg shrugged. "Well, okay ..." The microwave beeped, and he retrieved his steaming drink. "Go ahead—what else can I tell you?"

"What's in it for you?"

Greg blinked. "What do you mean?"

"This." Jay said, indicating the room around them, "*Me.* Why are you helping me? What are *you* getting out of it?"

Greg sat down and sipped his tea, grimacing at the sweetness. "Well, maybe I just like to help people. I am a bleeding heart, after all."

"Yeah, right," Jason replied skeptically. "You just 'want to help.'"

"Well, sure. I mean, look, we're all victims here. We need to stick together."

Jay snorted derisively. "Right. You help a lot of people, do you?"

Greg shrugged. "Well, maybe not as many people as I used to," he said, the corners of his lips tugging upwards slightly even as his eyes expressed a deep sadness. "There was an … incident …" he continued, gesturing towards his face. "I guess you could say I've become a little more selective with my generosity."

*Oh, poor baby,* Jason thought, frowning. "All right," he said, "so give. Why me? What's in it for you?"

Greg sighed. "Fine—it's like this: I took you in because you're a Flasher. Also, you're a Flasher in the Rim, and that tells me you're probably not a very happy Flasher. Well, I'm not happy either. That being said, I think we can help each other."

"And why the fuck would I help a one-eyed faggot-ass Rimmer?"

Greg blinked. "Well," he said, his brow furrowing in bemusement, "out of gratitude for saving your life maybe?" Jason glared in silence. "Hm, well, maybe not … in that case, maybe because we have similar goals."

"Really? And what would those goals be?"

"Well, I think High Command is up to no good. I want to find out exactly what they've got the Research Division doing and help put a stop to it."

"You mean you want to get revenge for them throwing your ass in the Rim."

Gregory shrugged. "Well, that's not my *main* motivation, but ..."

"So you think I want revenge too?"

"I'm sure you do," Gregory replied, leaning forward. "I think you want revenge for what your friends did to you, but there's more to it than that. You see, I don't think the threat of punishment alone would be enough for someone like you to go running into the Rim." He leaned closer. "I think you saw something. Something secret. Something horrible. Something that made you feel you had nowhere else to go."

There was anger in Jason's eyes when he responded. Anger, and fear.

"Yeah," he said quietly, "Maybe I did."

## September 23, 2769

Greg played his flashlight over the stack of boxes by the window, then carefully scanned the rest of the room. The barricade across the back entrance seemed intact, and the bathroom to the right was empty (he had removed the door earlier, allowing him to see inside from his vantage point in the hallway). Chewing his bottom lip, he focused the beam on a glass beaker poking out from beneath the lid of the topmost box.

"Come on man, we gonna fucking do this thing or what?" Jason stood behind him, two large duffel bags hanging over his shoulders.

Irritated, Greg sighed heavily, then turned to face his companion. "Yes, Jay, we are going to do this thing."

"Well it's about fucking time," Jay replied, marching angrily into the room. "Being careful's one thing, but man …" He shrugged the bags off his shoulders, then unzipped them and pushed them next to the pile of boxes.

Sighing once more, Greg watched as the exiled Flasher began lifting the cartons and placing them in a row on the floor.

Gregory had grown to expect a certain kind of behaviour from his companion over the past few months (that being a grudging sort of cooperation mixed with an overwhelmingly huge dose of profanity and general asshole-ishness), but he still hadn't totally gotten used to it. There were still many times like these when he struggled to not lash out at Jay, reminding himself that he needed him if he was going to have any hope of succeeding in his plans. Besides, the kid *was* going through a lot right now …

"Listen, Jay," he said gently as he walked into the room, "I keep telling you, we *have* to be this careful. Believe me, you just can't predict how these people are going to behave."

"Yeah, well I can sure as fuck predict how *you're* going to behave," Jay grumbled. "Fucking back and forth, back and forth, back and forth. Wait, watch, leave, wait, come back, wait, watch … fucking waste of time!"

Greg opened his mouth to reply, then simply shook his head and turned his attention to the beaker which he had been studying from the hallway. Grasping it between his thumb and forefinger, he gently pulled it free and, after a quick dusting, held it up to the window for further inspection. Though the light coming through the filthy, dusty glass was diffuse, it was bright enough to confirm that the item was not only in good shape, but practically brand new as well. He placed the item next to the box, then gently pried the top all the way open, revealing a nice variety of test tubes and beakers, all apparently as pristine as the first. "Wow," he said quietly, "this is good." He turned towards his companion. "Be extra careful, all right? If the rest is anything like this, we've got some pretty decent stuff on our hands."

"*Be extra careful, all right?*" Jason mocked. "You'd think I was some kind of fucking retard or something."

"Okay," Greg said, raising his hands, "take it easy. I'm not trying to insult you. I'm just saying, this stuff could be really useful."

"Yeah, whatever. It all looks the same as the shit back at the apartment."

Greg chuckled. "Ah, well, my friend," he said, wagging a finger in the air and smiling, "that is where you are wrong. A little bigger, a little smaller, a little flatter, a little rounder … it all makes a big difference in how I use it. Besides," he said, bending forward and peering at the treasure before him, "the markings on these are nicer than most of the stuff at home."

"Whatever." Jason mumbled, reaching into one of the smaller boxes and retrieving a tiny glass funnel. "Hey, look!" he exclaimed, thrusting the object in Greg's direction. "This one looks a little gayer than the other ones! That should come in handy."

"Uh huh."

"And look!" he continued, turning the funnel upside down. "It's nice and tapered. You could lube it up and give yourself a fucking vitamin tea enema!"

"Hmph," Greg said, shaking his head. "Nice. Just keep sorting so we can get out of here."

"Okee dokee!"

The next little while was spent in relative silence as the two men continued poking through the boxes. Having sorted and packed the contents of the first carton, Greg set it aside, then froze. The lid on the box underneath (which had apparently once held NicoStix refills) was spattered with some kind of dark, reddish-brown substance.

The memory hit him like a sledgehammer: the pain in his face, the blood pattering down onto the electronic supplies so carefully laid out in the centre of the room, the way his hand had skidded through the gore as he had tried to break his fall after the second strike. He straightened, emitting a strange kind of gasping sob.

Jason, who had been waxing eloquent on how a common test tube could best be used to perverse effect, spun around to face him. "What the fuck's your problem?" He demanded, a mixture of irritation and concern on his face.

"We're leaving," Greg replied, quickly zipping up his backpack and slinging it over his shoulder. "Close up your bags, we'll come back later for the rest."

"What? What're you talking about? We can carry way more than this!"

"Never mind," Greg said, marching towards the door. "Pack it up and let's go."

Jason watched as Greg poked his head through the doorway, nervously peering from side to side. "No fucking way, Science-Boy," he said, shaking his head. "It takes forever to crawl through this shithole building. I'm not fucking leaving till my bags are full."

Greg glared at him from the entrance. "We're leaving. Now. I'm not gonna say it again."

"Good!" Jay exclaimed. "Cause I don't wanna *hear* it again. So why don't you quit being such a faggot and get your fucking candy ass back in here." He turned away and nudged a box with his foot. "Fucking grow a pair already," he grumbled. "I can smell your pussy from here. Maybe if you'd just—"

Greg was on him in an instant, grabbing his upper arm and spinning him around. Jason looked up, blinking in surprise, then slowly looked down at the older man's hand. "Get off me," he growled.

"Fuck you!" Greg snapped, tightening his grip on Jason's arm. "You're gonna pick those fucking bags up and we're gonna leave, and if you think—" Jason quickly yanked free of him, causing Greg to stumble forward. Recovering immediately, he cocked his fist back, then paused as the kid stood his ground, eyes smouldering. The two stared at each other for a moment, Greg finally letting his arm drop and taking a small step backward. "Sorry," he said, his anger tempered somewhat by a growing sense of sadness and shame. "I'm just … sorry."

"Yeah," Jason replied through clenched teeth, "I guess you fucking are." He glared at Greg for a few seconds longer, then slowly turned away, shaking his head. "Fucking crazy old queer," he mumbled, pushing boxes around as Greg watched in silence. "No wonder I'm still fucking stuck in this shithole. Asshole."

Greg opened his mouth to speak, then paused, shoulders slumped. The kid was being a prick, but that didn't excuse what he had almost done. Truth was, he would probably be less than civil himself if he were in Jason's predicament.

He took a deep breath, then released it slowly. "Listen, kid," he said as Jason slung a bag over his shoulder, "Maybe we can stay a little longer. At least get the best stuff out of here."

Jason bent to retrieve the second bag. "Nah, fuck it," he said. "Let's just get out of here before you fucking start crying or something."

Greg shrugged, then quietly began collecting his things.

"Tell you what," Jay said, smiling sardonically. "On the way back you can tell me what it's like to be a faggot."

★ ★ ★

The artificial sun was nearing the horizon as the pair emerged from the building, its slanting rays glinting brightly off the imposing power arches straddling the Moat. Beneath the structures' spherical brass emitters were tremendous billboards, most of which displayed a non-stop series of cheerful propaganda films, starring handsome young Flashers, sexy young Booster Girls, and a healthy sampling of the well-adjusted, society-minded families who benefited daily from the selfless efforts of the Flasher Corps and the Council which oversaw them. On the Core side, the arches were clean and bright, a result of the rigorous cleaning and maintenance program to which they were subjected on a weekly basis. The ones on the Rim side sparkled just as brilliantly on top, but showed increasing signs of neglect the closer they got to the ground; in most cases their bases were reduced to peeled, graffiti-ridden hulks, serviced just to the point of basic usability, and no more.

Jason walked in silence, staring distractedly at one of the billboards in the distance, where he could just make out a young blonde Flasher grinning broadly, as behind him the shield's light show went off in all its patriotic glory. He shrugged his packs into a more comfortable position, then looked down at his right hand, which at the moment sported a filthy, threadbare, yet fairly serviceable work glove. He flexed his knuckles.

"How're they feeling?" Greg asked.

Jay blinked, then looked up. "What?"

"Your hands ... how do they feel?"

Jay frowned. "All right, I guess," he mumbled. "No fucking thanks to you."

Greg frowned, then looked down at the crumbled pavement passing beneath his feet.

Jason tugged on his glove, frowning. He knew there was no way he could have kept his implants in the Rim; they would have fallen out eventually, and he probably would have died from infection. Truth was, he owed Greg his life. Still, he was angry, and the old guy was a good target. Maybe that wasn't fair, but fuck it, life's like that.

Jason glanced at Greg and sighed. The old guy had a pretty good pout-on happening. "So," Jay asked, making a small effort to sound a little more convivial, "you figure we got some useful stuff?"

Greg walked silently for a moment before answering, "Yeah, pretty good. Should be able to use it for a lot of things."

"Really? That's good. Old queer like you should keep busy. Reduce your stress and shit."

Greg smiled a little. "So ..." he said a moment later, "guess what?"

"You're really a woman?"

Greg chuckled. "No ... actually, what I was *going* to say is, I'm trying out a new recipe tonight."

"Oh, fuck no!" Jason exclaimed, feeling both alarmed and amused at this revelation. "Last time I was shitting for a week straight! C'mon, man, have a little fucking mercy!"

Greg shook his head, laughing. "You are sorely lacking in faith my young friend."

"Yeah, well you're sorely lacking in cooking skill, you fucking old bugger."

Jason glanced at his companion, who was now grinning broadly. He shook his head and tried to conceal the little smile tugging at the corners of his mouth.

"Trust me," Greg said, raising a finger in the air, "you'll be laughing out the other side of your mouth once you've tried it."

"More like shitting out the other side of my ass." Jay replied, adding after a slight pause: "And I think you're using that phrase wrong."

"Oh, is that so?" Greg said, smirking. "So you figure you're some kind of grammar expert now?"

"Whatever ... Just don't put any of those fucking cockroaches in there, all right? I fucking hate those things."

"All right," Greg replied, "tell you what—I'll make the soup without, and whoever wants the roaches can add them after. Sound good?"

Jay snorted. "No, it still sounds like I'm gonna puke, but ... thanks."

"Hey, no problem."

The two walked along amiably for a while, keeping an eye out for anything useful while navigating the streets's cracked and pothole ridden surface.

"Hey, speaking of problems," Jason said as they neared their destination, "what the fuck was that all about back there?"

Greg sighed, then slowly shook his head. "You know, kid, it's something I don't really like to talk about."

"No kidding?" Jay replied, frowning. "Well whatever it is, you need to fucking get over it. I mean, we left a lot of shit back there. Not that I give a fuck about your little bottles and shit, but we go to a lot of trouble to get that stuff. And what if we get into trouble and you go all fucking weird again?"

"Well …" Greg said, chewing his lip, "yeah, maybe you're right … I just don't want to talk about it right now."

"*Wahhh!*" Jay exclaimed mockingly. "*My name's Gwegowy and I don't want to talk about it. Wahhh wahhh wahhh!*"

Greg frowned slightly. "All right, very funny."

"Seriously man, get over yourself! Besides, you know what they say about keeping that kind of shit bottled up inside. Makes you all fucked up and gay and shit, then one day all the gay comes shootin' out your ass like some kinda big fuckin' fagstorm."

Greg shook his head, then glanced at Jay. "You, my friend," he said, once again smiling broadly, "you are definitely one of a kind."

"Yes I am," Jay replied. "And you … you are definitely an old homo bastard."

★ ★ ★

"Hey Shaky," Greg said as he and Jay strode into the building's dilapidated lobby, "what's shakin'?"

In the far corner hunched a small, elderly man with long, wavy grey hair. He wore a stained sleeveless undershirt half tucked into ragged denim shorts, his outfit smartly accessorised with a mismatched pair of women's sandals. "Ha!" the man exclaimed joyfully. "My cock! Hey, Greg, my cock is shaking! Ha! Greg is funny!"

"Yeah, that's right," he replied kindly. "Greg is funny." He knelt down and rummaged in his pack as the old man approached in a strange, hunched-over, sideways fashion. Greg pulled out a small beaker, studied it for a moment, then tossed it over. "Here," he said, winking, "Merry Christmas."

Shaky made a grab for it, mewling pathetically as it bounced off his hand and smashed against the marble tiles which lined the building's entrance.

"Hah! Missed!" Jason crowed. "Serves you right you fucking old knob gobbler."

"No!" the old man squealed. "Why did Greg throw? Greg is bad! Jason is bad!" Shaky made two awkward hops to the side, then squatted down, screwing his face up in a bizarre display of abject misery and questionable sanity. "My friends! My friends!"

"Shut the fuck up!" Jason turned to face Greg. "Why do you even talk to this guy? Man, I wish I could just punch him in the head."

"Noooo!" Shaky cried, wrapping his arms around his face. "No! Greg!"

"Relax Shaky," Gregory said quietly. "No one's gonna punch you in the head. Here." He approached the old man, once again rummaging in his sack and pulling out another little beaker. "Here, take this one. This one's even better." Shaky reached out tentatively, tears flowing along the deep grooves in his cheeks. He took the beaker and held it to his forehead, then glared accusingly at Jason.

"What are you looking at me for, you old fuck? I didn't break your fucking ... whatever."

Greg stepped closer to Shaky and knelt beside him. "I'm sorry I threw the first one. I shouldn't have done that."

"Shouldn't."

"Yeah. You okay?" Shaky nodded, then stuck a glistening, lumpy tongue out at Jason.

"Seriously?" Jay turned to face Greg. "Can we just fucking go already?"

Gregory held up a hand. "Yeah, hang on."

Jason rolled his eyes then shrugged the bags off his shoulders. When Gregory had first introduced him to Shaky, Jason had assumed it was some kind of joke; the old guy was certifiably nuts, and he smelled like piss. Before long he real-ized that Greg actually liked the old guy, and had decided to take care of him, kind of like a family would adopt a fucking retarded baby or something. Though Jason had made no at-tempts whatsoever to hide his disdain for the old weirdo, Shaky had initially made several enthusiastic, though ulti-mately vain attempts at gaining his friendship. Since then they had settled into a familiar pattern of bully and victim, each hating the other for their own reasons.

"Go," Shaky said to Jason. "Gay-Jay can go now." The old man's voice was quiet and quavery, childlike in a creepy sort of way.

Greg smiled. "Okay, we're leaving in a minute. You good?"

"Good. My friend. Good."

"Okay. Did you have a good morning?"

Shaky grinned. "Good morning."

"Good, good. Did you see anything interesting?"

*Ah, fuck. Here we go …* thought Jason, teeth clenched. Listening to Shaky was bad enough at the best of times, but these little information gathering sessions were the worst; how anyone could trust anything that came out of the crazy old bastard's mouth was beyond him.

"Funny rocks," Shaky jabbered. "Big rocks, a man with blood on his feet and rocks. Two girls with their titties hanging out. Claimer truck. Black rocks. Two piles …"

Greg, who had been listening patiently and nodding his head, interrupted. "Claimer truck? The reclamation truck went by yesterday. Did you see one today too?"

"Claimer truck yesterday. Saw truck and rocks."

"Right. Yesterday. No truck today?"

Shaky grinned, revealing a few crooked, brown teeth. "No. Today rocks. Girls with titties. Big church with no doors."

"Oh for fuck's sake!" Jason exclaimed, his patience ex-hausted. "Let's go! This guy's just spouting out crazy old fag-got shit like he always does!" He kicked a small chunk of concrete in Shaky's direction. The old man raised an arm and cried out.

Greg frowned. "Cut it out, kid!" Jay gave him the finger, then sat heavily next to the bags, scowling. "Okay, Shaky," Greg said, placing a hand on the old man's shoulder, "don't worry about him ... you're all right."

"All right," Shaky croaked, a bead of snot forming under his nose. "Shaky is all right."

"All right ... No claimer truck. How about soldiers? Did you see any Green-Heads today?"

"Green helmets," Shaky muttered. "Green helmets, green heads ... no Green-Heads. Rocks and titties and no Green-Heads."

"Good, Shaky, you did good," Greg said, giving the man's emaciated shoulder a squeeze. "We'll see you later, okay?"

"See you later! With Rim-juice?"

"Sure buddy, I'll bring you some Rim-juice. But just a little."

"See Greg later. Rim-juice. Okay." Shaky crouched down even lower, and turned his eyes towards Jason. "Jason eat shit. Shit and farts and my cock!" Apparently caught off guard by this unusual display of bravado, Greg burst out laughing. Encouraged, Shaky continued. "Shit and my cock and piss in my ass! Right Greg? Jason will eat my fart and ass! Right?"

Greg stood up, holding a hand palm-out towards the old man squatting on the floor. "That's enough, Shakes, I get it." He glanced over at Jason, who was now standing next to the bags, hands balled into fists. He gave the kid a quick wave, then looked down at Shaky. "Okay Shakes. Look at me. What's shakin'?"

"My ass! And shit and cock and Jason will—"

"No, Shaky," Greg said, kindly but sternly. "Remember? What's shakin'?"

Shaky paused, glee-filled eyes darting from Greg to Jason

and back again. He looked uncertain for a moment, then his face lit up with joy. "My cock! Right Greg? My cock is shaking!"

Greg smiled. "That's right Shakes. You got it."

"I got it! Right? My cock! I got it! My friend!"

"You bet. We're going now. Take care of yourself Shakes."

"Take care of Shakes!" the old man replied, hopping back a step. "All right! Right Greg? All right."

Jason hefted the bags back onto his shoulders, scowling. "So what's the deal?" he said, glaring at Shaky. "Are we fucking going or what?"

"Yeah. Let's go," Greg said, casting one final glance toward the old guy before turning and walking away.

"Fucking old knob," Jason grumbled. "Seriously, why do you bother with him?"

"Give him a break already," Greg replied, frowning. "He's helpful. And besides, we all gotta watch out for each other. We're all victims here."

Jason snorted; he had long ago grown sick of the old guy's 'We're all victims here' routine. "Yeah?" he said. "Well I'd like to make him a victim of my foot up his nuts."

Shaking his head, Greg mounted the rickety staircase at the far end of the lobby, carefully navigating the loose and rotted boards to the third floor. Abandoning the stairs (which beyond this point were completely impassable), he and Jay walked down the hall and into the last apartment to the right, manoeuvring past piles of debris and discarded furniture until they reached the kitchen. There, Greg stepped through a window onto a small ledge which had once been connected to the fire escape, but now hung isolated above the side lane.

Jason watched irritably as Greg dug through his bag, searching for one of the many safety-related items he lugged around on every outing. After a moment he retrieved a piece of coat hanger whose end had been bent into a rather complex hook form. Pulling a brick from the wall by the window sill, he inserted the hook into the wall, poked around a bit, then yanked. A second later a rusty metal ladder clanged noisily down from three stories up, coming to a rest a foot away from the ledge. Tucking his makeshift tool back into his pack, Greg carefully put the brick back in place, then proceeded to climb to the ledge above, Jason in tow.

"Get the ladder," Greg said as he unlocked the steel door mounted across the window. Reaching over the ledge, Jason grasped the ladder and pulled it back up on its rails, giving it a good yank at the end to secure it. The two men crawled over the windowsill into a bathroom, Greg yanking the door shut and locking it from the inside. Exiting through the living room, they marched down to the end of the hall, where a large cast iron radiator sat askew beneath a window. Greg pivoted the radiator on its pipe, moving it away from the wall, then stuck a finger into a gap in the baseboard and yanked off a panel about two feet square. After they had squeezed themselves through the opening, Greg pulled the radiator back and replaced the panel, using a pair of handles he had affixed to its back. A large, ragged hole led from the cramped space between the walls to a small room littered with debris. On the far wall stood another steel door, this one larger, and festooned with half a dozen padlocks, some key, some combination. After a few minutes they were inside the apartment proper. As Greg locked up from the inside, Jason tossed his bags onto the floor, shoving them next to the wall with his foot.

"Hey, Jason," Greg said, frowning, "careful with those. You're gonna break something."

"Yeah, well I'm tired of carrying this shit," Jay replied irritably. "It'd be a lot easier if we didn't have to go through a million fucking doors and locks every day." Of all the things that annoyed Jason about the old guy, this obsessive caution of his was the worst. And it wasn't just the excessive vigilance while searching strange buildings, it was practically all the time! Twenty steps to leave the apartment, twenty steps to come back in, left turns, right turns, doubling back, secret locking mechanisms … seriously, it was a real fucking wonder they managed to get anything done at all.

"Better safe than sorry," Greg replied, snapping the last padlock shut and carefully placing his own bags on the floor.

"Yeah, like you fucking keep telling me," Jay said, scowling. "Seriously, there is no fucking way some retarded Rimmer could ever even *begin* to figure out that ladder thing. You don't need all this other shit!"

"And I also keep telling *you*, you'd be surprised what those 'retarded Rimmers' are capable of."

"Well, from what I can see, they're a bunch of pinheads and burnouts, but whatever."

Greg sighed heavily. "Yeah, whatever …"

Jason marched across the room and flopped onto the couch.

"Jason! For crying out loud!"

Jay looked up quickly. "What?" Frowning with exasperation, Greg pointed at Jason's crotch, drawing attention to the alarmingly tented condition of his pants. "What?" Jason exclaimed. "It's called a boner. Guys get those sometimes. What the fuck do you want from me?"

Greg's shoulders slumped as yet another heavy sigh escaped his lips. "All right," he said wearily, "just … go take care of yourself, okay? I'm going to get Shandra."

★ ★ ★

"Come on, Greg, I'm *horny*." On her knees, legs apart, Shandra lifted her dress and yanked her stained, threadbare panties down with her thumb, exposing her vagina. She had spent the past five minutes or so gently trying to entice Greg into having sex with her, and as a last resort had gone into full Booster-Girl mode, brandishing all the weapons at her disposal. Greg had to admit, her technique was effective, and as the front of his pants began to tighten, he considered giving in and indulging himself with a quickie. He quickly thought better of it though; in his experience, "quickies" had a strange way of turning into "longies". Besides, it was usually a good idea to find out what she wanted first.

"Sorry Shan," he said, adjusting his crotch. "I'm starving—I really want to get supper started. Besides, we found some good stuff today, and I don't want the kid messing around with it while I'm not there."

"Oh, poo!" Shandra exclaimed, yanking her dress down theatrically. "I hate it when Jason ruins our fun."

Smiling, Greg held out his hand and helped her up. "I know, honey," he said, drawing her near. "I'll make it up to you." He kissed her left cheek, stroking the back of her head, then lightly brushing his fingers over the tangled mass of scar tissue where her ear used to be. She pulled back, shyly covering the area with her shiny blond hair. "C'mon," he said, "let's go."

Shandra waited in the tiny hallway as Greg padlocked the door, then concealed it behind a sheet of drywall. A few feet away, another locked door led to a larger hallway, which in turn led to a steel door similar to the one at the main entrance to Greg's apartment. He undid the locks on the outside, ushered Shandra in, then locked up again from the inside.

"Well look who's here!" Jay exclaimed, grinning. Greg frowned at the young man, who was sprawled out on the sofa with a big wet spot on his crotch. "Hey, why the long face?" Jason asked, sitting up to make room for Shandra. Greg simply shook his head, then stepped silently into the kitchen to start dinner. Behind him Jason said, "What'd I do this time?"

"Oh, never mind him," Shandra replied. "He's just a little tense." After a moment of silence, Shandra giggled, and Jason shushed her. Frowning more than ever, Greg spun around to face them. Jason and Shandra both raised their hands in a "what, we're not doing anything" gesture, mischievous smiles pulling at the corners of their mouths.

Greg was used to a certain amount of flirtation going on between his two young charges. He didn't like it, but he felt he had to cut them a little slack if he wanted everything to keep running smoothly. Sometimes, though, he just wasn't in the mood for their shit, especially that little prick Jason's. This was one of those times.

Gritting his teeth, Greg turned back to his work. "Shandy," he said quietly, "come help me."

"Help you with what?" she replied, a hint of a giggle still in her voice. "You're just cutting up some protein bricks, right?"

"Now."

Shandra sighed theatrically, and a moment later she was next to Greg as he stood hunched over a cutting board. "Here I am," she said blithely. "Use me as you will."

Gregory glared at her, then pointed to a small canister on a shelf. "Grind some of that for me."

"Ok." She reached up for the tin, then twisted the top off and sniffed. The yellow pellets inside had a strong savoury scent. "Mmm. This smells good. Where did you get this?"

"It was part of the last drop," he replied, carefully slicing into a protein brick. "Kingman couldn't fill my order this week, so he topped me up with a few spices."

"Fucking yes!" Jason exclaimed. "Just make sure you put enough on there. That ass flavour's pretty hard to cover up."

"Yeah?" Greg replied testily. "Well if you ever had to fight your way through a food grab, you might not be so quick to complain."

"I keep telling you I want to come along!" Jason exclaimed from the couch. "I'll fucking do the food run myself even!"

Shandra poured a few pellets into a heavy ceramic bowl,

then began pounding on them with a short piece of broom handle. "Yeah, c'mon Greggy," she said playfully, "let him have a little fun."

Gregory silently unwrapped a brick of slimy grey gelatinous material and laid it on the counter next to the one he had just sliced. He regretted bringing up the food run thing; the topic had been covered several times before, and it generally ended with a heated argument. *Me and my big fucking mouth.*

Shandra looked down at her handy-work and said, quietly, "Maybe I can go with him. He can watch over me."

Greg slammed his knife down on the counter and turned toward her, jabbing a finger at her face. "That's enough," he growled, his voice low. "I don't want to hear another word about this." He turned to face Jason. "Same with you. Just shut the fuck up."

"What's the big fucking deal?" Jay persisted. "Sure, leave Shandra here. I can take care of myself! I'll wrap a scarf around my head, wear my gloves. Who's gonna recognise me? Everyone thinks I'm dead anyway!"

"The *public* thinks you're dead," Greg said, for what felt like the thousandth time, "but somewhere out there *someone* knows you're not. And it's pretty likely they've figured out you're in the Rim."

Jay rolled his eyes. *Yeah right.* He had worried at first that he might be tracked going into the Rim, but the fact that he had gotten by the guards so easily had set his mind at ease somewhat. In his opinion, the whole Rim-job Work Program thing was one big cluster-fuck; the people in charge didn't seem much brighter than the fucking Rimmers themselves. Of course he had used that girl's ID, and they probably found her quite a while ago. Still, those guards were fucking morons; they couldn't possibly remember or care who went in and out that day. And besides, who would believe a Flasher would go into the Rim on purpose; he sometimes found it hard to believe himself.

"Yeah, you can roll your eyes all you want," Greg continued, "but it's true. And who can guess what the Green-Heads know? They've gotta have orders to keep an eye out for you, whether they know you're here or not."

Jay snorted. "Yeah right. Those guys are a bunch of retards. They couldn't find a pile of shit if they stepped in it. And it's been three months now! Do you really think they'd still be looking for me?"

Greg glared at Jason for a moment, then turned and sighed. The kid was an asshole, but he wasn't stupid. "Maybe not," he growled. "But we can't take any chances, so just forget it. Both of you." He reached into the ceramic bowl and removed a pinch of the yellow spice. "You guys go sit at the table, I'm almost done here."

"Fuck that," Jason mumbled, arms crossed. "I'm not eating that shit."

"Fine," Greg said, tossing the spiced protein slices in a bowl. "More for us."

"Oh, come on you guys," Shandra said as she pulled up a chair, "play nice."

Greg poured a few ounces of vitamin tea into the bowl, then put it in the microwave. Everyone waited in silence as the appliance whirred noisily, finally beeping a few minutes later.

"Come on kid, let's go," Greg said as he served the steaming concoction onto mismatched plates. "Last call."

"Mmmm, smells good!" Shandra exclaimed brightly as Jay petulantly walked over to the table and took a seat.

"Smells like ass," Jason said, studying the contents of his plate. "Seriously, couldn't I just starve to death and get it over with?"

"Oh, Jay," Shandra said, giggling, "You're always so dramatic!"

"Shandra!" Greg barked, dropping a small container of crispy baked cockroaches onto the table. "Just shut up and eat." He glanced at Jay. "You too."

"Yes Daddy," Jay replied, stirring his stew. He lifted the spoon to his mouth and took a tentative bite. "Oh, for fuck's sake!" he exclaimed, screwing his eyes shut in disgust. "This is really fucking objectionable. Seriously, is this shit? Did you fucking shit in this?"

Greg glared at Jay as Shandra sat giggling into her bowl. "Please," he said wearily, "Just shut up and eat."

"Yeah, yeah, okay," Jay said, grimacing at his spoon. "At least you kept your promise about the fucking cockroaches."

The meal proceeded in relative silence, Jay pulling the occasional odd face for Shandra's benefit. When they were done, she cleared the table and served them all water from the tap.

"Shandra," Greg said as he stirred a pinch of sugar into his glass, "you're going to have to go to your room early tonight. Jay and I have to work."

"Oh, Greg, no!" she pleaded. "Not again! I'll be quiet, I swear! You'll never even know I'm here."

Greg frowned. Why did these kids have to be so fucking difficult? "No Shandra," he replied sternly, "I want you out of here in half and hour."

She glared at Greg, then looked at Jay, who shrugged apologetically. "Fine!" she said, pushing her chair back. "I'll just go now."

"Man, why are you always sending her away like that?" Jay asked as Shandra stomped towards the door. "She wouldn't bother us."

"Yes she would," Greg replied as he stood, fumbling in his pocket for his keys. "Sometimes she just doesn't know when to shut up."

Jay looked towards the door, where Shandra stood, arms crossed, hair dangling in her face. "Yeah, that's true ... but still ..."

"Never mind," Greg said as he headed towards the door. "I'll be back in a minute, then we'll get to work. We've got some important stuff to talk about."

"Yeah, don't we always."

Jason didn't *really* care what happened to Shandra; she was just a used-up Booster-Girl, really nothing more than a play-thing for Greg, as far as he was concerned. Sure, she was fun to flirt with (and it was fucking great to watch the old guy get pissed off about it) but he couldn't actually *do* anything to her. Still, he couldn't help but feel at least a *little* empathy toward her situation; she was stuck here just like he was, and she had even less control over her life. At least he got to go out once in a while …

He looked down at his bandaged hands, and experienced an all too common mixture of misery and astonishment. He had lost ten pounds, most of it muscle, and his skin had taken on an unhealthy yellow hue, dark rings growing ever more apparent under his eyes. He now stooped noticeably, and was often out of breath, despite the exercise he got tramping around in the Rim. He shook his head. How had his life come to this? He was a fucking *Flasher*, for fuck's sake! A veritable rock-star of the military set, with the whole fucking world at his feet. A few short months ago he had been on the verge of actually flashing up to a Squelcher ship, actually fighting the enemy he had been raised to hate. Now he wasn't sure just who the enemy was. The only thing that kept him going (apart from the occasional healthy dose of Rim-juice mixed with a dash of denial) was the hope, however dim, that Greg might, just *might*, actually find them a way out of this.

Jay watched grimly as his "saviour" sorted through a stack of old, mismatched paper. "Why do you write on that shit anyway?" he asked. "Don't you have something electronic you can use?"

"Security, my naive young friend," Greg replied, displaying a wrinkled, water-stained sheet of paper which had, in another life, been part of an installation manual for a bathroom fixture. Though one side was unusable, the other was mostly blank—Greg had scribbled out the original text on top, and had used the rest for his notes, filling the empty space from edge to edge with neat, tiny script. "Electronic devices are too easily compromised."

Jay shook his head and snorted. "Dr. Paranoid strikes again," he mumbled as Greg glared at him. "All right, whatever. So," he said, sitting up in mock excitement, "what incredibly interesting things are we talking about today?"

"Well, I think ..." Greg paused, shuffling through a few more sheets of paper. "Hang on a second, I've just got to find ..."

"Oh, for fuck's sake!" Jay barked in frustration. "Let's fucking get on with it already!"

"All right, kid, settle down. Just give me a second."

"Give you a second ..." Jay mumbled under his breath. "I'll give you a fucking second." He slumped in his chair, then sat up again a moment later. "Oh, oh! I know!" He said, thrust-ing a hand in the air. "Why don't I just tell *you* what we're gonna talk about! Yeah, yeah, I know! You're gonna tell me how you've got plans to get us out of here, and how we're gonna fix the High Command's wagon, and how there have been some unfortunate delays on the other end, and how you can't actually tell me anything about *what the fuck's really fucking going on*!" He pounded a fist on the table, then slumped once again, arms crossed. "There, fucking meeting's *over*! Huh? How's *that* for fucking efficiency?"

Greg studied the young man for a moment, apparently struggling to contain his irritation. A few seconds later he got up, sighing, and headed for the kitchen counter.

"Oh, great! Where the fuck are you going now?" Jay said. "I thought we had some *very important secret shit* to attend to."

"Just getting Joe," Greg replied softly, carefully grasping the little tin and carrying it back to the table.

"Oh, of course ..." Jay mumbled. "Joe! I mean, seriously, how could we possibly fucking get anything done without a scrawny-ass little plant on the table, right?"

"Joe relaxes me," Greg replied, placing the plant between him and Jay. "He helps me remember what we're fighting for."

Jay crossed his arms. "Fine. Can we please just fucking get on with it?"

"Yes, yes, just a second." Greg poured a little of his water into the can, then leaned back. "First of all," he said, "you're right—I haven't really been telling you much, and you deserve to know more. I'm sorry about that, but it's just the way it had to be; this is serious stuff, and it was important for us to get to know each other a little better. Besides, I had to work some stuff out with my contacts before I really had anything concrete to talk about."

Jay blinked. The apology had caught him off guard. "Yeah, well, we're best of buddies now, aren't we?" he grumbled. "In fact, I've been seriously thinking about letting you suck my dick."

Greg chuckled, then sighed. "Ok, then," he said. "Here's the plan. We're going to do an extraction, followed immediately by a press conference in the Transitional Zone. So far, we've got three Green-Heads to get us out, and two reporters ready to meet us on the other side. We've also got my connections in the Reclamation Centre, so there's a slim chance they'll find a way to get us into the Research lab and bust this whole thing wide open in one fell swoop."

Jay's eyes went wide; apparently Greg's plan involved both of them getting killed. "Are you fucking nuts?" he exclaimed, leaning forward. "They'll fucking shoot us the second they realize who I am!"

"No, no ... they won't," Greg replied, hands forward, palms out. "The cameras will be rolling the whole time, with a simultaneous feed to multiple locations. Nobody will know who you are till we tell them, and by then it will be too late. They wouldn't dare do something that stupid on the air."

Jay blinked. The old guy was fucking delusional! Did he really think they would survive a stunt like that? "Fuck you man!" he shouted. "This is way, way fucking bigger than that! I don't know if you're looking to be some kind of martyr or something, but I'm telling you right now, you can fucking *sign me out!*"

Greg fidgeted with his notes. "Look Jay," he said quietly, leaning forward, "I don't want to get killed any more than you do. And neither does anyone involved. We all know the risks, and if we do this right, the only casualties will be the High Command and their fucking Flasher system ... and maybe a councillor or two."

Jason blinked. "Councillor? What's the Council have to do with it?" Like most of the ship's citizens, he was well aware that the elected Council basically took orders from High Command. Whether they would willingly take part in what he had seen in the Transitional Zone though ... that seemed unlikely to him.

"Well, of course the Council's under a lot of pressure from High Command to support the war," Greg said, "and the public's largely sold on it, so I can't blame them *too* much. But I'm pretty sure there are at least a *few* of them who know about the shenanigans going on in the Research Division. At least the Council Head would know, anyway."

Jay frowned. "Are you serious? Why would *anyone* on the Council have to know?"

"Come on, kid. Think about it. Even though the Council follows pretty much everything High Command says, there are times when they just *don't* want to cooperate. The High Command needs someone in the know to facilitate things, move things along when the rest of the Council balks. Who better than the Council Head?"

Jay glared silently for a moment, then glanced down at his

knuckles. "Yeah, I guess that makes sense." He crossed his arms and sat back. "Okay then, back to your awesome plan —tell me exactly how we're going to do this without getting our brains blown out."

Greg pursed his lips. "All right," he said after a moment's thought. "We're going to hitch a ride on a reclamation truck just before it goes into the Zone. We're gonna go in body bags, same way you went in from the Core."

Jay winced. The memory of waking up in a plastic bag still filled him with dread, not to mention shame and embarrassment. "I gotta tell you," he said, "so far your plan's not doing much for me."

Greg smiled sympathetically. "Yeah, I know," he replied. "Not exactly an experience you'd like to revisit, right?"

"No shit."

"Yeah, well, I hear ya. But truth is, it's a good idea, and it's already been tested." Jay snorted and looked away. "Okay, listen," Greg continued after a moment. "The claimer trucks in the Rim always have two Green-Heads plus a driver, so those'll be the three soldiers I mentioned, right? We'll roll up to the front of the Reclamation Centre, just shy of the gate, where the press will be waiting for us. We'll all jump out and start the show immediately, under the protection of our soldiers. It'll take everyone totally by surprise; by the time any-one figures out what's going on, it'll be too late."

"Yeah!" Jay exclaimed. "Too late for us! No matter how long it takes for them to figure it out, they're *gonna fucking shoot us!*"

"Not with our guards there. The Green-Heads watching over us will add just enough confusion and doubt to stop them from acting rashly; they'll have to think about things a little, and that will give everyone a chance to cool down." Greg shrugged. "Sure, they'll take us into custody, but things will already be in motion, and we'll be safe."

Jay shook his head. "I don't know …" He paused as a

thought occurred to him. "Hey, why would these Green-Heads want to be involved with this anyway? They have to know this could get them killed too."

Greg gave him a look that was both disbelieving and slightly condescending. "Come on, kid ..."

"What?"

Greg looked away and sighed. "Okay, look," he said, turning back to face Jay. "You and I both know the shit that goes on. Bad things happen to people. The High Command makes sure the Council glosses it over, but there are always people, victims and those close to them, who know exactly what's going on. Maybe a Booster Girl gets roughed up, and a parent wants some kind of justice. Who's to say that a parent can't be a soldier?"

"Why would the High Command let someone who knows be a Green-Head? That's crazy!"

"Sure, it sounds crazy on the surface, but the High Command has different ways of keeping people in line. And they need soldiers. Maybe they threaten their families to keep them quiet, then force them to stay in the military so they can keep tabs on them. Who knows? The thing is, they can't just get rid of anyone who might know too much; too many people would disappear, and things would get out of hand."

"I don't know man," Jay said, crossing his arms. "All I can say is, if we get shot, I'm gonna fucking kill you."

Greg leaned back, the little smile on his lips belying the hardness lingering in his eyes. "Fair enough."

After a moment of silence, Jay leaned forward, elbows on the table. "So when's this crazy suicide mission gonna happen?"

"Well," Greg replied, flipping through his notes, "we've still got a few details to iron out, but it looks like we should be ready to go within a month."

"A fucking *month*?" Jay exclaimed, slapping a palm to his forehead. "It'd better not be any fucking longer than that; living with you's a fucking nightmare."

Greg chuckled. "Duly noted."

"Yeah. *Duly noted.*" Jay groused. "How about you *duly note* my foot up you ass?"

"Right. Mind if we move along to the next topic?"

Jay spread his hands. "Hey, you're in charge of this clown fest. Fire away."

"All right then." Greg leaned back with his hands behind his head, studying his friend's face. "So," he said after a moment, "your turn."

"My turn for what?"

"Your turn to talk."

"I am talking, you fucking retard."

Greg sighed. "Ok, let me be more specific. What exactly did you see in the Reclamation Centre?"

*Ah, shit.* Jay's shoulders sagged and a small shudder ran through him; this was a topic he had no inclination to revisit. "I fucking told you what I saw in the Reclamation Centre."

"Well, yes, you did," Greg continued patiently. "And I know it's hard to talk about. But you didn't tell me very much. I need more details."

Jay pushed his chair away from the table. "I fucking told you what I saw!" he barked. "Flashers hooked up to a bunch of medical shit! Half-dead guys full of tubes and machines sucking shit out of them!" His voice cracked, and he grit his teeth. "What the fuck else do you want to know?"

"Like I said, I know this is hard," Greg said quietly. "And I'm sorry. I just really need more details to help prepare our case for when we get across."

"What, can't your so-called 'contacts' get this info?" Jay grimaced and looked away, flexing his knuckles compulsively. "I'm already part of your crazy 'let's all go get killed' extraction mission. Isn't that good enough?"

Greg leaned forward. "You being there *is* important. Your presence will get us more attention than we could possibly get otherwise. But we need to have the whole story. We need to know exactly what you saw so we can all be on the same page when the real questions come. And no, my contacts can't get this stuff; we don't have anyone who's actually been in the Research lab." Jay shook his head and swore under his breath. "Look," Greg continued, "we've suspected this stuff for quite a while now. We've got a lot of credible information, but it's mostly second and third hand. We need to know what we're really fighting against before we attack."

Jay sat silently for a moment, then sighed heavily. He really didn't want to talk about this. "Fuck," he said, his voice nearly a whisper. "All right, what do you want to know, exactly?"

"Good," Greg said, pen poised above his notes, "thank you." Jay responded with a sneer and a dismissive wave of his hand. "Okay," Greg continued gamely, "let's start with the machinery. Can you describe the different parts, how they connected to the patients, what the devices looked like, readouts ..."

Jay hesitated, then threw his hands in the air in frustration. "Well, no! I mean, I was just in there for a few minutes, and I was kind of freaking out! Like I told you, there were tubes and machines and fluids and ... fuck man, what more do you want?"

"Okay, that's all right," Greg prompted gently. "You said they were harvesting something from the bodies, and that Flashers, or at least some of them, are ... like *offspring*? What exactly did you see that gave you that impression?"

"I told you before, I looked at the charts. All the guys in there had Flasher call signs. Fuck, one of them was Hep Leipsic for fuck's sake!"

Greg's eyes widened. "Hep Leipsic? Holy shit, you didn't tell me *that* before." Jay shrugged, frowning. "Wow," Greg continued. "Hep Leipsic was supposed to have been killed in action ... he was definitely alive when you saw him?"

"Yes, he was fucking alive!" Jay barked. "He was …" he paused as a shadow of pain flitted across his features, "messed up … but he was alive."

"Wow," Greg whispered, quickly jotting down notes. "And what about the 'offspring' thing? Was that in the charts too?"

Jay looked down at his hands. "Yeah," he said. "Every patient had a list … all Flasher call signs. Some of them were people I know … fuck, I even trained with some of them!"

"Hmmm … okay." Greg paused a moment, chewing his pen as he reviewed his notes. "So … you said you saw your name on someone's 'offspring' list?"

"Yes," Jason said, glaring, "I did say that. I thought you were after *new* information here."

"Yeah, yeah, sorry. Just bear with me … did the file specifically say that this person was your father, or did he donate something that was given to your father before you were conceived, or …"

Jay stood up abruptly, hands balled into fists at his sides. "How the fuck should I know?" he shouted. "Maybe he's my father, maybe not, I don't fucking know! I don't even know if my mother is really my mother! Did they give her this guy's sperm? Did they fertilise someone else's eggs and put them into her?" He froze, eyes wide, as a heretofore unexplored thought entered his mind. "Holy shit, am I a fucking *clone*?"

"Kid," Greg said quietly, "it's okay. Calm down."

"Calm down? Fucking *calm down*?" Jay stepped forward, tearing the bandages from his right hand. "Look at this!" he shouted, pointing to the scars on his knuckles.

"Jay, I'm sorry, I …"

"Look at this, and tell me something!" he cried, thrusting his hand towards Greg's face. "Who the fuck am I, *Gregory*? Huh? *What* am I?"

Greg spread his hands helplessly. "Jason," he said quietly, "I really am sorry."

Jay stood silently for a moment, breathing heavily, before

finally dropping into his chair. "Yeah," he said, "I fucking bet you are." He shook his head, then reached down to retrieve his discarded bandage. *Fucking old queer*, he thought as he wrapped the stained fabric around his knuckles. He tied the bandage tight against his palm, then glanced at Greg, who was fiddling with his pen, a hangdog expression on his face. Jay looked away, sighing. The old guy was a pain in the ass, and like pretty much everyone in his life he was using him. Still ...

"It's all right, kid," Greg said, interrupting his thoughts, "let's take a break. We can finish this later."

"Nah," Jason said, calmer now. "Let's just get on with it."

"No, no, let's cool it for a bit. This can wait."

"I said let's fucking get on with it." Jay repeated, a little more loudly. "Just fucking tell me what else you want to know."

Greg studied his companion for a moment, then once again referred to his notes. "Okay then," he began cautiously. "Just one more question, really." Jay nodded tersely. "The message you sent to ..." he paused, flipping through his notes, " to Claude ... what did you tell him, exactly?"

Jay flinched. "How did you know about that? I never fucking told you about that!"

Greg cleared his throat. "It was ... intercepted."

"What the fuck are you talking about?"

"Well, to put it simply, the High Command *does* know you're in the Rim."

"Fuck!" Jay cried. "Are you fucking kidding me? So you're saying they're actually, *really* searching for me now?"

"No, no," Greg said, raising his hands. "Well, maybe, I don't know. Truth is, they've probably known you were here the whole time, like I said. If they had the resources to search the whole Rim, they would have probably found you by now."

Jason glared incredulously at Greg. "And you fucking took

me out with you to do your little fucking errands? When you *knew* they knew I was here?"

"I didn't know they knew for sure until just recently. Besides, would you have preferred being locked up in here the whole time?"

"Well, I don't know," Jay replied through clenched teeth. "You seem to think it's good enough for your girlfriend."

Greg balled his hands into fists, struggling not to lose his temper. "Listen," he said after a moment, "I know for a fact there's no way the High Command could manage to search the Rim well enough to find you—there are just too many places to look. And even if they walked right by you, it's unlikely they'd recognise you. I mean, without your fancy Flasher clothes and high-end hairstyle, you could easily be just another Rim-dweller. And with your implants gone, you probably don't even have to wear gloves. Now I'm not saying you shouldn't wear them, but truth is almost everyone here has scars of some kind—without taking a close look, yours are not much different from anyone else's."

"Seriously?" Jason growled. "Then what was all that shit about me not going to the food dumps?"

"Jay, that's different. People are crazy at food dumps. There's twitchy Green-Heads everywhere, just looking for an excuse to shoot somebody. And if the soldiers *are* keeping an eye out for you anywhere, it would be there, considering it's the only place where Rimmers have to come to *them*." Greg paused, shaking his head. "Trust me Jay, you don't want to be anywhere near a food dump."

Jason struck the table with his fist. "Fuck. So first you try to convince me they're looking for me, and now you're trying to make me believe they're probably not, but maybe they are at the food dumps. So what, is everything you say just a pile of shit now? Is this fucking plan of yours even real?"

"Kid, listen," Greg said, obviously fighting to keep his patience. "Everything I've told you is basically true. I just didn't tell you about the message intercept before because I didn't want to freak you out. You needed enough time to adjust to your situation. And like I said, we needed to get to know each other a bit more before you got all the info."

"Fuck," Jay said under his breath. Though he knew that Greg was the only game in town, he had never fully trusted him; it was just too obvious that the guy was working on his own agenda. Still, to his credit, Greg had never really tried to hide that fact. Jason crossed his arms and took a deep breath, struggling to sort out what had just been said. After a moment he leaned back and sighed. Though what Greg was saying did initially seem to contradict what he had said before, in truth it all made sense, more or less. He *was* pissed off that the old bastard hadn't told him about the message interception, though.

"So listen, *Gregory*," Jay began, frowning, "you keeping any other information I should know about?"

Greg paused. "Look," he replied, "I'm sorry it had to be that way. But it's different now; we've been together long enough, and now we're both fully invested. I swear I'll answer any of your questions as best I can from now on."

"*Fully invested*," Jason mocked. "How about I *fully invest* my boot up your ass?"

"Okay," Greg said, sighing. "So, how about that break?"

Jason looked away angrily. "No," he mumbled after a moment. "Let's keep going."

Greg nodded wearily. Truth was, he was ready for a break himself. He scrubbed his face with his hand, then looked down at his notes. "All right then," he said, "what *did* you say in that message?"

Jay sighed heavily. "Not much, really ... I was pretty freaked out. Basically something like 'You gotta help me! They're using Flashers hooked up to machines in the Reclamation Centre—I'm hiding in the Rim and I can't come out.' Something like that."

"Okay ... did you send it to anyone else, other than Claude?"

"No. I was in a fucking hurry!" Jay paused and shook his head. "I figured he was the only one I could trust." He shook his head again. "That little twerp's actually a pretty good guy. I should've been nicer to him."

Greg cast his companion a sympathetic look. "Don't worry," he said quietly, "I'm sure he's okay."

Jay sat up suddenly. "Fuck!" he blurted, eyes wide. "What do you mean? Is he in trouble?"

Greg cringed slightly. "Well," he said, shrugging apologetically, "they *did* intercept your message to him."

Jason blinked. "Well, yeah, but ... fuck! *He* didn't do anything! I mean, he might have helped those other fuckers send me over the Shit, but that couldn't have been *his* idea ..." He paused for a moment, then put his head in his hands. "Aw, man ..."

Greg sighed. "Look, Jay," he said, "I'll be honest ... your friends were taken in for questioning, but they're probably okay. We would probably have heard something ..."

Jason raised his head and cast his companion a frightened, angry glance. "You really think so?"

Greg hesitated. "Well ..."

Jay quickly looked away, nodding. "Yeah, of course they're okay ... like you said, you would have heard something, right? Bunch of assholes anyway ..." He looked down at the floor, then whispered: "My family ..." When he looked up again, Greg was shaking his head sympathetically. "Oh, fuck," Jason breathed, tapping his foot nervously on the floor. "It's okay ... they'll be fine ... *they* didn't do anything. They'll be fine ..." His thoughts racing, Jay lowered his head into his hands. He had always viewed his friends with a certain amount of disdain, and his reaction to their situation was confusing, especially considering what they had done to him. Even more jumbled were his feelings for his family; no longer certain of his biological lineage, he couldn't help but feel suspicious towards them. Were they willing participants in a system that would see their son ultimately hooked up to a machine like some kind of freak? Still, he couldn't deny the love he felt, that all children felt, even under the worst circumstances, for the people who held him close and protected him when he needed protecting. He took a deep, shuddering breath, then let out a small, strangled sob.

"All right," Greg said quietly, "that's enough for now. I'm gonna work some more on my own."

"Fuck," Jay mumbled. "Just … fuck." He tapped his foot a few more times, then abruptly threw his hands in the air. "I wasn't thinking straight!" he cried, a tear running down his cheek. "I had to get rid of my phone so they wouldn't track me … it was my last chance to use it. I was freaking out! I just wanted to get the fuck out of there!"

"Of course," Greg replied sympathetically. "You couldn't let them catch you; you knew too much."

Jay laughed humourlessly, almost hysterically. "Oh, I fucking knew too much all right," he said, swiping angrily at his cheek. When he spoke again moments later, his voice was low, haunted.

"I knew they were going to put *me* into one of those beds."

"Shaky come with Greg?"

Greg paused on the way to the door, a bemused look on his face; Shaky, well-known for his odd body language, was doing a particularly strange dance, shuffling from side to side with his hands tucked under him armpits. "Uh …" Greg blinked, then smiled and shook his head. "No, sorry buddy," he said kindly. "I've got work to do."

"Shaky can help!" the old man persisted, now grabbing his long greasy hair with both hands and pulling it towards the sky. "Shaky can guard Jason!"

Jay raised his hands and turned towards Greg. "What the fuck …"

Greg laughed, looking down fondly at the old man. "It's all right, Shakes," he said, "I don't need anyone to guard Jason."

Jason glared at Shaky, prompting him to step back, cringing. "Shaky can *help*," he mewled, "and … Jay can eat my ass!"

Greg glanced at Jason, then looked back at Shaky, frowning. "Okay, that's enough, Shakes," he said sternly. "Just chill, and I'll see you later."

Shaky shrank back into a corner as Greg turned to leave.

Jason considered the old man for a moment, then shook his head and laughed. "Ah, what the fuck," he said amiably. "Let's bring the old bastard with us."

Greg turned. "All right Jay," he said irritably, "quit fucking around. Leave Shakes alone."

"No, seriously," he persisted. "It might be fun. Maybe he can carry our stuff or something." Shaky took a small step forward, looking anxiously from Jay to Greg, then back again.

Greg sighed. "Jay ..." he said, now smiling a little but looking like he was trying not to. "C'mon, you're giving the poor guy false hope."

"No, really," Jay said. "Let's do it." He sat on his haunches and held a hand out to the old man. "Whaddya say, Shakes? Ya wanna come? Huh? Ya wanna go outside with Greg and Jay?"

Greg glanced at Shaky, who had begun hopping up and down in anticipation, a small stream of drool dribbling down his chin. "Ah, shit," he said, shaking his head, "I can't say no now, can I? C'mon Shakes, let's go."

Grinning his big, lopsided, and mostly toothless grin, Shaky hopped over to Greg's side. "Shaky go!" he crowed happily. "Shaky help Greg and piss on Jay's balls!"

Greg turned to Jason and smiled. "Just remember," he said, "you asked for it."

Greg knelt by the base of the power arch and rummaged through his bag as Shaky hovered excitedly over him. Keeping an eye out for trouble, Jay glanced up and down the street, pausing a moment to study a small group of Rimmers who were presently looking up at their apartment building, only a few blocks away. One of them turned and pointed towards Jay and his group and, after a short discussion, began walking towards them, fellow Rimmers in tow. Jay frowned. "Who are *these* fuckers?"

Greg looked up, squinting. "Don't worry about it," he said. "Just some juice heads. Harmless."

Jay watched the group approach as Greg carefully laid out his tools. "They look like a bunch of assholes," he said. "You sure they're okay?"

"Assholes!" Shaky exclaimed. "Fucking cock suckers, right Greg?"

"All right Shaky," Greg said, "keep it down for a minute." He turned towards Jay, who was watching the group with a strange intensity. "Relax, kid," he said quietly. "They're okay. Just let me handle it." Moving his tools aside, Greg stood up and waited for the Rimmers to arrive.

At the head of the group was a young bald man in a tattered grey trench coat, his left eye largely hidden by a ghastly chunk of scar tissue. His clothes hung loosely off his frame, partially concealing his swollen, malnourished belly. "Hey Greg, old buddy," he croaked, "what's the word?"

"I'm busy right now Pete," Greg replied sternly. "I'll see you tomorrow."

"Yeah, sure," Pete said, shifting nervously from one foot to the other, "I hear ya. It's just that me and my friends were hoping maybe you could give us a little juice, you know, just to hold us over till then. You know, since we're already here and everything ..." Greg looked from Pete to the others, one of whom he recognised. The third, a short woman with long, filthy, matted brown hair and dirty pink dress, he had not seen before. She had wandered over to the side, and was presently staring at Greg's tools. "Hey, listen," Pete said. "We found some stuff for ya." He quickly turned to the man behind him, a large-boned mental deficient by the name of Gap. "C'mon, show him the stuff."

"Who's that looking at my tools?" Greg asked, nodding towards the woman. Startled, she looked up at Greg, then quickly looked away.

"What?" Pete said, turning away from Gap to look at the

girl. "Oh, no … nobody's lookin' at nothing … no, yeah, that's Gitch. She's all right, man. Hey, tell you what, she's got no teeth, so she can suck you off like nothin!" Before Greg could respond, Pete quickly reached back and took a handful of electronic bits and pieces from Gap's outstretched hands. "Here's the stuff, man. Good stuff—see? All kinds of wires and shit. Good for a couple of shots, right? Or maybe you wanna fuck Gitch's mouth first? Whatever you want, man." Shaky poked his head out from behind Greg and giggled. Pete glanced at him, then quickly looked back at Greg. "Hey, she'll do all of you if you want. Whatever you want, no problem!"

Jay stood a few feet away, watching the exchange. He and Greg ran into people like this fairly regularly when they went out, and they rarely had any real trouble. Still, he couldn't help but feel anxious when strangers were around. Though the average Rimmer was weak, malnourished and stupid, the truth was they had gotten the best of him once before, an experience traumatic enough for him to have blocked it from his memory. It stung his pride to admit it, but fighting humans out in the street was nothing at all like fighting Squelchers in the familiar, cramped confines of an alien spaceship.

He glanced uneasily from one stranger to the other, finally locking eyes with the woman. She winked at him, and pistoned a closed hand suggestively in front of her open, toothless mouth while squeezing a saggy breast with the other. He felt himself redden as his pants tightened, adding a strange kind of shameful sexual frustration to the already uncomfortable mix of fear and anxiety he was feeling. *Fucking Rimmer filth.*

"Get out of here," Greg said, interrupting Jason's increasingly volatile thoughts. "See me tomorrow, and don't bring her."

"But hey …" Pete looked down at the treasures in his

hand, then gestured towards the woman. "C'mon, just a little taste ... hey, aren't we your friends?"

"Fuckin pussy!" Gitch rushed forward and gave Pete a shove, spilling the electronics from his hand. "Let's just take it!" she yelled, her voice rough and hoarse. "Are you scared of these losers?"

Gap stepped between Greg and the girl, his face twisted into an alarming mask of fear and misery. "No, Gitch!" he wailed, his voice deep and thick. "No, no, no!"

Stricken, Pete looked down at the spilled offering, then back up at Greg. "Oh, boy," he croaked. "Look, Greg, she's ... she's ... I don't know man, we weren't gonna to do nothin'." He turned towards the girl, who was glaring angrily at Gap. "You fucking cunt!" he yelled. "I'm gonna fucking kill you, you skanky fucking bitch!"

"Pete," Greg said, the steely anger in his eyes belying the calmness in his voice. "Leave now. Come back tomorrow. Do not bring her."

"Right. Right," Pete said as he scrambled to pick up the bits and pieces scattered on the pavement. "Tomorrow. You got it." Stuffing the electronics in his pocket, he turned and gave Gap a shove. "C'mon, c'mon ..." he breathed, "let's go!" The three of them hurried away, Gitch grumbling and complaining about her new companions' apparent lack of genitalia. A few yards away, Pete slammed his fist into her head, knocking her to the ground. He kept walking as Gap hovered uncertainly over the girl, finally helping her to her feet and following Pete from what he apparently believed to be a safe distance.

"Wow ..." Jay muttered as the Rimmers retreated down the street. The people they had run into in the past were generally deferential to Greg, or at the very least fairly civil. These people, though, they actually seemed to be scared of him (with the exception of the woman, of course, who didn't know him.) Maybe he could afford to feel less anxious the next time they met up with a group of Rimmers, considering the effect Greg seemed to have on them.

He looked down at his companion, who, having selected what appeared to be some kind of home-made wrench, was carefully sliding it over one of the two bolts which secured the access hatch at the tower's base. "Huh, fucking shit stains," Jay said with a forced air of bravado. "They better fucking take off! Am I right?" Greg glanced down the street, then turned back to his work. Behind him, Shaky giggled. "Yeah. Fucking right." Jay chewed a fingernail, watching the Rimmers as they turned down an alley. "So, Greg," he said, attempting to sound casual, "like, what the fuck was that all about, anyway? Was that little Pete fucker actually scared of you? I mean, those guys were pretty lame but still, *you're* a fucking pussy. Why the fuck would they be scared of *you*?"

Greg twisted the bolt clockwise until it clicked, then studied a small bank of coloured lights on the wrench as they flashed on and off in sequence. He furrowed his brow in concentration, then pressed a small stud below the lights three times in quick succession. The bolt clicked again, and Greg began twisting it counter-clockwise. "They're not afraid of me," he said, "they're afraid of not getting their juice."

Shaky hopped up and down, shuffling his feet in what looked like some kind of weird jig. "Get the juice!" he cried. "Get the juice! Shaky's gonna get the juice!"

"Are you shitting me?" Jay said, ignoring the old man's antics. "They seem pretty fucked up. Have they ever actually tried to jump you?"

Greg removed the bolt and placed it carefully next to his tools. "They have. But they don't any more."

"What's that supposed to mean?" Jay asked, furrowing his brow.

"Shit in their pants and cry!" Shaky exclaimed. "Screaming and shitting and pissing!" Grinning madly, the old man spun around twice, finally squatting and doing his best imitation of someone crying and screaming and shitting and pissing.

"Shaky!" Jay shouted. "Shut the fuck up!" Looking chastised, the old man waddled towards Greg, then sat on the concrete, frowning.

"If they want juice," Greg said, sliding the wrench over the second bolt, "they have to follow the rules." He paused to study the lights as they once again flashed on and off. Quietly, he added: "If not ... there are consequences."

Jason blinked. *Consequences?* "Ha!" he exclaimed, grinning. "Consequences! Ya hear that Shakes? There are *consequences.*" He snorted, then looked down at Greg. "What, are you some kind of fucking bad ass now?"

"Whatever," Greg replied. He had the second bolt off, and was presently wiggling the plate free. "Just shut up for a while."

Jason snorted again. "Shutting up, sir!" he said, snapping off a crisp salute. He watched Greg for a moment, then turned to face Shaky. The old man was squatting by the curb, drawing circles in the thin layer of dust covering the road. "Watcha doin' there, Shakes?" Jason said, taking a step towards him. Shaky looked up, then quickly rubbed out his drawings and hopped back a few feet. "Aw, c'mon Shaky," Jay said, stepping even closer, "don't be like that. I just wanted to see what you were drawing."

"Jay eat fuck and die," the old man muttered, grimacing.

"Oh, for fuck's sake ..." Jason grumbled, shaking his head. At moments like these he actually kind of regretted giving Shaky such a hard time. Truth was, the old guy actually wasn't all that bad; sure he was weird and smelly, but he was also pretty entertaining at times, which was more than he could say for old Beardy-Boy. More than that, though, Shaky was the only person he knew who didn't seem to want anything from him. Old, sickly and demented, with nothing to show but a few rags and a little collection of knick-knacks, all Shaky really seemed to want was to be included in Greg and Jay's activities.

Jay watched the old man for a moment, then smiled mischievously. "Hey Shakes," he said, playfully kicking a chunk of concrete in his direction, "think fast!" The old man squawked as the projectile bounced off the pavement and struck him square in the jaw, knocking him flat. "Oh, shit!" Jason exclaimed, hurrying over to where Shaky lay, his face a study in confusion and abject misery. "Sorry! Sorry!" The old man cringed as Jay reached down to grab his sleeve. "No, no, it's all right," Jay said, yanking Shaky to his feet and dusting off the greasy rag that passed for his shirt. "I didn't mean to hit you."

"Jay hurt me!" Shaky cried. "Greg, make Jay eat dead shit and piss!"

"Ah, man," Jay sighed, frowning. If he was hoping to make friends with Shaky, this wasn't the way to do it. "C'mon Shakes," he said, holding the old guy by the chin and inspecting his grimy face, "quit being such a fucking old pussy! There's barely even a mark."

Greg shook his head as he pulled a package from the tower's access hatch and stowed it in his pack. He replaced the plate, then screwed the bolts back on with his fingers. They easily spun all the way in, coming to rest with a loud click.

"Gay-Jay go shit now!" Shaky barked, struggling to his feet. "Jay leave now!"

"Fine," Jason mumbled, turning away. "Fuck you too." He wandered over to where Greg knelt, ignoring the continuing stream of insults and obscenities coming from Shaky's direction. "Can't your *contacts* give us more than this?" he asked as he knelt down to study the package poking out of Greg's bag.

"They do what they can."

"Yeah, well, seems kinda stupid to go to all the trouble of smuggling stuff in, just for a little package like that."

"It's enough."

Jay sighed, then glanced over at the base of the arch. "So what's with those fucked-up bolts, anyway?"

"They keep the Rimmers from messing with the towers," Greg replied as he gathered up his tools. "The Council had them put in about a year before they locked up the Rim. Told everyone it was part of a ship-wide upgrade."

"Weird ..." Jason said, reaching out and touching one of the bolts. "They don't have 'em on the Core side." He knew this for a fact; Isaac's father was a technician for the Department of Power Distribution and Maintenance, and he would sometimes take the two of them along on his route when they were kids. One time, he had actually let them take the bolts off of a maintenance hatch. There had been no electronic doodads involved at the time, just a regular old wrench.

"Well," Greg replied as he carefully zipped up his pack, "turns out the ship-wide upgrade wasn't so ship-wide after all."

"Yeah," Jason said, frowning down at the cracked, broken mess that had once passed for a road, "I guess not."

Greg stood up and slung his bag over his shoulder. "All right," he announced, "let's go. Where's Shaky?"

Jason looked around for a moment, finally pointing to a broken-down storefront a few buildings away. "There he is."

Greg turned to look at the old man, who was peering into a window and grinning. "Hmm ... figures." He put two fingers into his mouth and whistled. "Hey, Shakes," he yelled, "let's go!"

"Delicious!" Shaky called back cheerfully. "Greg and Shaky go in delicious!"

Jay blinked. "Delicious? What the fuck's he talking about?"

Greg shook his head and sighed. " 'Delicious Deviance'. It was one of the classier sex shops back in the day. Shaky says his parents owned it when he was a kid." He whistled again. Shaky stared at him a moment, then peered into another section of the window. "I keep telling him there's nothing in there; I checked out all the buildings around here years ago, and they're all cleaned out." As they watched, the old man began to hop up and down, apparently unable to contain his enthusiasm.

"Did his parents really own the place?" Jay asked, frowning skeptically.

"I don't know … the guy says a lot of weird stuff. Still, I guess anything's possible."

Jason watched Shaky for a moment, then turned towards Greg. "What the heck," he said, grinning. "Let him take a peek. We'll go in with him."

Greg shook his head, smiling despite himself. "Jason, *there's nothing in there.*"

"Yeah, yeah, whatever … we'll just go have a quick look, get it out of his system. Besides, I want to make up for kicking a chunk of concrete at his head."

Greg gave him a quizzical look. "What? Did you just say … did you just say you want to do something nice for Shaky?" He paused, then gripped his young companion by the shoulder, a stern look on his face, "Okay," he quipped, "who are you and what did you do with Jason?"

"Yeah, hee-fucking-larious," Jay snapped, shrugging off Greg's hand. "C'mon, let's just fucking go already!"

Greg watched Shaky for a moment, then sighed. "Well," he said slowly, "I guess we can go in for a minute or two … but we'll have to be careful; most of these buildings are pretty unstable."

Jason clapped his hands and began jogging towards the shop. "Yo Shaky, my man!" he called out. "Hold on to your cock, cause the fun times are about to begin!"

"Hold up!" Greg shouted as he hurried after Jay. "Let me go in first!"

Joining the others at the doorway, Greg pulled a flashlight from his bag and pointed it into the store, illuminating a series of smashed display cases and nude mannequins. Satisfied that there were no immediate dangers lurking within, he slowly stepped inside. "Ok guys," he said, "follow me. Just let me stay in the lead."

"Hear that, Shaky?" Jason said, nudging the old man with his elbow. "Nothing to worry about. Our fearless fucking leader is gonna show us the way."

Pushing past Jay, Shaky made a beeline for a dusty, torn lace undergarment he had spotted peeking out from beneath an upturned shelf. He held it over his face, peering through the sheer spots in the red lace, then held the ratty garment over his crotch and danced around in circles. Greg continued searching the room's corners and crevices, then disappeared into the back room, leaving his friends to enjoy themselves up front.

"Wow, man," Jay said, tossing aside a pink cardboard box which had once contained a large vibrating dildo of some kind, "Beardy-Boy was right. There's really nothing in here." Ignoring him, Shaky tucked a corner of his new found treasure into the front of his pants, letting the rest swing back and forth over his crotch. He began gyrating and making bizarre squeaking noises. "Shaky," Jason said, grinning, "you are one fucking strange son of a bitch."

"Shaky got sexy Mamma clothes!" the old man crowed. "Sexy Mamma clothes and Jay is gay!"

Jason's smile faltered slightly. "Shaky old boy," he said amiably, "I would punch your fucking ugly faggot face if you weren't so damn entertaining. Still, watch your fucking mouth."

The old man gave Jason the finger, then walked across the room to where a pair of dismembered mannequins lay sprawled on the floor. He squatted down next to them and began running his hands over their plastic breasts. Jason watched for a while, then wandered off in the opposite direction, idly readjusting the front of his pants. He kicked aside a piece of wire shelving, then bent down to pick up a small cellophane package lying in the dust. "Hey Shaky, check it out!" he called, holding it up to a shaft of sunlight. Within the clear wrapper was a piece of green plastic moulded into the shape of a nude couple, the woman bent over so as to facilitate the insertion of the little man's erect plastic penis. Jay ripped open the cellophane and inspected the toy as Shaky wandered over for a closer look. Much to his delight, Jason discovered that part of the toy's base was actually a lever which, when pulled, caused the plastic man's hips to thrust forward, plunging his little green manhood into the grinning woman's butt. "Oh, man," he said quietly, "this is fucking awesome ..."

"Mamma Papa!" Shaky cried, reaching for the toy. "Mamma Papa! Give Shaky Mamma Papa!"

"Fuck off!" Jay said, yanking his treasure out of the old man's reach. "Find your own shit!"

"Mamma Papa *is* Shaky's!" he bleated. "Shaky's Mamma Papa! Give to Shaky!"

Greg walked back into the showroom, a bemused expression on his face. "What the heck's going on in here?"

"Mamma Papa!" Shaky cried. "Greg make Gay-Jay give Mamma Papa!" Hopping up and down, the old man grasped spastically at the thing in Jay's hand, the old red panties flapping about over his crotch.

"Oh-oh! Can't have it!" Jay crowed triumphantly as he easily evaded Shaky's grasp. "It's mine! My Mamma Papa!"

"Oh, for crying out loud ..." Greg said wearily. "What is that?"

Jay placed himself between Shaky and Greg and held up his new toy. "It's two green people fucking. See?" He grabbed the little plastic handle and pumped it a few times, smiling. "I don't know why Shaky calls it 'Mamma Papa'. Do you think his parents posed for it?"

"Oh, man," Greg breathed, shaking his head. "Well, that's what I get for bringing you two into a sex shop." He turned to look at Shaky, who, thoroughly defeated, was wandering sadly back to his mannequins. "Come on, Jay," he said, "why don't you just give it to him? Hey, it'll be a good chance to practice your sharing skills."

"Well hey," Jay replied matter-of-factly, "why don't you suck my dick? It'll be a good chance for you to practice your fag skills." He nodded towards the back of the store. "Besides, he found something too."

Greg glanced once again at the old man, who was sadly stroking a smooth mannequin crotch. "What, you mean those dummies? No. We're not taking those back."

"No, not *those* things. The fucking panties hanging out of his pants."

Greg sighed heavily. "For the love of Earth …" he mumbled. "All right, whatever. Let's get outta here."

"What about the back room?" Jay asked. "Anything good in there?"

"Nah, it's flooded out. The floor's already half caved in."

"Okay, whatever." Jay turned towards Shaky, who was now full-on humping one of the mannequins. "Shakes, my man," he said, "let's go. We're heading out." Frowning, the old man gave the plastic woman one last hump for the road, then wandered sadly towards the door. Jason studied the dummies for a moment, then looked down at the little sex toy still in his hand. "Hey Greg," he said, "maybe we *should* take one of those."

"What? The mannequins? Forget it! I don't want those in my apartment."

Jay snorted. "Well, of course *you* don't fucking need one, do you?"

Greg shot him a glare. "And what exactly do you mean by that?"

Jason opened his mouth to reply, then paused, frowning.

He was tempted to give Beardy-Boy an earful regarding the whole Shandra situation, which had been preying on his mind with ever-increasing frequency. He would love to tell him how he resented the way the old guy let her prance around the apartment in sexy outfits, then fucked her in the back room while poor old Jason had to resort to whacking off in the toilet. He was even starting to genuinely feel bad for Shandra and the way Greg kept her locked up all the time; he was really just using her, the way he used Jason (despite his repeated assertions that "we're all victims here"). What kept him from speaking his mind, though, was the maddening feeling that he *owed* Greg something; he *had* saved his life after all, and probably Shandra's for that matter. Even worse was the knowledge that Jason *needed* the old queer—the knowledge that without Greg's help, he would probably be stuck in this shit hole for the rest of his life. In a way, he supposed, they were all using each other.

"Whatever," Jay grumbled, pushing the complicated mess out of his mind. "Let's just fucking get out of here."

Greg studied him for a moment, his expression challenging Jay to elaborate on his comment. Jason raised his arms. "What? I said let's just fucking go!"

Greg watched silently for a few more seconds then, apparently satisfied that the kid wasn't going to push the matter any further, turned towards the mannequins. "Well," he said slowly, hands on hips, "maybe we *should* bring one of those things back. We could always leave it in the lobby, I suppose …"

Shaky, who had been listening near the entrance, rushed back into the room. "Yes! Yes!" he cried triumphantly. "Shaky have plastic girl in the lobby!"

Jason grinned. "Hey, now you're talking! Shaky hardly ever leaves that place anyway."

"All right, fine," Greg said, giving his head a quick nod. "Shaky, go pick one out and we'll bring it."

Shaky hopped over to the most recent target of his affections. "This one!" he exclaimed, running a gnarled hand over its smooth, glossy breast.

"See?" Jason said, still grinning. "The old fucker's in love."

Greg smiled. "It would appear so ..." He watched for a moment as Shaky struggled to lift his new prize. "Hey kid," he said, "why don't you carry it for him?"

"What?" Jason replied, frowning. "Why don't *you* fucking carry it? Do I look like some kind of fucking slave or something?"

"Listen, Jay, I've got my bag, and that thing's obviously too heavy for Shaky. We've got to share the load here."

"Yeah, well, you can just *suck* my load," Jason groused as he stomped over to the mannequin and wrestled it onto his shoulder. "Can we *please* just fucking go already?"

"Yes, we can." Greg patted Shaky on the back. "C'mon old buddy, let's go home."

The three men walked out the door and headed back towards the apartment, Shaky running ahead and giggling.

"It's too bad the back room was flooded," Jay said, shifting the mannequin on his shoulder. "Shakes would've probably enjoyed poking around in there."

Greg shrugged. "Yeah, well, we're lucky we got to go in there at all. Won't be long till the Council orders the Safety Commission to come and finish the job."

Jay frowned. "What? What the fuck are you talking about?"

"The Safety Commission," Greg replied. "They come in and flood buildings—open up a pipe, let everything soak for a while, then declare it a hazard to the residents of the Rim. Before you know it, there's a fleet of Claimer trucks hauling it away piece by piece."

Jay snorted. "Yeah, right."

"I'm serious. Why do you think there are so many empty lots in the Rim?"

"Well, I don't know ..." Jason said uncertainly, "I'd guess

Rimmers don't worry too much about maintenance, for starters."

"Well, sure, there's that," Greg said, glancing at his companion. "But it takes a long time for buildings to come down just from neglect. No, you need something more serious to make it happen this quickly."

Jason thought about it for a moment, then shook his head. "I don't know, man," he said. "I knew you were paranoid, but this seems like a bit much, even for you. Maybe you should lay off the juice a while."

Greg studied Jay for a moment, then bent down and scooped up a chunk of road material. "Look at this," he said. "Do you think roads just break up for no reason? They put special blades on the front of the reclamation trucks that dig into the streets. One day the whole Rim will be just one huge expanse of bare metal."

Jay blinked. "Seriously, Greg," he said, "that's fucking *nuts*! They have to keep Rimmers somewhere. They can't just take *everything.*"

"Sure they can. As long as they kill off the population as fast as they can reclaim the infrastructure."

Jay stopped in his tracks. "All right, now you're fucking with me, right? Greg, the Council's *not fucking killing anybody.*"

"Sure they are!" Greg shouted. "Listen, the High Command puts a *huge* amount of pressure on the Council for resources. Add to that the fear and hysteria being peddled to the Core, and *this* is what you get. People being forced to live in horrid conditions, being fed shit the Core won't touch … You think that's gonna help them thrive? Most of these people are sick and malnourished, and the Council isn't lifting a finger to help them. I'm telling you, I've seen—and I mean I've *seen*, with my own eyes—Green-Heads pulling sick people off the streets and shipping them straight to the Reclamation Centre!" Greg tossed aside the chunk of concrete. "I'm telling you, kid," he said as he turned to leave, "this is seriously fucked up."

Jay hung back a moment, frowning. He shifted the mannequin from one shoulder to another, then jogged to catch up with Greg. "Well okay, so even *if* you're right," he said, "what's the big fucking deal? These fucking Rimmers are mostly retards and drug addicts—the ship's better off without em."

Greg glared at his companion. "Really?" he snapped. "Like the ship's better off without *me*? Without *you*? Let me tell you something, kid. The people here are the way they are because of the environment they've been put into. Sure most of them had something going against them, like low IQ, or physical disabilities, behavioural problems. So what does the Council do? Do they try to help these people, or at least give them some kind of decent life? No, that would require pulling resources from the 'Cult of the Almighty Exalted Flasher.'" Greg picked up his pace. "No more expensive Booster Day parades. No more plants for well-connected Core dwellers. No more hypocritical bureaucrats smiling out their ass, assuring us that the Rim dwellers are all really very healthy and happy despite the sacrifices they've had to make. And you know something else?" he said, eyes burning with intensity. "They poison our food. That's right. Those fucking protein-bricks they throw off the trucks? They're full of psychotics and chemical birth control agents."

"Whoa!" Jay exclaimed, grabbing Greg by the arm and pulling him to a stop. "Are you fucking kidding me?"

"C'mon, kid! We both know what kind of messed up shit goes on here, you most of all."

"And you've been letting me *eat* that shit?"

"Well sure!" Greg replied. "What else are we gonna eat? I don't know if you've noticed, but there's a pretty serious restaurant shortage in the Rim."

Dropping the mannequin by his feet, Jay stepped forward,

his hands balled into fists. "I'm gonna give you one fucking chance to tell me you're joking."

Greg opened his mouth to speak, then hesitated as Jay's eyes began to truly smoulder. "Well," he said, his anger apparently giving way to caution, "I don't *really* know if it's true ... I guess it's more of an educated guess than anything." He looked down at Jay's fists, then cleared his throat. "Anyway, I always freeze the stuff, then cook the shit out of it just in case, to neutralise whatever might ..."

"Fuck!" Jason shouted, punching the air in front of Greg's face. "You fucking prick! Tell me right now, am I being fucking poisoned or not?"

"Well, all right kid, take it easy," Greg said, hands raised. "Probably not. I mean, I've been eating the stuff way longer than you have, and I don't have any *real* proof that anything's wrong. It's just ..."

Jay backed away a step, then bent down to pick up Shaky's mannequin. "Man," he said between clenched teeth, "you really are a fucking piece of work, you know that?"

Greg studied the young man for a moment, then sighed, "Well," he replied, "I'll guess I do get a little worked up sometimes, but ... c'mon. You know I'm not *completely* out in left field. Like I said, we both know the Council's doing the High Command's dirty work."

Jay shook his head and snorted. "Yeah ... whatever."

"Truth is," Greg said slowly, "they're probably doing worse things than putting additives in our food."

"You don't say?" Jay sneered as he resumed his march towards home. "Like what, pray tell?"

"Well," Greg continued hesitantly, "you know your Jabbers?"

Jay frowned fiercely. "What about my fucking Jabbers?"

The older man paused, choosing his words carefully. "Well ... you know ... how they put psychotics in them to make Flashers more aggressive—I mean, everyone knows that, right?"

Jay came to a sudden halt, once again balling his hands into fists. "Are you fucking gonna call me *psychotic* right now?" he snapped, "Seriously, do you *want* me to fucking punch you in the face?"

"No, no, hang on now," Greg said, taking another step back, "I'm not calling you anything! It's just ... you don't really believe there's nothing in those shots but Phenylbutalol and a few nutrient supplements, do you? I mean, seriously, you've gotta admit Flashers tend to be a little ... well ... tightly wound. And it might also explain this raging sex drive business."

"Hey, fuck you, man!" Jay shouted, eyes blazing. "My sex drive's right where it's supposed to be!"

Greg raised his hands, palm-forward. "All right, all right, maybe I overstated things a bit. Just take it easy."

"I'll take it easy with my foot up your ass!" Jay snapped, stepping closer to Greg. "I don't need some fucking limp-dick old homo to tell me about my fucking sex drive!"

"Okay, fine," Greg replied hastily, stepping back yet again, "that's cool. I guess what I mean is—"

"What you mean," Jason growled, once again closing the distance between them, "is that you have no fucking idea what you're fucking talking about! Cause if you *did*, you'd know that Flashers *have* to be tightly wound! Because of the whole Squelcher thing, remember? Fighting the aliens before they fucking kill everybody? But I guess you just don't know about any of that, since you spend most of your time playing with your fucking chemistry set, or ... jerking off on that little faggot plant of yours!"

"Okay, Okay, I surrender," Greg pleaded anxiously. "I'm sorry! Really ... I just ..." He paused, suddenly frowning and tilting his head to one side. "Did you just call my plant a faggot?"

The two men stared at each other a moment, then suddenly burst out laughing.

"Oh, man," Greg said as the laughter and the tension between them subsided. "You, my friend, take the term homophobia to a whole new level."

Jay shook his head, smiling. "Well, hey ... it's not my fault your plant's gay."

Greg sighed, and for a moment the two men smiled at each other in silence.

"So," Jay said, nodding in the direction of the apartment, "I guess we'd better get going. Shakes must be home by now."

"Quite true, my friend," Greg replied amiably. "Let's go."

"There he is," Greg said as Shaky emerged from the apartment building, barely a block away. "I'm guessing he's anxious to get his little plastic girlfriend set up."

Jason shook his head and smiled as the old man waved and did a pirouette before scurrying back into the building. He felt good; the confrontation with Greg had given him a chance to vent some of his pent-up anger and frustration, and the emotional release of laughter had left him feeling pleasantly calm and buoyant. "So, hey, tell me something," he said, glancing amiably at Greg. "What's with the "Shaky" business? That's not really his name is it?"

Greg looked at his companion and smiled. "Well, kid, let me tell you. Shaky is a mysterious man of unknown origins, and I have absolutely no idea what his real name is. As for the "Shaky" business, well ... let's just say he likes to give his wiener a particularly long and enthusiastic waggle after he takes a piss."

Jay's eyes widened as a grin spread across his face. "What? Seriously? That's where he got the name?"

Greg smiled. "It is indeed."

"Did you give it to him?"

"I most certainly did."

They came alongside the apartments, and Jay led the way

down the small path to the entrance. "So what," he said, "you just happened to be watching him taking a piss one day, or what?"

Greg opened the door and held it for Jason. "I'd, uh … rather not discuss it."

"Yeah," Jay replied jovially as he wrestled the mannequin through the doorway, "I guess I probably wouldn't want to either."

In a corner of the foyer, Shaky was hopping up and down excitedly, his red panties flapping about like a flag. "Here!" he crowed with delight. "Put Shaky's girl here!"

Chuckling, Jay dropped the thing next to the old man, pushing the base down into the debris until it was fairly stable. "There you go, Shakes old boy. Have at 'er!"

"Ah, good! Good!" Shaky yanked the lingerie from his pants and pulled them over the mannequin's crotch. He adjusted them once or twice, then, apparently satisfied, bent down and sniffed loudly. "Ah, good! Smells nice! Ah! Ah!"

"You know what?" Jay said, grinning. "Something tells me those fuckin' things are gonna be white and sticky before too long."

"Okaaaayyyy …" Greg replied. "I think I've had enough excitement for today." He waved at the old man, who was now sniffing *and* fondling the mannequin's butt. "Pace yourself Shakes," he said. "You're not a young man, you know."

"Ah, good!" Shaky cooed. "Mamma nice."

Shaking his head, Greg crossed the lobby to the staircase. Jay followed shortly after, idly fingering the green plastic toy in his pocket. As he reached the base of the stairs he stopped and turned to watch Shaky a moment longer. His face buried between the mannequin's plastic breasts, the strange little man was the picture of unfettered, perverted bliss.

Jason Crawford smiled. "Hey Shakes!" he said, tossing his prize in the old man's direction. "Merry Christmas!"

## October 12, 2769

Jason handed the dropper to Greg, then leaned back on the couch, sighing deeply as his tension melted away. Gregory took two doses beneath his tongue, then screwed the dropper back into the bottle and shoved it into his pocket. A moment later he joined Jay on the sofa.

"Greg old chap," Jason mumbled, "you can't cook worth shit, but you are a *genius* with the juice."

Greg chuckled nervously. "Hey, what can I say? I aim to please."

Eyes closed, Jason smirked. "Well in that case, could you *aim* to *please* give me some more?"

"Would if I could kid," he replied quietly. "Gotta keep some for my friends outside."

"Your friends outside can blow me sideways," Jason quipped, sinking deeper into the cushions. "Speaking of," he said, opening his eyes and leaning over with a lopsided smile, "if I suck you off would you give me Shandra's share?" Greg tensed visibly, crossing his arms and frowning at the floor. "Okay, okay, sorry," Jay said, quickly raising his hands. "No Shandy jokes. Got it."

"Who's telling Shandy jokes?" The young woman in question asked as she glided in from the kitchen, glass of water in hand. "I like jokes. Tell me!"

Greg scowled. "Nobody's telling jokes about anybody."

"Oh, Greggy," she said as she climbed onto his lap and caressed his face, "what's wrong? Are you all grumpy today? Do you need a hug?" Twisting around to straddle him, she wrapped her arms around his torso and rested her head on his shoulder. Her tattered skirt rode up on her thigh, expos - ing part of the garter belt which was holding up her mis - matched stockings. Jason got hard immediately. He glanced down at his crotch, then looked up at his friends to see if anyone had noticed. Shandra, still in mid-hug, caught his eye, then looked down at his tented pants. She gazed seduct - ively at him and winked, slowly wetting her lips with the tip of her tongue.

"Oh, shit," Jason mumbled, quickly crossing his legs.

"What? What's wrong?" Greg said, gently pushing Shandra off his lap. "What's going on?"

"Nothing," Jason replied, hastily grabbing a tattered cush - ion and squeezing it against his abdomen, carefully conceal - ing the erection which already strained against his pants. "Just got a bit of, uh … intestinal discomfort, you might say. Probably that fucking bug soup you fed us this morning."

"Hey, there was nothing wrong with that soup," Greg replied amiably, his eyes beginning to droop. "That was a total soup-de-force."

"Yeah, more like soup-de-fart," Jay said, squirming be - neath the cushion.

"Oh, Greg," Shandra cooed, stretching a leg over Gregory's lap and pouting playfully. "Did you make poor Jay sick?"

"Well, I sure hope not," he replied, his eyes drawn to Shandra's breasts as they strained mightily against her too small t-shirt. Sighing wearily, he let his head drop to the back of the couch. "Didn't I tell you not to dress like that out here?"

Jason blinked, then glanced at Greg, eyebrows raised. He was well aware that Greg gave Shandra instructions on how to dress outside of her room, but this was the first time he had actually heard him do it. He figured the juice must be hitting Greg pretty hard today, making him a little more careless than usual.

"What are you talking about?" Shandra replied, frowning. "You found these clothes for me! And besides," she said, arching her back, "I look marvellous!"

"Whatever," Greg grumbled, eyes closed. "Go back to your room."

Scowling, Shandra turned to face him. "What?"

"Go back to your room, I'll come by later."

"But I just came out a little while ago!" Her scowl giving way to a look of misery and fear, Shandra looked pleadingly at Jason, who shrugged his shoulders sympathetically.

"I don't care," Greg mumbled. "Go. Now."

Shandra's face turned red as tears welled up in her eyes. "No!" she cried. "I can't stand it in there! It was bad enough being locked up every time you went out, but now you're keeping me in there almost all the time! You can't do that!"

"I can do whatever I want," Greg said, rising from his seat and grasping her by the wrist. "You're going back!"

"Whoa, Greg," Jason said, sitting up quickly. "What the fuck are you doing?"

"Stay out of this!" Greg barked as he yanked Shandra off the couch, eliciting from her a small cry.

"Fuck, man … c'mon!" Jason shouted, jumping to his feet, ignoring the cushion as it tumbled to the ground. "Take it easy!"

"Stop right there!" Greg bellowed. Jay hesitated; he had never seen the guy this angry before. "Stay where you are! I'll handle this myself!"

Looking wounded and defeated, Shandra sobbed quietly as Greg led her away. For a few moments, muffled shouts could be heard from the direction of her room, followed by the sounds of a door slamming and several locks clicking into place. Finally Greg stormed back into the living room, banging the door shut behind him.

Jason watched in silence as Greg walked over to his workbench, grabbed a small bottle of clear fluid, then wandered over to the kitchen. "Come sit at the table a while," he said, opening a cupboard and retrieving two small glasses.

Jay hesitated a moment then slowly bent down to pick up the cushion.

"Oh, don't worry about that," Greg said, smirking. "We all know about your present state of arousal. Go ahead and jerk off if you want to."

"Fuck you," Jason replied, tossing the cushion onto the couch. He paused for an instant, considering whether he should, in fact, go relieve himself, then thought better of it; something weird was going on—he should probably just stay here. Besides, his hard-on seemed to be flagging on its own. "What the fuck's wrong with you, anyway?" he said, walking slowly towards the table. "You're acting like a real douche."

"Oh, that's rich," Greg said as he sat down, a tired smile on his face. "A douche … You know, there's an old Earth saying: 'the pot calling the kettle black'. You ever heard it?"

Jason stood before the table, frowning, "What the *fuck* are you talking about?"

"Yeah, that's what I figured," Greg replied, slumping into his seat. "A little obscure, that one." He sighed wearily, then suddenly brightened up. "But hey, why the long face? C'mon, sit down," he said, waving Jason towards a chair. "Let's have a drink." He popped open the top of the bottle and carefully poured a small amount of liquid into each of the glasses.

Jay hesitated, then slowly took a seat, all the while keeping an eye on Greg. After a moment he picked up the glass and peered at the contents. Unlike the Rim-juice Greg produced, which was cloudy and viscous, this liquid was perfectly clear and thin, like water. He held it up to his nose, then pulled his head back quickly, face puckered. "What the fuck *is* this shit?"

"Good old-fashioned alcohol," Greg replied. "I like to keep it for medical reasons, but, hey, what the heck, right? You only live once!"

Jay swirled the contents of his glass, a plainly skeptical look on his face. "Yeah, sure. Thing is I'd like to *keep* living, you know what I mean?"

"Oh, c'mon!" Greg exclaimed, chuckling. "Where's your sense of adventure?" He raised the glass to his mouth and took a slug, then hissed through his teeth. "Whoo! That's what I'm talking about." He poured himself another shot, then held his glass in the air. "Go on, kid, have a drink. Bottoms up!"

" 'Bottoms up'? What the fuck is that, another one of your retarded Earth sayings?"

"Jason," Greg replied with mock sternness, "*drink!*"

Jay once again swirled his beverage, trying to wrap his head around the situation. Greg was acting weird, and it was making him nervous. Then again, life in the Rim wasn't exactly a picnic, and it would be strange if Greg *didn't* act kooky once in a while. And he *was* offering him a drink, after all ... Steeling himself, Jay raised the glass to his lips and took a gulp. The alcohol was strong, and it burned like fire all the way down. There was a strange aftertaste that made him frown.

Greg laughed. "Not quite what you're used to out in the Core, huh? Well, don't worry, it'll get the job done."

Jay blinked. The combination of alcohol and juice suddenly hit him like a sledgehammer, leaving him surprised and more than a little pleasantly high. He looked up at Greg. "Wow."

Greg laughed again. "Yeah, *wow* indeed." His speech was slurred; he was obviously feeling it too.

"What's in this stuff?"

"Moshtly … just alcohol. I distill it from, um …" Greg paused, smiling. "Well, let's just call it a proprietary formula."

Jay snorted. "Whatever."

"Whatever indeed." Greg refilled the young man's glass, then leaned back with his eyes closed.

Jay picked up the bottle and held it up to the light, then put it down and took another, smaller gulp. "So, Greg," he said after a moment, "what was all that shit with Shandra about?"

"Oh, don't you worry about Shandra," Greg replied, smirking. "I got that covered." Opening his eyes, he reached over and clinked his glass against Jay's, then emptied it in one loud swallow. "Aah. That really hits the spot."

Jay took another small sip, then pushed the glass away. He was already feeling pretty hammered.

"C'mon, kid!" Greg exclaimed. "Don't be a little cry baby! I'm sure you used to pound 'em down pretty good out there in the Core, eh? Out with your Flasher buddies, carousing around the town?"

Jay hesitated a moment, then picked up the glass, but didn't drink. He glanced at Greg, then looked down at his bandaged knuckles.

"Okay," Greg declared drunkenly. "You want to hear about Shandra? Well let me tell you a little shumthing about Shandra. She's weak." He wagged a finger in the air. "She's frail. Yep. She needs to be *protected*, but she doesn't know it." He shook his head, then reached over to pour himself another drink. "But *I* know it."

Jay pushed his glass aside once more and frowned. "But Greg," he said, "c'mon … you've gotta fucking let her out more. How would you like to be locked up in that tiny-ass room all the time?"

"Oh, listen to you," Greg said mockingly. "Have you suddenly become a defender of poor young women?" He reached forward and filled Jay's glass to the brim, then pushed it towards him, sloshing half its contents onto the table. "Go on, kid," he said, "drink up! What, you don't like my booze?"

"No thanks ... I think I've had enough for now." Though he was no way near as wasted as Beardy-Boy seemed to be, Jay was starting to regret having drunk as much as he had; something was definitely not right with Greg, and it would've been easier to deal with the situation had his head been a little clearer. "Seriously, Greg," he said quietly, "what the fuck's going on?"

Greg leaned back and laughed. "Oh, relaksh, pal. Everything's fine."

Jay frowned. "I don't know, man ..."

"You don't know?" Greg drawled between sips, "Okay, fine. You don't know about what?" He waved his hand over the table with a drunken flourish, nearly knocking the bottle over. "Ask and you shall reshieve!"

Jay hesitated, pushing his chair back a few inches. "All right then. It's you ... you and this weird fucking paranoia. All these fucking locks and secret entrances ... and the way you treat Shandra, I mean, that's fucked up. And that time you went all weird and left all that good shit out there. And you're just getting worse!" Jason shook his head in frustration. "And the fucking weirdest part is, I've never once seen anyone even try to *touch* you. Fucking Rimmers are either your buddies, or they're scared shitless of you. I mean, the way you act, it just doesn't make any fucking sense!" He stared at Greg for a moment, then slumped back in his chair. "I just don't get it."

Greg turned his head and laughed derisively. "Yeah, I don't suppose you *would* get it, would you?"

"What the fuck?" Jay said, scowling. "Why are you being so fucking *weird*?"

"Oh, I'm sowwy," Greg replied, pouting. "Am I making little Jay-Jay angwy?"

Jason leaned forward, hands balled into fists, "Well yeah, now that you mention it, you fucking *are* making me angry."

Greg chuckled, then shook his head and sighed. "All right, little Flasher," he said, crossing his arms and looking up at the ceiling. "I'll tell you a little story ... a little parable, or no ... a *caushionary* tale about life in the Rim.

"Once upon a time, not *too* long ago, I went scrounging around in this beautiful palace down the street. Big, majeshtic structure ... whatever. So I'm looking around, peering about every dark and dushty crevice when suddenly, bam! There's this big pile of treasure just sitting there in the middle of the room. Electronics, shum tools, and glass stuff, you know, like that stuff we left behind that time ..."

Jay snorted. "You mean the stuff *you* left behind that time."

Greg clenched his teeth. "You want to hear this story or not?" He stared silently for a moment, then continued. "Anyway, my lucky day, right? So I ran up to the stuff and started digging around. Mostly shit, but there was shum good stuff in there too. So I was marvelling at this magical labelling machine, trying to figure out what kind of shpell or incantation I would need to unlock its secrets when POW! An evil troll shtruck me from behind!" Greg faltered then as a complicated mixture of emotions travelled across his features. He was silent for a moment, then continued, more slowly, all attempts at embellishment apparently forgotten. "So I'm standing there," he said, shoulders slumped, "like stunned ... I could see blood dripping on my shoes ... and then BAM! I get hit *again*, and I fell down. When I looked up, there's these two assholes looking down at me. These two guys ... these two *fucking guys* ... I *knew* them! I had acthually helped them out once! Huh! Like I fucking helped *you*! I fucking brought them into my house ... *my house* ... and gave them food, patched them up." He paused, shaking his head. "They musht have seen the kind of stuff I keep here ... the kind of shtuff I'd probably go out looking for. So these *bastards* actually went out and found some shit they thought I'd probably like, piled it up in a room, then fucking hid shumwhere and waited." He sighed heavily, then slumped lower into his chair.

"You know," he said, "I always thought these fucking Rimmers were harmless. Dirty, vulgar, shtupid ... but, you know ... harmless. I never thought they could do shumthing like this. Anyway, they took my clothes ... my fucking *clothes* ... and they took all my other stuff too. And the junk they planted for me? Didn't even fucking *touch* it—it was just bait." Greg toyed with his glass a moment. "One of them pissed on me."

Frowning, Jason looked down at the table, saying nothing.

Greg chuckled sadly. "Sucks, eh kid?"

"Yeah," Jay replied quietly, "I guess it does." He sat in silence for a moment, then leaned forward. "I don't get something, though."

"Oh, really? Whatsh that?"

"Well ... how did they know you were gonna go into *that* building?"

"Well, I ushed to search in, like, shquares. You know, like a grid, whatever. I guess they just ... I don't know ..." Greg paused, waving his hands above his head, "*watched* me for a while, and kinda figured out where I'd go next."

"Yeah, I guess that makes sense," Jason said, then pushed his chair back and stared at the floor, considering everything Greg had just said. When he had been attacked upon entering the Rim, it had traumatised him so much that he had blocked it out of his memory. He wondered how messed up he would be if could actually *remember* everything, especially in the kind of detail Greg did. "Well," he said, looking up at his companion, "I suppose that kind of shit *could* really fuck up your world view."

Greg smiled sadly. "Huh. 'Fuck up your world view'. Yeah, I shuppose it could."

Jason reached out and grabbed his glass, then took a small sip as he thought more on the subject. Though he understood where Greg was coming from, he couldn't help but be irritated by the old bastard's behaviour. They were in a shitty situation here, and shit happens in shitty situations. If he kept up this pattern of increasing weirdness, their whole escape plan could get fucked up.

"Well, all right then," Jason said, his tone stern and businesslike, "I see why you're acting kind of flaky, but you've got to get over this shit. We've got to keep our heads in our plans, or we'll be stuck here forever."

Greg blinked, then began chuckling softly. A moment later he was full-on laughing, and not long after had given himself over to a near-maniacal fit of hilarity. Jason watched in a kind of horrified wonder as Greg's guffaws eased off, leaving him gasping and wiping the tears from his eyes. "Okay, kid," he said once he had gotten his breath back, "tell me … just how do you shuggest I 'get over this shit'?"

"Oh man," Jason said, shaking his head. "You're really starting to lose it."

"No, no, I'm fine. Perfect. So go 'head, tell me. I'm all ears."

"Ah, fuck," Jay replied nervously. "How the fuck should I know? I'm not a fucking shrink …" He paused, then threw his hands in the air in frustration. "I don't know! Maybe do a little fucking positive visualisation or something!"

Greg laughed out loud once again. "Poshitive visual-isashun?" he said between gasps. "*P-poshitive visualisashun?* Holy shit! Where'd that come from? They teach you that at Flasher school, do they?"

Jay stared at the floor, angry and embarrassed. "Fuck you! Whatever … I still think you need to fucking ease up on Shandra."

Greg downed his drink and stared dully at his friend. "You want to fuck her, don't you?"

Jay looked up suddenly, his eyes wide with indignation. "What the fuck?"

"Oh, c'mon, little buddy. Don't look so shurprished. Did you really think Shandra wouldn't tell me?"

"Tell you what?" Jay barked, scowling. "What are you even fucking talking about?"

"Oh, I don't know ... maybe how you're always trying to get her attention when I'm not looking ... lewd gestures and what-not."

"What ... are you serious?" Jay's speech faltered and he looked away. Of course he wanted to fuck her, that much was obvious to anyone. But he wouldn't actually do it. Not under these circumstances anyway; there was too much at stake. But what did the old queer *think* would happen? He wasn't dead, and that little whore kept cavorting around like queen of the cock teases ...

Jason clenched his teeth. "Well, yeah," he said a moment later, "we flirt a little ... but she's way worse than *I* am! Talk to *her* if you've got a fucking problem with it!"

"So," Greg said, raising his eyebrows, "it'sh all her fault, I guess is what you're saying."

"Well ... yeah!" he shouted. "What did you expect? She's a fucking Booster Girl!"

Greg glowered drunkenly. "I see ..."

Jay threw his hands in the air. "For fuck's sake, man... *come on!*"

"Okay, kid," Gregory said, leaning forward. "Sho tell me ... what should I ekshpect from a Booster Girl? Hmm? Should she be, I don't know ... a happy and well-adjusted member of society? Huh? Cause I really want to know: when you're beating the shit out of them in the Booster Suites, should they smile and shay 'thank you'?"

"Greg," Jay said, a maddening pang of guilt lending a pleading tone to his voice, "come on ... please ..."

"Or when they get pregnant," Greg continued, nonplussed, "do they look forward to having their babies ripped out of them and *fucking covered in plastic*? Huh? And tell me this: when they present you a dead foetus to put on your mantel, should the Booster Girl be invited to the ceremony?"

"Fuck you, Greg!" Jay said, teeth clenched, furious tears stinging his eyes. "Booster Girls are *volunteers* … And they make a lot of money …"

"Volunteers?" Greg shouted, pounding a fist on the table, knocking over Jay's glass. "Did Shandra *volunteer* to get her *fucking ear ripped off*?"

"Fuck you, man!" Jay barked, tears now flowing freely down his face. "I'm fucking sorry about what happened to Shandra, but I didn't fucking rip her ear off! And you know what? Being a Flasher is fucking *stressful*! You have no fucking idea!" He faltered as a strangled sob escaped from his throat. "Sometimes things get out of hand! Don't you fucking get it? That's *just the fucking way it works*!"

Greg stared at Jay for a moment, then sighed wearily as some of the anger left his face. "Yeah," he said, the hint of a sad smile touching his lips. "That's just the way it works."

The two men sat in silence for a while, Greg staring grimly at his glass while Jay struggled to get his emotions under control.

A few minutes later Greg stood up, teetered over to the kitchen, and fixed his eyes on his little plant Joe. "Ok, enough of this," he exclaimed, shambling over to his workbench. "I've got a little shumthing here that should improve our moods greatly."

Jay looked up and frowned. "Fuck you."

Greg pulled a key from his pocket and unlocked a small cabinet. "No, no," he said as he clumsily retrieved a small glass vial, "I'm sorry … got a little carried away there. This'll make ush feel better." He plopped down next to Jason and unscrewed the cap. "My deluxe juice formulation. Just for shpecial occasions. Open up."

Jay pulled away. "Fuck off, man! I don't want any more of your fucking shit."

"Pshaw!" Greg exclaimed. "Look, I shouldn't have gone off on you like that … let me make it up to you! Trust me, this'll mellow you right out—make you feel like the universh is giving you a blow job."

Jay chuckled despite himself. "Huh. How fucking eloquent."

"Hey, I try. Now c'mon, open up."

Jay crossed his arms, scowling. He was still pissed at the old faggot, but it seemed like the confrontation was pretty much over; at least if he allowed it to be. Besides, a little shot of juice probably wouldn't hurt …

"Fucking prick," he mumbled as he turned towards Greg. "All right. Fucking go ahead."

"That's my boy!" Jay tilted his head back as Greg squirted a generous dose of the drug beneath his tongue. "There ya are," he said, smiling. "How'sh that working for you?"

Jay swallowed, then coughed. "What the fuck? That's kind of a big shot, isn't it?"

"Nah, this stuff is subtle. You need more, but the ride's a lot smoother. You'll see."

Jay smacked his lips experimentally, then leaned back as his eyes glazed over. "Wow …" he said, his voice sleepy, "that fucking *is* nice."

"Hey, what'd I tell you?" Greg replied, grinning. "I wouldn't steer you wrong now, would I?"

"Well, you *are* a genius with the juice." Jay closed his eyes and sighed. "You gonna have some?"

"Oh yeah," Greg said, chuckling, "in a while. Don't you worry about your old friend Gregory."

"Hmm … well, your loss, man." Jay scrubbed his hands over his face and yawned. When he opened his eyes Greg was looking at him, smiling. "Quit fuckin' staring at me," Jay said sleepily. "Take a hit … or go make out with your plant or something."

"Nope. I'm good right here."

"Yeah, well you're creeping me out. More than usual. Why don't—unh!" Eyes wide, Jason put a hand to his stomach.

"Oh oh!" Greg said quietly, leaning forward with mock interest. "Shumthing wrong?"

"I don't know … I …" Jason paused, then suddenly doubled over and cried out in pain as a series of brutal cramps shot through his belly.

"Aww, what's the matter, buddy?" Greg asked. "Got a tummy ache? Huh? You got some nasty cockroaches diggin' around in there?" Jay looked up accusingly, his face contorted in pain, tears once again streaming down his cheeks. "Ooh," Greg said, frowning, "I guess that was a bad batch, huh? Oops." He stood up and walked over to where Jay sat, clutching his stomach in agony. "Maybe we should put you somewhere a little more comfortable." Lurching forward, he grabbed Jay by the shoulders and dragged him unceremoniously into the bathroom. "There you go. You just shtay in here and rest a while."

Jay curled up in front of the toilet, crying. "Fuck you," he moaned between sobs. "You fucking prick! Fuck you …"

"Oh hush, now," Greg soothed. "You'll probably pass out for a while, but then you'll be just fine—right as rain. Except you don't know what rain is, right? Poor little guy …"

"You fucking faggot cock sucker! I hate you!"

Greg raised his hands. "Whoa, c'mon now. That'sh a little harsh. But whatever … just don't think I didn't warn you." With this he spun on his heel and lumbered away, not bothering to close the door. After a few steps, he paused and turned back to glare at the young man writhing on the bathroom floor. "There are consequences."

★ ★ ★

Jay leaned heavily against the sink, head throbbing dully. He had no idea how long he had been unconscious, but thankfully it had been long enough to get over the worst of the stomach pain. He turned on the faucet and splashed cold water on his face, shocking himself into a slightly higher state of wakefulness, then stood motionless for a while, struggling to sort out the tangled mess of emotions he was feeling.

Of course he was angry (very, *very* angry), but he was also worried, and most of all, frightened. He had no hope of escaping the Rim if Greg went off the deep end—in fact, as much as it pained him to admit it, he wasn't sure he could survive at all without the old queer's help.

Though a large part of him wanted badly to *beat the living fucking crap out of the crazy, paranoid, cock sucking homo bastard*, he knew the smartest thing to do right now was to figure out what was going on then, if possible, work at steering Greg towards some semblance of stability.

Jay grasped a towel and clumsily wiped his face, then, steadying himself against the door frame, peeked around the corner. Greg sat at the kitchen table with his eyes closed and his head lolling. Before him sat two bottles of alcohol, one empty, one nearly so. A vial of juice lay on its side by his hand, the dropper forgotten on the floor, next to a bright yellow sheet of paper.

Shandra sat a few yards away on the couch, eyes red and wet. Jay cleared his throat and croaked, "Shandra, are you okay?"

The young woman rose from her seat and took a quick step towards him, before pausing and looking back nervously at Greg. "Jay," she whispered, "what's going on?"

"Hummf?" Greg raised his head and slowly focussed his bleary eyes on Jason. "Oh, Jay my boy," he said. "Glad you could make it." Leaning forward drunkenly, he gestured towards the bottles before him. "We're having a … a party, but the little fucking shlut here doesn't want to play."

Jay walked unsteadily to where Shandra stood watching

him, her red eyes pleading. "You all right?" he asked quietly. She nodded glumly, nervously tugging a strand of hair across her scarred face.

Half-walking and half-staggering, he made his way to the table and sat a few feet away from Greg, who seemed to have nodded off again. "Hey man," he said, carefully shaking the edge of the table, "what the fuck's going on?"

Greg sat up with a start. "Umff? Huh? Oh, my pal the Flasher. D'you shay something?"

Jay studied the items strewn across the table, then wiped sweat from his forehead. "What's happening, man? What the fuck is all this about?"

"Whaa … this?" Greg replied, giggling drunkenly. "Just havin' a little shelebration is all. Whassa matter, Flashers don't like to have fun?" With a grunt, he raised his arm then let it drop heavily to the table. "Shandra, you like to have fun, right? Oh, shorry … I forgot. Yer a fucking slut." He closed his eyes and chuckled.

"What did he do to you?" Shandra asked, stepping forward to place a tentative hand on Jay's shoulder.

"Never mind," he said, pushing her hand away. "I'm okay." He glanced down at the items on the floor, then bent to pick up the slip of paper.

"No!" Greg cried, lunging toward the yellow sheet. Jason pulled away as the other fumbled about on the floor, finally grasping the paper and clutching it to his chest. A moment later he laid the document on the table. "Remember this?" he asked, trying awkwardly to smooth out the crumpled sheet.

"Yeah, sure," Jay said cautiously. "That's a note from one of the supply drops."

"Yeah … yesthterday's." Greg smiled and let out a little sob, pushing the paper aside and grasping his glass. He took a clumsy slug, alcohol dripping down his beard and pattering onto the table.

Jay frowned. "Well," he asked irritably, "what about it?"

Greg gazed dumbly into the distance. "It's off."

"What? What's off?"

"Everything. It'sh over ... pulled the plug."

Jay glared at the document. "What do you mean?" he asked. "Did they postpone *again*?" Though Greg's reaction seemed to suggest something more serious, Jason allowed himself to believe that a delay might indeed be all that they were facing; as troublesome as these postponements were, they at least left room for hope.

Greg chuckled sadly. "No ... no. This time it'sh for real. Pulled the plug. Not. Gonna. Happen. Never."

A lead ball dropped in Jay's stomach. "No," he said quietly. "No, that can't ... you've gotta be fucking with me ..."

"Nope," Greg drawled, spreading his hands. "It ish what it is."

Jason reached across the table and grabbed the paper, quickly scanning the handwritten note until he found the relevant passage:

*Recent developments have required us to cancel next month's planned extraction and press conference. Unfortunately it will not be rescheduled. We'll do our best to keep this line of communication open and to supply you with whatever we can, until the time comes when this is no longer feasible.*

*May Earth's healing light shine upon you.*

Four short sentences ...

"What the fuck are we gonna *do*?" Jay demanded, his eyes wide with panic.

"Ha! I don't know what *you're* gonna do. Me, I'm just gonna keep on keepin' on."

Jay looked at Shandra, who was standing by the sofa with

her hand over her mouth. "But ... but there has to be some-thing ..." he said, turning back towards Greg. "We can't just, just ..." His voice broke and he looked away, angry tears streaming down his face.

"Oh, poor baby!" Greg mocked. "What? You really want me to tell you what to do?" He sighed theatrically, then struggled out of his chair and stumbled towards the sink. "How about you go fuck yourshelf?" he said, grabbing his little plant. "Better yet, why don't you fuck Shandy? I mean, hey, howdy! It's business as usual on the good ol' USS McAdam!" Shandra made a small gagging sound, then threw herself on the couch and began crying hysterically. "Chill out, ya little slut," Greg said, turning the tap on and holding Joe unsteadily beneath the stream of water. "Hey, you should get yershelf a plant! Does wonders for the nerves."

Jason dropped the note, then stormed across the kitchen and struck the can from Greg's hand. "You fucking prick!" he yelled, eyes blazing. The older man blinked, then slowly turned to look at Joe, who was now lying in several pieces on the floor.

"Hey kid, ya wanna know something interesting?" Gregory said, eyes fixed on the remains of his plant. "Go have a look at that note again."

"Fuck you!" Jay shouted, struggling not to strike him. "Fuck you and your fucking little shitty-assed plant!"

"No, really," Greg continued, unperturbed, "have a look. You won't regret it." He knelt down and began collecting the ruined pieces of his little weed.

Shandra, whose bawling had diminished to the odd whimper, got up and walked over to the table. She picked up the note and glanced over its contents.

"What am I looking for, Greg?" she asked quietly between sniffs.

"Well look at that!" Gregory announced, chuckling as he

placed the can back onto the counter. "Flasher's little friend is gonna read him a bed time shtory. Isn't that fucking *sweet*?"

Shandra flinched as Jay grabbed the note from her hand. He scanned it quickly, then started again from the top, reading more carefully. He stopped part way down the laundry list of items included in the shipment and looked up at Greg. "I, I don't understand ..." he said weakly.

"What's not to understand?" Greg replied, leaning against the counter. "I got shum Phenylbutalol. No big deal. And I'll tell you something else ... I got *lots* of Phenylbutalol. I get some with every shipment. Always have. Use it in the juice ... well, some of it, anyway. The rest I store in that cabinet over there. Stuff's really starting to pile up, actually."

Jay went pale. His voice wavered. "Are you saying you could have saved my implants?"

"Meh, probably. Well ... most of them anyway."

Jay's stomach clenched. All at once his head swam, and he had to thrust a hand onto the table to keep from falling over. He glanced over at Shandra, who had opened a drawer and was now slowly rummaging through its contents. He slowly turned back towards Greg. "But ... why?"

"Why didn't I save your implantsh?" Greg shrugged. "Bah, why bother? I figured you didn't need them anymore."

Jay was totally dumbstruck. "But I did need them ..." he croaked. "I ... I *do* need them."

"What?" Greg blurted. "What on Earth for? *I* don't see any Squelchers around here. Do you?"

"But ... we were gonna go back to the Core ..."

"*But we were gonna go back to the Core,*" Greg mocked. "Well now we're not, are we? And beshides, d'you really think they'd let you keep those fucking ... *things*? Wake up, kid! *We were going to expose the Flasher system!* Remember? Flasher heroes hooked up to machines? Human gene farms? Jay's daddy is not really Jay's daddy? Ish any of this ringing a bell?"

Jay began to tremble uncontrollably. He felt disjointed, totally surreal. He flinched as Shandra walked up to him, one hand behind her back, and caressed his shoulder with the other. "I ... I would have kept them," he whispered, staring dumbly into her eyes. "It was my choice ... "

Greg laughed out loud. "Your *choice*? I'm afraid you're mishtaken there, my little Flasher friend. When I found you, you were in no position to *choose* anything." He cocked a thumb at his chest. "*I* chose to shave your life. *I* chose to ushe up my supplies for you. *I* even chose to clean the cum off your asshole before you woke up." He shrugged. "Figured you'd be hard enough to handle without knowing you'd been ass-fucked to within an inch of your life. So ... you'll have to forgive me if I didn't really feel like wasting my time on your little party-zappers, 'specially since—"

With an insane shriek, Jason launched himself at Greg, knocking him to the ground. "You son of a bitch!" he cried, shaking him by the front of his shirt. "You fucking faggot cock sucker! I'm gonna fucking kill you! I'm gonna fucking kill you, you fucking homo queer!" Gasping, he sank to the floor, eyes closed. "I'm gonna fucking kill you ..."

Jay released him, then sat motionless, head down. Moments later, there came a rustling sound to his right, and Greg spoke. "Sorry, kid," he muttered, his wavering voice tinged with amusement, "I think somebody beat you to it."

Jay opened his eyes. Shandra knelt next to him, a bloody kitchen knife held tightly in her grip. She was smiling.

## October 25, 2769

Jay scratched nervously at his knuckles, eyeing the vial of juice on the table before him. He had taken a hit half an hour ago—just enough to keep the shakes down, but not enough to really dull his senses. It was taking everything he had to not take more.

He got up and walked across the kitchen to where two bodies lay propped against the cupboards. Leaning forward, he gave the air an experimental sniff. Though the apartment was still fairly rank, it was nowhere near as bad as it had been earlier; either the stink was diminishing, or he was becoming acclimated to the smell. "Well, I hope you're fucking happy," he growled, kicking the cadaver on the right. "Fucking cunt." He reached down and pulled the knife from Shandra's corpse. It came out as easily as it had gone in.

He felt little remorse for what he had done; the little whore had ended any hope he might have had of getting out of the Rim, and ending her life seemed more than fair. His only regret was the way he had beaten her before killing her, not because she didn't deserve it, but because the blows had further damaged his knuckles (which had never really healed to begin with). Now, with no protein bricks and no alcohol to clean his infected wounds (he had run out of both days ago), Jason was forced to go out on a food run, with only a faint hope of locating some alcohol along the way.

Placing the knife on the table, Jay walked over to the workbench and retrieved one of the bags he and Greg had used on their scavenging runs. He dumped the contents and put the blade inside, then slung the sack over his shoulder. *Well,* he thought, taking one last look around the dingy little apartment, *here goes nothing.*

Jay sorted nervously through Greg's keys, eventually managing to open all the deadlocks on the heavy steel door. Lacking the combinations for the padlocks, he beat at them with a metal lamp until the clasps gave way, falling noisily to the floor. The effort reopened one of his wounded knuckles, and a vile mixture of blood and pus oozed through the fabric of his glove. He studied his hand a moment, then hurried back to the table. Grabbing the bottle of juice, he stuffed it into his pocket, then marched out into the hallway.

Shaky lay on the floor by his mannequin, an emaciated arm draped across his eyes. He would only sleep for a minute, he told himself; he had to be awake if Greg came down.

Shaky had not slept well since Greg's visits had stopped. He was lonely, and he was worried about his friend. He was also juice-sick, having not touched a drop since running out a week ago. He still held out hope that Greg would show up eventually, but a large part of him doubted it; everyone left.

Just as sleep threatened to overtake him, Shaky was aroused by the sound of footsteps from above. He quickly jumped to his feet, then scurried into a dark corner where he could watch without being seen. His breath caught in his chest as a moment later Jason appeared, alone.

"Shaky, you old fucker!" Jay called out as he hurried down the stairs. "Where the fuck are you?"

Shaky froze, suddenly terrified. Jason had been nicer to

him the last time they were together, but Jason was still bad. Greg was good, but Greg was not here.

"What the fuck are you doing over there?" Jason demanded as he stomped towards the old man. "What, do you think you're hiding or something? I can totally see you!"

Shaky shrank away, pushing his back into the corner. "Jay go away ..." he muttered urgently. "Jay doesn't see Shaky ..."

"Come here, you old fucker," Jason said, grabbing Shaky by the arm and dragging him out into the light. "I need your help."

Shaky struggled in vain to escape Jason's grip, finally dropping to the floor, arms over his head. "Where is Greg?" he mewled miserably.

"Never mind Greg," Jason replied. "Do you have any alcohol?"

Shaky glanced up at Jay, then wrapped his arms tighter around his head. "Where is Greg?" he repeated in a thin, quavery voice. "Shaky want Greg! Jay is gay!"

"I told you to fucking forget him!" Jason shouted, kicking dust in the old man's direction. "Alcohol! Do you have any fucking alcohol?"

Shaky scooted back a few inches, whimpering. Shaky was scared. Shaky's head throbbed from juice withdrawal. He looked up warily. "Jay got juice?" he whispered.

"Yeah, figured as much," Jason replied derisively. "Yeah, I got your juice. But only if I get alcohol."

Shaky put his hands on the floor. "Jay wanna get drunk?" he asked, frowning.

"No! Or yes, whatever! Fuck, Shaky, I swear ..."

The old man blinked, then looked pointedly at Jay's gloves. The right one was half-soaked with a viscous, foul-smelling fluid. "What did Jay do to his hands?" Shaky asked, the tiniest hint of mischief in his eyes. "Did Jay hurt his hands jerking off?"

"Quit fucking around!" Jay shouted. "Alcohol!"

Shaky rose to a half-standing, half-hunching position, then shuffled quickly towards his mannequin. "Where is Greg?" he demanded, nervously clutching the dummy's arm.

"Greg's back home," Jason said between clenched teeth. "He didn't want to come out today. Alcohol."

"Greg not come out for long time," Shaky whined. "Greg always comes out." He glanced at Jay's hands again. "*Greg* has alcohol ..."

Jay rushed forward and knocked the mannequin to the ground. Shaky knelt on the floor, hands in the air. "Help!" he wailed, tears gathering at the corners of his eyes. "Greg help Shaky!"

Jason reached down and grabbed him by the hair, eliciting a strangled yelp from the harried old man. "There's no fucking alcohol!" he shouted. "*I* don't have any! *Greg* doesn't have any! *It's all gone!*"

"Jay eat my ass!" Shaky wailed, tugging feebly at the young man's hand. "Help! Greg help Shaky!"

"Fuck!" Jay released his grip on Shaky's hair, then knelt down, bringing his face to within a few inches of the old man's. Shaky tried to turn away, but Jay grabbed him by the chin and twisted his head around. "Listen, you old, fucked up piece of shit! Greg's not gonna help you! You wanna know why?"

"No!" Shaky wailed, clawing at Jason's sleeve. "Greg help Shaky! Greg is coming!"

Jason tightened his grip. "Greg's *not* coming!" he shouted. "Cause he's dead! Shandra killed him!"

"No!" Shaky wrapped his arms around his face. "No! Greg not dead! No! Shandra!"

Jay gave the old man's head a shove, then stood up, eyes smouldering. "Yes he is! And guess what?"

Shaky, who had fallen backwards onto his hands, pushed himself forward onto his haunches and covered his ears.

"No," he moaned, squeezing his eyes shut. "Shaky not guess! Jay not talk!"

"I killed her!" Jay bellowed, suddenly bursting into tears. "I fucking stabbed her to death! Right after I busted my knuckles open on her stupid fucking cunt face!"

Shaky rocked back and forth, mewling pathetically. He hated Jay. He missed his friend Greg, and Jay was crying. Shaky didn't want Jay to cry. He missed Shandra, even though he had never met her. Shaky felt confused. Shaky felt bad for Shaky.

"Now my hands are infected," Jason raved between sobs, "and I can't clean them because I drank all the fucking alcohol! So I'm gonna ask you one more time, you *fucking useless old fuck*, do ... you ... have ... any ... *fucking alcohol*?"

"Jay leave Shaky alone," the old man whimpered, snot dangling off the tip of his nose. "Jay killed Greg."

Jason slapped Shaky hard, knocking him onto his back. Stepping back, he reached into his pocket and pulled out the small glass vial of drugs. "I got your juice right here, asswipe," he cried, throwing the bottle onto the floor and crushing it with his heel. "Merry fucking Christmas!"

Shaky watched in anguish as Jay marched out of the lobby. A moment later he was alone.

Sitting up, the old man reached into his pocket and pulled out the little plastic sex toy Jason had given him. He wiped his nose on his filthy sleeve, then pulled the toy's handle, chuckling sadly as the tiny green people fucked. "Momma Poppa," he whispered compulsively, "Momma Poppa ..."

After a while he put the toy back into his pocket and crawled over to where his mannequin lay. "Greg is gone," he whispered as he gently stroked one of the smooth plastic breasts.

Everyone left.

★ ★ ★

Jay reached the edge of the crowd just as the armoured truck was pulling to a stop, its roof-mounted speaker blaring. "Consumables disbursement will begin in 60 seconds. Citizens are reminded to line up in an orderly fashion and to only approach the truck when instructed to do so. Failure to behave in accordance with food disbursement regulations will result in withdrawal of food disbursement privileges and/or summary execution." He clutched his bag tightly against his side, trying in vain to control the trembling which had taken hold of him the moment he had spotted the vehicle. Try as he might to convince himself that everything would be fine, he just couldn't shake the feeling that things were about to go very, very wrong.

*Fucking get a grip*, he told himself. *These fucking stupid-ass Rimmers do this all the time …*

A hatch opened on the roof of the truck and a large man in riot gear emerged, machine gun in hand. "All right, people," the speaker blared, "you know how this works. Line up behind the vehicle and leave a space." As Rim-Dwellers began jockeying for position near the truck's big double doors, three more armed soldiers exited from the passenger side, two of them taking up defensive positions on the left and right while the third shoved people back, effectively clearing a space about ten feet deep behind the truck. Pulling a can from one of his uniform's many pouches, the Green-Head then sprayed a crooked red line on the pavement, heedless of the half-dozen Rimmers' shoes he painted in the process.

"Hey, fuck you, you fucking fascist!" a middle-aged woman called out, angrily wiping at her boot with a grimy sleeve. The soldier quickly stepped up to her and thrust the butt of his machine gun up under her chin, sending her reeling into the crowd.

"Anyone who doesn't want their shoes painted," he shouted, "should back the fuck up!" A low murmur of dissent rippled through the throng as the people at the front stumbled backwards, tripping over each other. Jason stepped back himself, careful to avoid those who had gathered behind him since his arrival. The crush of Rimmers around him made him feel claustrophobic, yet at the same time he was grateful for the confinement; had there been an opening, he may very well have given in to his fear and made a run for it.

Once everyone had regrouped in a more or less orderly fashion, the Green-Head walked back and rapped on the side of the truck. The double doors clanged open and two men in riot gear rolled out a large ramp, the end of which came to rest about two feet short of the red line. Seconds later, hungry Rim-Dwellers were scrambling for the brown packages which piled up at the ramp's base.

"Citizens are allowed one package each," the speaker blared. "Failure to behave in accordance with food disbursement regulations will result in withdrawal of food disbursement privileges and/or summary execution. Citizens are allowed one package each. Failure to behave in accordance with food disbursement regulations will result in withdrawal of food disbursement ..."

After successfully retrieving a package, most Rimmers sprinted away as fast as they could, either alone or in small groups. Occasionally a fight would break out nearby as desperate and/or unscrupulous individuals attempted to increase their take at some other poor soul's expense. Though the soldiers kept a careful eye on the combatants, they did nothing to intervene.

Jay's heart thudded in his chest as he approached the front of the group. When his turn finally came, he had a terrible moment when he thought he might actually faint. Someone gave him a shove from behind, and he marched forward on numb legs, reaching a trembling hand down towards the nearest package.

Though he had managed so far to not make eye contact

with any of the soldiers, Jason couldn't help glancing up as his sweaty, gloved hand hovered over the little parcel. The two Green-Heads on the truck, having already loaded the ramp to capacity, stood idly watching the crowd, waiting for more packages to be retrieved. One of them looked down and locked eyes with him.

Time stood still as Jay, despite Greg's earlier assurances that he was not likely to be recognised, mentally reviewed all of the possible ways that he might be seen for who he really was: His hair, though free of the styling products and colour effects he had sported in the Core, could still be a give-away to anyone who knew his natural hair colour … but then again dirty-blond was not all that uncommon, even here in the Rim where darker shades were more prevalent. Though his implant scars were hidden, covered with gloves and bandages, the oozing spots over his knuckles could still give him away. However, a lot of Rimmers had injuries, and—

"What the fuck are you looking at?"

Flinching, Jay snapped his head toward the other guard. As the soldier stepped forward, Jay noticed virtually every detail of the weapon held across his armoured chest: the dull grey metal, the small glints of silver where the coating had worn away, the sheen of oil poking through the crevices of the moving parts, the light grey fabric sac hanging over the chamber. His chest tightened as he had a very vivid and very unnerving vision of the sac twitching and inflating as spent shell casings were caught inside it.

The Green-Head took another step forward, this time pointing the weapon directly at him. "Fucking move!"

Jay blinked, then grabbed the package and turned away, bumping solidly into the person behind him. Flustered, he ignored the exit route most of the Rimmers were taking, and pushed his way upstream amidst a flurry of angry shouts and expletives. When he reached the edge of the group, he veered off to the side and leaned against a wall, the small brown package hugged tightly to his chest. After a moment he un-zipped his bag and dropped the food in next to his knife.

"Hey, whatcha got there, little buddy?"

Jay blanched as Pete laid a hand on his shoulder, smiling. Gap stood nearby, nervously shuffling his feet. "Greg never did give us that juice he promised," Pete said cheerfully. "Maybe you could, you know, make up for it."

Eyes wide with fear, Jason pulled away from Pete's grasp and took a step backwards. "Leave me alone," he said lamely.

Pete chuckled. "Okay, we'll leave you alone. Just give us your bag and we'll go. Promise."

Jason glanced at Gap, then back at Pete. He took another step back. "Fuck you!" he said, trying his best to put on a brave face despite his distress. "I'm not giving you shit!"

Pete laughed out loud. "Oh, for fuck's sake," he said. "Do you really think we're fucking scared of you? Just give us the bag, and we won't hurt you." Jason clutched the sack tightly against his chest and scanned his surroundings, looking in vain for a way out. Pete marched forward and grabbed him by the front of his shirt. "Where ya gonna go, you fucking little shit?" he growled.

"Okay, wait … wait …" Jason stammered, his voice weak and plaintive. "Greg's on his way … he'll give it to you when he gets here."

"You know," Pete said, pulling Jay closer, "I actually haven't *seen* Greg in a while. Now I don't want to have to beat the shit out of you, so just *give me the fucking shit!*"

Seeing no other option, Jay shoved Pete away and made a frantic grab for his knife. He had barely wrapped his hand around the handle when Gap lumbered forward and punched him in the back of the head, toppling him to the ground. Bending forward, Pete gently slipped the sack off Jay's shoulder, then stepped back and delivered a well-aimed kick to his jaw, knocking him out cold.

★ ★ ★

The crowd had mostly dispersed by the time Jay came to, the few remaining Rimmers either wandering about aimlessly or lying unconscious on the pavement. The guards, though significantly more at ease, maintained their positions by the truck as the remaining packages were stowed away. Pete and Gap were nowhere to be seen.

Struggling to his feet, Jay leaned against a wall, frowning painfully as the reality of his situation oozed its way into his dazed mind. Slowly turning his head toward the truck, he watched in dismay as the guards slammed the doors shut, finally taking one last look around the perimeter. "No," Jason croaked. "Nooooo!"

The guards turned as Jason launched himself toward the vehicle, eyes wild with panic and fear. "Stay right there!" the Green-Head on the left shouted as the others quickly stepped forward, guns raised. Ignoring them, Jay sprinted frantically forward, desperately reaching out as he neared the back of the truck. Steadying themselves, the Green-Heads took aim.

"No, wait!" Jay gasped, finally coming to a halt. "Please, I lost my food ... you have to ... *please!*" Cursing, the guard on the left stepped forward and struck him savagely with the butt of his gun, tearing open a gash over his right eye. Jay fell to the ground, then immediately struggled to his knees. "Please," he cried plaintively as blood and tears flowed down his cheeks, "you don't understand ... I'm all alone ..." A loud sob escaped him then, and he clasped his hands before his chest. "I need *help!*" The guard raised his weapon to strike him again, but paused as the young man began crawling forward on his hands and knees.

"Just fucking shoot him!" the soldier on the right bellowed. The Green-Head hesitated, then flipped his weapon around and once again took aim.

"Noooo!" Jay cried in utter desperation. "I'm a Flasher!" A grisly mixture of blood and pus smeared across Jason's knuckles as he tore away the gloves and bandages, thrusting his hands towards the guard. "See? See? I'm Jason Crawford! Please ... I'm a Flasher!"

The Green-Head paused, frowning uncertainly.

"What the fuck's going on down there?" the guard on the roof shouted.

"Just hang on a minute!" the soldier replied. Edging carefully forward, he peered down at the wounds on Jason's hand, then looked up into the young man's bloody, tear-stained face.

"Holy shit ..."

PART III

## March 3, 2802

Claude gazed up in wonder. Never in his life had he seen anything so beautiful, so extraordinary, so … right. Warm, golden light filtered through the canopy, collecting in brilliant little pools amidst the brightly coloured leaves on the forest floor. A heady, almost intoxicating scent wafted through the air, carried by a light breeze. Though he had never experienced a real forest, he somehow knew this scent was right …

He wandered amongst the trees, smiling broadly and breathing deeply, even weeping a little as a small winged creature flitted by, emitting the most amazing, bizarre, beautiful little tune one could ever hope to imagine. A deep sense of peace and comfort enveloped him; pain and worry became abstract concepts … dreamy, smoke-like memories drifted away on the wind. This was right. He was right.

Off to his left Claude caught the sound of running water. He jogged over, joyfully kicking aside sprays of multicoloured leaves. Standing at the edge of the stream (surely that was what this was: water travelling across the ground in a small channel not created by human hands), he stared in wonder at the clear liquid, delighted by the way it wound itself in and around the rocks and pebbles beneath, skewing the light so that the little stones appeared to bend and dance. He closed his eyes and breathed deeply, as a warm wetness began to spread around his groin.

He opened his eyes and staggered backwards, gazing in horror at the wet spot expanding on his crotch. His chest became tight, his breathing fast and shallow. He was urinating. He was urinating into his clothes, piss trickling down his legs and dripping onto his shoes, finally flowing onto the ground to disappear between the leaves.

A tree spoke to him. "Will you look at that?" it rumbled. "Pissing on the ground like a fucking Rimmer. What kind of a fucking little asshole would waste resources like that? Maybe we should get your mommy in here, teach you how to use the reclaimer." Claude looked on in dismay as the tree pulled itself up by its roots and shambled towards him. He tried to turn and run, but his feet were heavy, mired down amongst the leaves. He fell slowly backwards, landing on his ass. He was scared, confused, and ashamed for what he had done. He was also afraid for his mother. The tree continued its monstrous approach, extending a branch into the stream and flinging a heavy shower of cold water into Claude's face. "Here. Let's clean you up a little. Might wake you up a bit too, eh?"

Gasping, Claude shook water from his head, then looked down in confusion. He was naked except for his underwear, which was covered in blood, vomit and piss. His legs were bloody and swollen, the left one bent unnaturally at the knee. Filthy water ran down the reclamation drain beneath his chair.

★ ★ ★

Claude sat on the edge of the bed, hands clasped, head down. Jeanine leaned against him, her long red hair spilling down his shoulder. "You okay?"

Claude sighed. "Yeah. I'm good."

She studied his face a moment, then stroked his hair affectionately. "More nightmares?"

"Yeah."

"What was it?" she asked.

Claude turned toward her with a small, sad smile. "I dreamt of trees ..."

His wife held him for a moment, then kissed him gently on the forehead. "I'll get breakfast started."

Claude squeezed her hand and waited until she had gone before hobbling over to the dresser. His cane rested against the edge of the mirror, next to a small framed photograph of three young men in Flasher uniforms. He was once again struck by how out of place he looked next to his friends; with dark hair and gangly, awkward-looking limbs, it was a wonder anyone could have imagined him as a Flasher. To think he had come so close to actually joining the elite squad still filled him with a wondrous sense of dread. Claude grabbed his cane and headed for the washroom.

The sky to the west still showed traces of the Squelcher's nightly light show as Councillor Claude Creston began the long walk from his apartment to the Research Facility. He had a nifty two-seater supplied by the City Council, complete with custom pedals to accommodate his gimpy leg, but he preferred to walk as often as possible; not only did this benefit his health, but it also gave him a chance to study the neighbourhood.

He and Jeanine had moved to New Haven eleven years ago, a year after the Rim's population had officially been liberated. At the time the neighbourhood had really been nothing more than an extension of the Transitional Zone, the wall between it and the Rim proper having been moved a few blocks space-ward to accommodate a small low-income housing project. Though travel in and out of the Rim had still been heavily regulated at the time, citizens of the sector had been, for the first time in decades, allowed to enter the Core without fear of reprisal.

As the area was expanded, improvements to New Haven's infrastructure proceeded at a brisk pace; streets were resurfaced, housing units were repaired or replaced, businesses took root and eventually flourished. With as much of the work as possible being given to Rim dwellers (now more often referred to as "citizens"), along with the implementation of a well-organised health and nutrition program, the ship's heretofore abandoned population had begun to heal.

Incentives were given to the Core dwellers to move "Space-ward", and though the influx of new residents had been understandably slow at first (mostly people driven by political and ethical issues, such as Claude himself), New Haven had recently developed a sort of bohemian charm, attracting a new generation of young, idealistic and highly motivated people. Over the past few years, several government services were relocated to the Rim, a move which not only helped to give the area a sense of legitimacy, but also forced reluctant Core dwellers to cross the channel and see the improvements for themselves.

At present, New Haven spanned across nearly one quarter of the Rim, the border between it and the rest of the sector marked only by a short decorative fence manned by a small contingent of police officers trained in non-violent conflict resolution. Those still residing outside of New Haven were, for the most part, healthy and free, and though their quality of life still paled in comparison to the rest of the ship, the improvements they had seen, coupled with the very real prospect of New Haven eventually spreading across the entire sector, gave them hope enough to move forward.

Claude took his time getting to the Reclamation Centre, stopping here and there to chat with construction workers, reclamation crews, and business owners opening up shop for the day. He found that this personal contact invariably lifted his spirits, helping to validate the work he had done as a councillor while keeping the worst of his inner demons (many of which were particularly active today) at bay.

As he neared his destination, Claude's attention was seized by the wonderful scent of fresh-baked, sweet carbohydrate desserts. He stopped in front of the shop window and gazed longingly at the incredible array of delicious creations on display. Though Jeanine had often reminded him of the potentially dire consequences of overindulgence, he couldn't help but consider several good reasons why he should just march in and satisfy his sweet tooth. He would be supporting a local business, after all ...

Claude gave one last look at the heavenly cornucopia spread out before him, then sighing heavily, turned his attention to his own image reflected in the window, giving himself a quick once-over to ensure that he would still be presentable after his long walk. He quickly checked his hair, his tie, his shoes ...

His shoes. Comfortable, well-made, sensible shoes, carefully cleaned and polished to a brilliant shine. They had been purchased just a few blocks away, and had been modified by a cobbler a little further south. The shoemaker had done an excellent job matching the new sole to the original one; if not for the fact that the left sole was almost an inch thicker, you never would have guessed there had been any modification at all.

Claude spun on his heel and began the short trek to the Reclamation Centre, eager to finally reach the end of a very long, and very difficult voyage. As he strode purposefully toward his destination, he couldn't help but recall the toll this voyage had taken on his friends and family ...

Having intercepted Jay's message from the Rim, the High Command had apprehended, interrogated and tortured both Claude and Isaac. Claude's father had immediately sought out his connections in the Council, begging them to intervene. Though Claude had been left physically crippled and psychologically scarred, he had ultimately survived the ordeal, while Isaac had died screaming in the interrogator's chair.

Despite his success in saving his son's life, Claude's father had been left broken and defeated, ashamed at his inability to prevent the deluge of pain and suffering which had been visited upon his family. Claude's mother, a staunch Flasher supporter to the end, had been unable to cope with her loss of status after her son had been expelled from the academy. She had eventually turned to medicating herself with whatever substance was available, finally losing hope altogether and taking her own life. His little sister, completely blameless but tainted by association, had been banned from the Boosterettes. Though this in itself could not really be considered a bad thing, Angie had been left with a deep sense of betrayal which to this day cast a dark shadow over her life. His little brother had been the only family member left relatively intact; too young to have had any real involvement in the Flasher system before the trouble started, Raymond had grown up feeling a keen empathy for his wounded kin. As a result, he had spent years studying and researching the Flasher system and the society shaped by it, and was now well on his way to following in his big brother's political footsteps.

Claude shook the memories aside as he caught sight of a large group of reporters in front of the Reclamation Centre. Almost immediately, a woman wielding a large camera pointed, and the entire group turned to face him, a few hurrying forward to intercept. Claude paused to remove his coat, glancing as he did so at a power arch behind and to the right of the Reclamation Centre. Now clean and shiny from one end to the other, the arch sported a huge billboard featuring a happy family waving and smiling into the camera. Beneath them were the words "New Haven: Living on the Edge, and Loving It! Prime Retail and Residential Space Available Now!" A little smile crossed his lips as he squared his shoulders and hobbled into the fray.

"Councillor Creston!" The first to intercept Claude was a young man in a maroon suit, carrying a portable audio recorder. "How does it feel to see your years of hard work finally come to fruition?"

Claude slowed his pace but did not stop entirely. "Well, I'd say that ... though this is definitely a very important moment, it's not the end. We've made a lot of progress, but we still have a ways to go."

"But how does it feel?"

Claude was forced to stop as reporters and cameramen crowded in front of him. He targeted a reporter from Bidwell News and tapped the man's foot lightly with his cane, smiling his best diplomatic smile. "Excuse me, please," he said quietly. The man looked down at Claude's cane, then stepped back awkwardly, bumping his cameraman in the process.

"Councillor!" the young man persisted, following Claude through the newly-opened path. "How does it feel?"

Claude paused, leaning heavily on his cane as he considered the question.

It had been a long and difficult journey from Flasher trainee to ground breaking Councillor. After his torture at the hands of the High Command, he had spent five years recovering physically and emotionally, spending much of his time studying politics, more out of interest than any hope of actually making a career out of it. After all, it had seemed highly unlikely that the High Command would ever allow him to enter any kind of position of power.

He had been understandably shocked then when the Council Head, under direction of the High Command, had approached him with an offer to stand on the Council, effective immediately. It seemed there had been some concern that Claude would somehow manage to stir up trouble with the dozen or so anti-Flasher groups in the city, and that having him on the Council would be a good way to keep him under control. Though he had held no illusions that he would be able to effect any kind of real change, Claude had accepted immediately, hoping to make at least a small difference wherever he could.

Two years into his first term, Claude had caught wind of a small group of Flashers who had resigned their commission on unspecified ethical grounds. Unable to contain his curiosity, he had arranged a covert meeting with the group and learned that they had been alarmed by the high number of Flashers and trainees who had either been expelled or gone missing over the years, including Claude and his friends. Seeing this as a rare opportunity, Claude had quickly (and quietly) taken the group under his wing, encouraging them to band together with, and to help consolidate, the anti-Flasher groups. By the time the High Command had realized what was happening, the new coalition had gone public, their credibility bolstered by the actual one time Flashers among their ranks.

Unable to resort to their usual tactics of torture due to the coalition's outspoken public presence, the High Command had covertly arranged the assassination of two of the ex-Flashers, setting it up to look like a random crime. Undeterred, the coalition had redoubled their efforts, labelling the victims as martyrs and thereby attracting more citizens to the anti-Flasher cause.

As the coalition's momentum increased, Claude had for the first time felt safe enough to start looking into the Research Division's activities. He had worked slowly and cautiously at first, feeling his way around the system, learning who he could and could not trust. Eventually, having built up a network of allies, Claude had gathered enough evidence to actually uncover the horrific scenario which Jason had described in his message. Taking this new-found evidence to the ever-growing anti-Flasher coalition, Claude had arranged a massive press conference which had, in one massive stroke, begun the inevitable demise of the Flasher system.

And now here he was, poised to close yet another chapter in this long, sordid story ...

Claude sighed, then faced the reporter as he moved slowly forward. "Bittersweet," he said. "It feels bittersweet."

The reporter began to ask another question, but was cut off by a middle-aged woman holding a camera on her shoulder, "Councillor!" she shouted. "If all goes well today, will you be announcing your candidacy for Council Head?"

Claude frowned into the lens, suddenly wishing these people would all just leave. "Today has nothing to do with my political prospects," he said, moving more aggressively through the crowd.

"What's your reaction," the woman continued, undaunted, "to Councillor Blayne's assertion that disassembling the Flasher system has put the entire population at risk, as the Squelchers continue to target the ship's shields? Will this assertion hurt your chances in the next election?"

Claude grit his teeth, his anger growing despite his best efforts to calm down. "This topic has been covered several times before, but since it appears that not everyone has gotten the message, I will repeat myself.

"It is a well-documented fact that not one Squelcher beam had penetrated the shields since they had been shorn up following the initial attack, with the exception of those allowed through on purpose as part of the Flasher war effort. The only human casualties of the Flasher war were the young soldiers who were put in harm's way, the poor souls who died testing the transport system, and of course, the Rim-dwellers. Contrary to the reports of certain fear-mongering news stations aligned with the old Pro-Flasher vanguard, the

Squelchers' ongoing attack on the shields, though definitely worth monitoring, has for all intents and purposes had no negative effect on the ship whatsoever."

"Councillor! Councillor!" A third reporter called out from somewhere nearer the edge of the crowd. "Rumours persist that a message from Flasher trainee Jason Crawford was the impetus for your foray into politics, and more specifically, for your campaign to disassemble the Flasher system and liberate the Rim. Would you like to comment on that in light of today's anticipated events?"

Claude scowled. "No, thank you," he replied tersely.

"It's well known that Crawford was a friend of yours in the Academy," the reporter continued, pushing his way awkwardly through the crowd. "It is also well known that some members of Council were against the dismantling of the Flasher system. Do you think today's events were delayed as a retaliation of sorts?"

Having reached the entrance, Claude paused and looked in the direction of the voice, finally lowering his head and reaching for the handle. He suddenly felt very tired. "My office will release a statement later today," he said as the door swung open and he stepped inside. "Thank you."

An attractive older woman in a lab coat stood waiting by the security desk. "Good morning, Councillor," she said, handing him his visitor's pass with a warm smile. Warm and … something else. Sympathetic? Defiant? "It's very nice to see you again."

Frowning, Claude snatched the pass from her hand. "Yes, well, if it's all the same to you, Vicki," he said, clipping the tag to his shirt pocket, "I'd just as well we forego the pleasantries and get right to it."

The woman's smile faltered, replaced by the slightest hint of a scowl. "Yes, of course," she said, looking over at the security guard, then down at a clipboard she had been hugging to her chest. She cleared her throat, then finally looked back up at Claude. "If you'll follow me, please." Claude sighed inwardly as she hurried off down the hall. Victoria Delenchek had been in charge of the experimental wing of the Flasher system for nearly thirty-five years. Though she and Claude had butted heads more often than he cared to remember, he couldn't help but feel some sympathy for the woman whose raison-d'être had been systematically disassembled before her eyes. Besides, this was going to be hard enough without him antagonising people by acting like a jackass.

The woman stopped a few meters down the hall, and held open a door marked: "Flasher Squad Special Operations: Asset Management". Though he had visited the room several times, he was still struck by how close to the main entrance it was. He guessed it was a case of "hiding in plain sight" … but then again, it could easily be just another example of the extreme arrogance which had been so prevalent within the Flasher system.

To the right of the door sat a small computer terminal surrounded by cabinets, equipment trolleys, and a compact wash station. To the left were six hospital beds, five of which were empty and dark, their equipment powered down and pushed neatly against the wall. Claude frowned. "Couldn't these be used elsewhere?" he snapped, raising his cane and waving it towards the empty beds.

The woman blinked, then looked away. "Well, yes, of course," she said quickly, a touch of anger coming through in her voice. "We're hoping to have these moved to the Rim … um, Space-ward … to one of the new facilities." She paused and cleared her throat, then looked back at Claude. "I'm very sorry Councillor, but as you well know, there exist regulations and procedures which I am in no position to circumvent. This equipment needs to stay here until the entire room is vacated, at which time an inventory will be made. Only then will we be able to pack it up and distribute it to the areas of greatest need."

Claude sighed, looking sadly at one of the darkened beds. "Yes, of course," he said softly, I understand." He paused, thoughtful, then turned towards the woman. "Listen Vicki … I'm sorry if I'm being a little gruff." Ms. Delenchek looked aside, frowning. Claude cleared his throat. "I know this is a challenging time for all of us. I'll try my best to be less cranky."

Vicki fiddled with her notes a moment, then sighed. "It's all right, Claude," she said quietly. "I imagine this must be very difficult for you in particular."

"Well, thank you, but that's no excuse."

The two looked at each other in silence for a moment, Claude finally glancing down at his feet. "Well," he said, tapping his cane against the tiled floor, "I guess we should get underway."

"Yes, I guess we should," she replied, looking down at her notes. "I'm afraid I'm not allowed to leave the room though … you know, regulations. But if you'd like a moment …"

"Yes, of course," Claude said, smiling sadly, "I understand. Thank you. I won't be long."

"Please, Claude, take your time."

He nodded, then turned and walked toward the small oasis of light where Jason lay. Claude's friend was barely re-cognisable, his yellowed, waxy skin drawn tight against his skull, dozens of festering sores and lesions scattered across his face and hands. All around him machines whirred and chugged, impassively sucking out the essence of what had once been Jason Crawford.

As he placed his hand on the shrivelled, wasted husk be-fore him, Claude felt the full weight of the grief and remorse which he had carried for so many years.

"I'm sorry … " he said quietly. "And thank you."

A moment later Claude turned and hobbled toward the door.

"All right," he said, "turn it off."

## March 3, 2802

Victoria Delenchuk rushed down the hall, a harried intern in tow. Her meeting with Councillor Creston had been difficult; she was having trouble reconciling her sympathy for him with her anger at having what practically amounted to her life's work yanked out from under her. Though she had been offered several new positions, she couldn't shake the feeling that even the best of them would feel like a demotion. And now, just when she thought this horrible mess was finally over ...

"You're absolutely certain of this?" she asked the intern irritably.

"Yes, ma'am," he replied quickly. "I was there. Benson was checking his foot reflex when it happened."

Victoria scowled. "What did he say?" she asked, turning the corner towards what had until a few minutes ago been Asset Management.

"Benson?" the intern asked breathlessly. Vicki shot him a glare. "Oh, no, of course ... um, I don't know. I didn't actually hear him. Benson did."

Ms. Delenchuk flung the door open and marched up to the bed, where Andy Benson and another nurse were busily adjusting equipment and monitoring vital signs. She looked down at Jason.

"How certain are you?" she asked.

"One hundred percent," Benson replied, nodding towards the heart monitor next to the bed. "His vital signs are weak, but there's absolutely no doubt. This guy is alive."

Vicki closed her eyes and sighed. *Oh, for the love of Earth, why?*

"I've got an IV drip going," Benson continued, "but we'll have to get him to a proper hospital soon."

"Yes, of course," Vicki said, her tone despondent. "You can arrange transport once you're sure he's stable." She shook her head, scowling fiercely. There was no logical explanation for this; the body on the bed had long since been ravaged far beyond any hope of recovery—he should have died the instant life support had been shut off.

Now that he was alive, however, they were legally bound to try and keep him that way …

"And he actually *spoke*?" she asked incredulously, watching the shallow rise and fall of Jason's chest.

"Yep."

"What did he say?"

Benson fiddled nervously with the IV drip, then turned to face his superior. "Well, I can't say with one hundred percent certainty." He looked down, apparently embarrassed. "I was checking his foot reflex when it happened … I was kind of caught off guard."

Victoria shot him an angry glare. "Benson. *What did he say*?"

The nurse paused. "Well, as far as I can tell," he replied, a hesitant smile pulling at one corner of his mouth, "he said … he said 'Get off me, you fucking faggot.' "

# About the Author

Gilles DeCruyenaere lives in Winnipeg, Manitoba, Canada with his wife Joanne and their fur-baby Yogi. In his spare time Gilles enjoys reading, watching movies, creating art and experiencing nature, as well as collecting rocks, minerals, antiques and Star Wars paraphernalia. A graduate of the Digital Media Design program at Red River College, Gilles recently served as film editor for the feature-length animated film "Emma's Wings: A Bella Sara Tale".

www.kreefax.com

47233347R00133

Made in the USA
Charleston, SC
05 October 2015